Praise for Clare Rhoden's *Chronicles of the Pale*

The Pale is a simmering read that never goes the way you expect it to … If you're into intelligent, innovative, feminist science fiction, you can find it in *The Pale*.
  —*Aurealis Magazine*

The Pale, in which many sentient species must, as they emerge from disaster, learn to rebuild together, is refreshingly nuanced and complex … The meticulous, deeply thought-out, and intelligent worldbuilding makes it shine.
  —Laura E Goodin, author of *After The Bloodwood Staff*

A gripping tale of resilience, survival, and how we define the 'other'— this is intelligent SF that speaks to our time.
  —Jennifer Mills, author of *Dyschronia*

The sign of good speculative fiction is that you can not only read it for the page-turning story and characters you will come to love and loathe, but also for the way it makes you think about issues relevant to your own world. Clare Rhoden captures both aspects excellently with this great read about a post-apocalyptic world and the four communities within it.
  —*Writer's Epiphany*

The Pale is a world of biomachines, talking and civilized canines, ferals and complicated futuristic technologies … that captivated me from the start.
  —*Reading Time Journal*

Rhoden demonstrates tremendous descriptive powers and impressive world building, *The Pale* reminiscent of the intelligent science fiction novels of old. I am reminded of my favourite science fiction author, Phillip K Dick. *The Pale* is filled with well-crafted and engaging characters—including dogs—in what amounts to a classy read with an important moral message, making the reader question where we are heading and whose side we are on and what it means to be fully human.

—Isobel Blackthorn, author of *Clarissa's Warning*

Rhoden's style is deeply humanist, showing people overcoming prejudices and learning from each other while they deal with dwindling resources and create a better world … It's a dense, poetic book and probably won't be for everyone, but if you're interested in layered world-building, nuanced plotlines, and complex characters, pay attention to *Broad Plain Darkening*.

—*Aurealis Magazine*

Some of the big questions in *Broad Plain Darkening* for me were to wonder at what it really means to be sentient? What is human? Why do some people fear difference? What is family and belonging? How far will artificial intelligence influence our decisions in the future? Will humans merge with machines? What gives rise to ultimate power? Why are people exiled? Surviving on Broad Plain is grim, but this is a warm heart of a story, with inter-species cooperation and care.

—*Reading Time Journal*

THE RUINED LAND

CLARE RHODEN

ODYSSEY
BOOKS

Published by Odyssey Books in 2019
www.odysseybooks.com.au

A catalogue record for this
book is available from the
National Library of Australia

ISBN: 978-1-925652-73-4 (pbk)
ISBN: 978-1-925652-74-1 (ebook)

Cover design by Elijah Toten (www.totencreative.com)
Map of Broad Plain and Schematic of the Pale by Bernard Maher

For all the believers and those with hope in the future

Character List

The Pale
Adaeze Patraena, the Regent
Jaxon Tangshi, Senior Forecaster
Hekili, Master of the Wereguard
Hokulani, a Wereguard, Head of the Service
Teiuc, Foremost Ingeneer
Quauhtli, Chief of the Teshniks
Ailani, Head of Recycling, former paramount
Arihi, a victualler, former paramount
Laylene, a service supervisor
Gavino, a serviceman

The Ravine Canini
Mashtuk, a scout
Hector, a human-humachine, formerly of the Pale
Callan, past leader of a canini pack that hunted with the Storm
Hippolyta, leader of the ravine guard pack
Thestia, leader of the deep ravine pack
Enis, son of Zélie and Mashtuk
Romulo and Remo, human infants
Tsendi, of Thestia's pack, Enis's chosen
Memandi, a hunter
Tillie, a hunter
Tanno, an old scout
Aled and Mared, Hippolyta's half-grown cubs
Niccolò and Rhosyn, half-grown cubs of Zélie and Mashtuk
Mishka, a half-grown cub of Thestia's pack

The Storm
Marin, Huntmaster
Willow, his partner
Freya, daughter of Feather and Jana
Paolo, a scout
Beris, an old wisewoman
Nita, an old wisewoman
Finn, an elder

Travelling on Broad Plain
Feather, son of Helm of the Storm
Jarli of the Owl, an outclansman
Daku of the Owl, Jarli's young brother
Various young men of the Owl, accompanying Daku
Wild men, human wanderers with no tribal allegiance

Newkeep Port
Valkirra Adelriksdottir, former chief of the Settlement
Talis, her partner
Jana, Feather's partner
Helm, tribesman formerly of the Storm, Feather's father
Rasti, a rat terrier Feather rescued from the Settlement
Iver, a former councillor
Ahrenkild, a former councillor
Branimir, a former councillor
Tammas, a shepherd
Cushla, daughter of Valkirra and Talis
Jasper, their son

The Settlement
Brettin, Lady of the Temple
Olinna, District Councillor
Anielka, District Councillor
Jenna, a Temple acolyte
Blazej, a Temple notary
Esteri, a Temple notary

Pirinna, a high-assessed matron
Denn, her partner, a high-assessed tailor

Equii
Pinto, a piebald cart-gelding
Violeta, a riding mare
Mateo, a young foal

Shaking Landers
Kohu, a man of the Shaking Lands
Kaihoko, Kohu's hearth companion
Kiri Ana Rea, a tribal leader

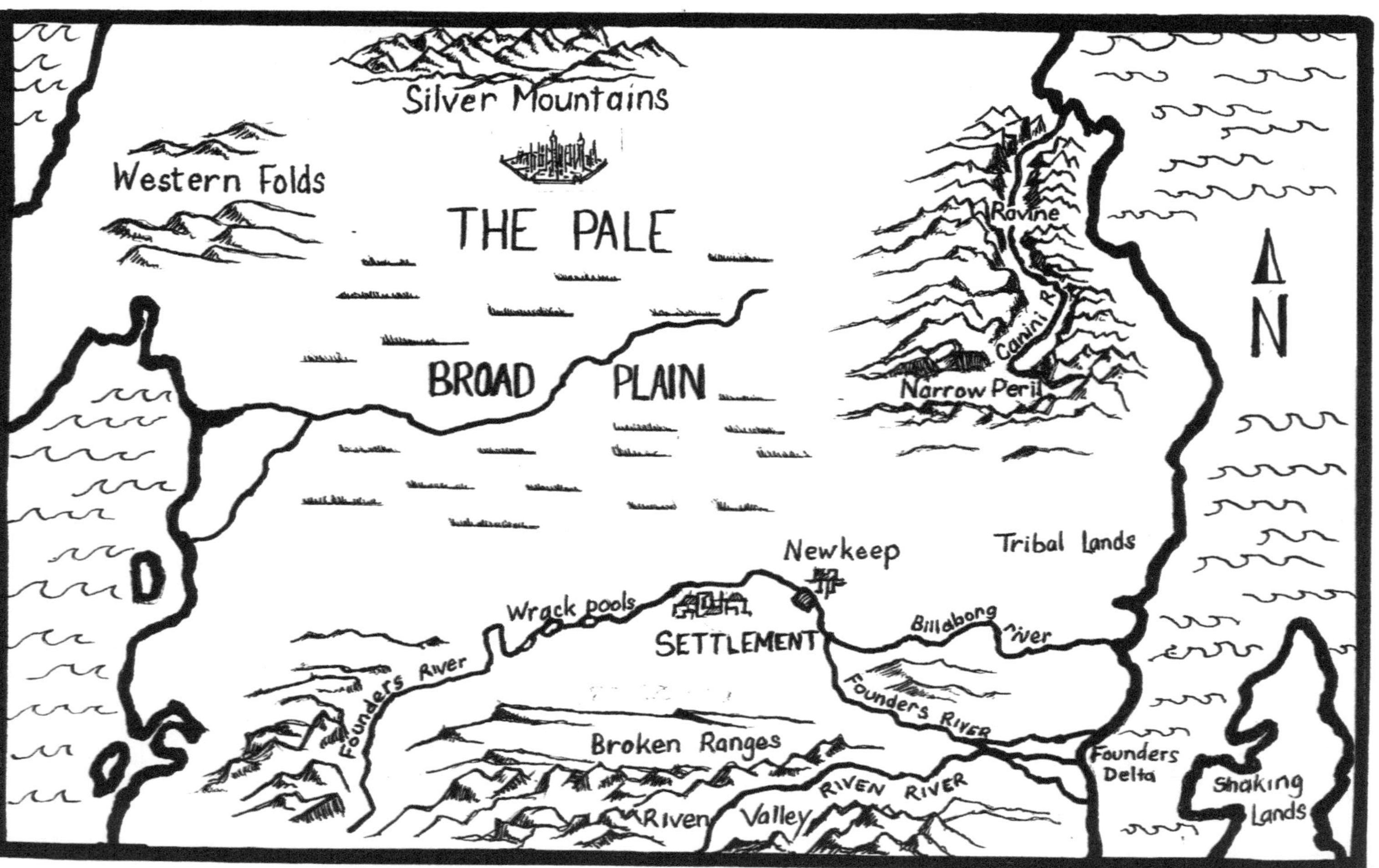

N
Silver Mountains
Western Folds
THE PALE
BROAD PLAIN
Ravine
Canini R.
Narrow Peril
Tribal Lands
Newkeep
Wrack pools
SETTLEMENT
Billabong River
Founders River
Founders River
Broken Ranges
RIVEN RIVER
Riven Valley
Founders Delta
Shaking Lands

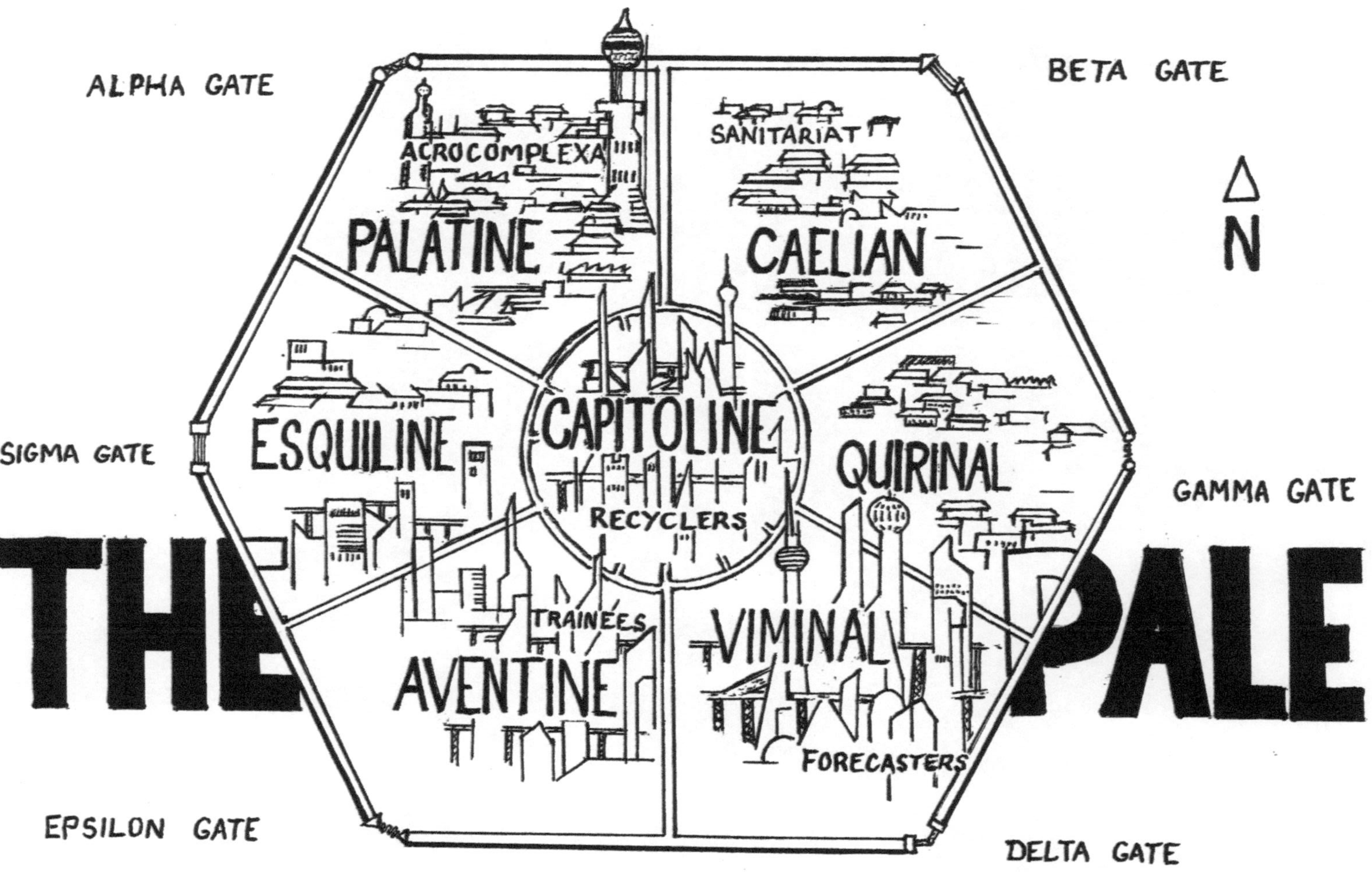

THE PALE
ALPHA GATE
BETA GATE
N
SIGMA GATE
GAMMA GATE
EPSILON GATE
DELTA GATE
PALATINE
ACROCOMPLEXA
CAELIAN
SANITARIAT
ESQUILINE
CAPITOLINE
Recyclers
QUIRINAL
AVENTINE
Trainees
VIMINAL
Forecasters

Autumn and Winter
the year 218pC

Chapter 1

Mashtuk kept his eyes closed. It was enough to be awake. He could hear so much, and feel so much, that anything more seemed an impossible burden.

He lay as still as he could, feeling every fibre of the dried grass that had been laid under him, as if his pelt had been stripped off and the indentations of leaf and stem and grain were being imprinted onto his bare muscles. He suppressed a moan. He should be grateful that he did not have the barren rock floor of the den for his bed. After lying motionless on his side for so long he desperately wanted to shift his position, but held himself immobile with an effort of will. He wasn't ready to let the pack know that he had regained his senses.

Truth to say, he wasn't ready to face a pack that no longer contained his beloved Zélie. She had been killed in the vulpini attack that had left him so direly wounded. She was a whisper on the wind, and he was hanging to life by a mere scrabble of claws. He could feel, with every shallow breath, the emptiness of her passing, the gaping abyss in his mind where her voice had been for so many years. Despite his best efforts, a shudder passed over him, and he could sense others stirring, looking at him, speaking to him. There was Callan, his great friend of many years, and young Enis, his son. His and Zélie's. The surge of his grief met the weight of their worry, the emotion pulsing against Mashtuk's mind, clouding his thoughts and blurring their words. He wondered if his ears had been damaged too, or maybe his mindspeech knocked completely out of his head. This foggy pushing of words without meaning was excruciating, and he could no longer pretend even to himself that he was unaware of his surroundings. Mashtuk yielded to the ache of his body. He stretched his limbs, pushing through the pain of his injuries.

His movement prompted more noise, more activity, and more mindspeech clutching at him. All of it was muffled into a formless wave of sound, empty of meaning, foamy and insubstantial. Mashtuk opened his eyes. Why could he not hear them properly? Every other sense said that Callan and Enis were touching-close.

The big white canine was leaning over him, a quizzical look in his eyes, while young Enis had reached forward to cradle his father's head in his hands. They were speaking to him, Mashtuk knew, but his mind could not separate the words they used. He let out a fretful whine, and Callan and Enis looked at each other. At last, thought Mashtuk, at last they know they can't get through to me with mindspeech. They must know that I can't hear them properly.

He struggled a little in Enis's arms, managing to drag himself into a sitting position, even if he leaned heavily on his son's strong body. The pain of his broken foreleg was less, he realised, if he rested the damaged paw on top of his other one. Callan and Enis continued speaking over him, around him, but nothing they said was clear to Mashtuk. He would have tried shaking his head clear, had it not felt so heavy and throbbed so much. He whined again, and his two supporters grew silent, their eyes meeting across him.

More canini entered the den, apparently alerted to Mashtuk's awakening. They smelled of cold and mud. With them came humans. Mashtuk recognised their scent. These were tribesmen of the Storm, old friends of Callan, whose pack had run with them for almost two decades. They, too, tried to mindspeak to him, but their words were fuzzy, faint. He couldn't hold them long enough to read them.

One of the women kneeled down next to him, and he realised that she was setting down two squirming infants. Within seconds, the two human babies had hitched themselves toward him, one flinging both arms around his neck, the other crawling close enough to take a gentle hold of his leg, just above the splint.

'Papa! Papa!' said the first twin in crisp mindspeech. It was Romulo, the one with the red birthmark over his lip and muzzle.

Mashtuk almost yelped in surprise, at last able to understand a mindspoken word. He leaned forward, licking the faces of both babies, his heart swelling again as he remembered how he and Zélie had saved the little humans from under the very gates of the Pale. So much love he and Zélie had given these two little ones, and now he felt it redoubled as they crooned comfort to him in perfect mindspeech, their little voices cutting through the haze in his thoughts, dragging him back to life.

* * *

Hector rose to his feet. At well over two metres tall with a width of shoulder to match, he made a superb target for anyone wishing to attack his sentry position from the plain below. His silvered skin caught every stray gleam of light that pierced the storm, reflecting off the tawny rock behind him like a misty halo, and the narrow pinch point he was guarding was perfectly bare of cover.

He knew he was quite safe, though. The strangers who were struggling up the steep track that led into the ravine were totally engrossed with their ascent, watching their steps on the rain-wet path. He could have blown them off their feet with one blast of his weaponised forearm before they had a chance to realise where the attack had come from.

Well, he corrected himself, maybe two blasts.

Since he had left the Pale and its steady diet of biofuel, all of Hector's in-fitted weaponry was slowly but steadily losing power, although his enhanced sensing was undiminished. Hector raised the viewfinder on his wrist to eye level and focused tightly on the pair approaching. He nodded, confirming his first impression that these fellows offered no threat to him or to the various members of his adopted pack.

He dropped to one knee, watching the two climbers curiously while he thinned his mindvoice to call his great friend Enis. He and the canine had an unusually close bond, and the range and inflection of their silent communication was greater than most of the pack could manage.

'INCOMING!" announced Hector, with a tone that called for attention but relayed calm.

'???' and 'On my way,' replied Enis immediately. Something in his mindvoice was edged with excitement and confusion, and Hector felt him pushing the emotions aside as he answered the call.

'Two humans,' added Hector. 'Tribal, I think. Footsore and hungry.'

He adjusted the viewfinder to scan the intruders from head to heel. On this precipitous trail where they needed to lift their faces into the rain to see the ground ahead of them, they were wide open to his inspection. The foremost was definitely a tribesman, thought Hector, and he guessed that the man may even belong to the Storm, the tribe that was currently camping in the ravine. The Storm had long been allies of the canini, and close contact with them had taught Hector something of their preferred markings—the specific way they braided their hair, the particular outlines of their face paint, their slender style of bow and arrow. The second man, though, made Hector frown. A young fellow, skinny and rather unkempt, this stranger had dark skin and hair bleached tawny by the sun. He wore a single mourning stripe of paint on his cheeks, and his gear looked makeshift, cobbled together from badly dressed skins and roughly woven reeds. Hector had never seen a human quite like this one, and though admittedly his experience of humans was small, he could find no exact match in his data sets either. 'A wild man' was what his data suggested, though why a wild man would be travelling with a tribesman was an anomaly he could not fathom, and the stranger did not wear the grotesque finery of the few wild men Hector had encountered. He continued watching as the pair slowly advanced toward his lookout post.

A tiny scatter of scree announced the arrival of Enis on the path above him, not that any such announcement was needed. With his mind so closely attuned to the young canine, Hector had been aware of him leaving the den, loping across the shared meeting space, and threading his way through the twisted paths of the thorn forest, his footfalls sure and steady. Enis would be here in a moment. The fact that the pack leader Hippolyta was coming down with him surprised Hector much more.

'Where?' asked Hippolyta, pushing past Enis to take up a position as close to the guard point as she could come.

Hector, being larger than any two canini put together, generally worked alone when he stood sentry duty, simply because he took up so much room. The fact that he had enhanced sensing was an added bonus. His mindspeech was so strong, too, that he was able to summon the pack with ease, even without the ability to howl a warning. He peeled back from the overhang that marked the narrowest waist of the trail, the place they knew as the pinch point, and stuck himself as close as he could to the rock wall so that both Hippolyta and Enis could look down on the visitors.

'I see,' remarked Hippolyta.

'You were right about one thing, brother,' Enis commented over his shoulder. 'These are no threat.'

'Bring them up,' commanded Hippolyta, turning to make her way back past Hector and up to the ravine. 'I will let the Storm know we have visitors. Likely they are known to the tribe.'

As the scrabble of her claws receded up the path above them, Hector and Enis looked at each other.

'So, brother,' said Enis, 'we had better let the visitors know we can see them.'

'Will you mindspeak them?' Hector dropped to his knees beside his friend, both watching the path below.

Enis tossed his head. 'Not all tribesmen can hear me,' he said.

Hector knew this was a matter of some annoyance to him, as he had always imagined a close connection with the tribes, who—in canini terms—were the most sensible humans left on the land. Hector had slightly different ideas, but these he mostly kept to himself. He caught Enis by the eye, the canini equivalent of calling for attention.

'Well, how about you give a yap to let them know we are here, and then I speak aloud to them?'

'Yes. One moment.' Enis cocked his head, his over-large ears pricked toward his friend. His eyes were steady.

Hector wondered why he did not immediately announce them to the travellers below. Then Enis spoke words that Hector had feared he may never hear.

'Hector, my father has woken.'

'Mashtuk is awake?' Hector jumped to his feet. He felt like running all the way back to the den immediately.

Enis raised a paw to stay him. 'He's awake. He isn't speaking yet, and we're not sure he can understand us. He seems rather confused. But Callan says it is a good sign, and that he will most probably continue to improve.'

'I—I hope so. Yes, that is good news. Yes.' Hector looked aside, a canini trick he had learned to hide the powerful emotion that bloomed inside him. After a moment he turned back to face Enis. 'Good news, yes. Now it's time to deal with these sorry two.' He tipped his chin toward the wet, weary travellers below.

'Yes. I will alert them, and then you speak.' Enis looked up at him, a wry twist to his lips. 'But, if you don't mind, you need to speak gently, and maybe crouch down a bit. The sight and sound of your ghastly self might just make them run all the way back down to the plain.'

Hector smiled. He rather enjoyed the canini sense of humour. Enis stiffened his forelegs on the crest of the pinch point and tipped back his head, emitting a sharp volley of stern yaps. Hector nodded approval. Friends though they might prove, no visitors to the canini of the ravine would escape a brisk challenge.

The two men froze on the trail, snapping their gaze to the place from where the sound ahead of them had originated. Enis shifted a little to allow Hector access to the crest. As he came into their line of vision, Hector noticed that both men seemed to shrink into themselves, shoulders tensing, hands straying toward their weapons. Recognising their fear, he felt something grow dull within himself. But he knew well that this was always what happened, here in the Outside, whenever a living creature caught sight of his metallic-looking bulk. Although he and his friends knew that his skin had paled, that his hair had grown thick and even more dense with curls, and that his offensive hardware had diminished with every day he spent Outside, to a stranger he looked every inch one of the Pale's monstrous humachines. He lifted his voice and spoke evenly, careful to use all the polite forms he had learned from the canini.

'Welcome, travellers on the land,' he said. 'I am Hector, of Hippolyta's pack that guards the ravine. My brother here is Enis. Do you seek entry to our den?'

He watched as the leading man stood straight, shoulders going back as he relaxed into a polite greeting stance. He also grasped his fellow by the upper arm in a gesture of reassurance. Hector's sensors, making instant calculations from the angle of his post, told him that the stranger was not quite as tall as most of the tribesmen. His newly honed canini perspective read the man's posture as confident and polite, quite different from the fearful, bewildered look of his fellow. Hector waited on their words, aware of Enis beside him tilting his ears this way and that, trying to hear whether the strangers had any mind-speech.

'Our thanks,' said the foremost traveller gravely. 'We are pleased to meet you, Hector and Enis of Hippolyta's pack. Our business is indeed with the canini of the ravine. I am Feather of the Storm, and this is my foster brother Jarli of the outclan Owl. We have travelled far in search of your den.'

The tribesman's respectful attitude, his careful use of their names, and his own name made Hector's heart warm. 'Feather! He is of the Storm. Freya's father, yes?' he asked in a private aside to Enis.

The young canine gave a tight nod, and then turned his attention to the strangers.

'You have found us,' said Enis in a brisk, broadcast mindvoice, watching with his eyes narrowed to see if there was any response. Hector felt him twitch with delight as he saw Feather's face break into a wide grin.

'And we are glad of that,' Feather responded in kind. 'We have a matter of the gravest importance to discuss with you.'

Hector saw him glance swiftly at his companion, and then up again at the two sentries. He saw wonder in Feather's clear grey eyes as he realised that Hector, too, could hear their mindspeech. Hector decided that it was time to confirm his position as a pack member.

'Approach, then, travellers,' he mindspoke them. 'Already the pack is preparing to greet you.' He rose slowly to his feet, aware again of their inevitable flinching as the Outsiders realised just how large and threatening a creature he looked.

'Be welcome to our den,' he said aloud, believing from his wide-eyed stare that Jarli was not as adept at mindspeech as Feather. 'You will find friends ahead.'

With his fingers clenched in Jarli's tattered cloak, Feather of the Storm led his companion up to the sentry point. Hector approved of the way the tribesman met his eyes without a shadow of fear. He stepped back to allow them to climb over the crest, and motioned for them to follow Enis up the last section of the trail.

He watched them go past, settling again to his sentry duty. There were some hours yet until he would be relieved. He wanted to see Mashtuk, and hoped that by then the old canine would have regained even more of his senses. He also hoped that by the time he re-entered the den, the two travellers would have discovered all that awaited them in the ravine. The presence of the entire tribe of the Storm, for example. Feather would be reunited with his daughter Freya. Jarli—Hector had no idea what Jarli's business was with the ravine canini, but he had detected a bio-echo that troubled him. Jarli's life-force, Hector's sensors told him, read very like that of the human twins the canini had saved from the Pale. Jarli must be, the twins must be, thought Hector in confusion, from the same gene pool. He shrugged off the unease that came with this thought.

And when eventually he went up to the den, he consoled himself, the strange circumstance of a humachine living with a canini pack would be a matter of complete indifference, and the new humans would no longer gape at him.

* * *

'I have never seen so much rain,' said the regent Adaeze in amazement, looking across the rooftop garden of her new home.

Renamed the regent's stronghold, the imposing building had until recently housed the Pale's forecasters along with their trainees, their precious archival storage banks, and their prodigious stocks of finely calibrated equipment. Extensive remodelling and redecoration had transformed the forecasting tower into a more gracious and impressive place, suitable for a queen's residence. Adaeze declared herself content with the changes, although she still expressed regrets about the superb views she had enjoyed from the regent's tower. All considered, though, her move to the forecasters' oikos had been a success.

The outcome for the forecasters was not quite as happy, mused Jaxon Tangshi.

The Pale's senior forecaster, who was also the regent's most powerful adviser, was at that very moment making plans to draw the plight of his colleagues to his queen's attention. He knew, for example, that she preferred not to have homeless forecasters underfoot when she took her daily exercise along the go-ways of the policosmos, and that she would rather not be confronted at every turn by layers of blinking, beeping equipment stashed under random porticos. She was young and vigorous, and easily affronted by signs of disarray and decay. Judicious—not to say more obvious—placement of these encumbrances, Jaxon was thinking, could readily prompt Adaeze to agree that other arms of the service might be ousted from their oikoi so that the forecasters could be housed in a manner more befitting their station. And out of her way, of course. He was considering the relative merits of various buildings when the regent spoke again.

'Have I? Jaxon, have I ever seen so much rain?'

The senior forecaster blinked, his own train of thought interrupted by her direct address. He suppressed the irritation that pinged through his biowires as they reacted strongly to the primacy of her question. Sealed into his very codes was his key directive to advise the regent, to place every scrap of his extensive data set at her instant disposal, no matter whether or not her request was fatuous. In more than two centuries, no other regent had interrupted his important thinking time with such inane wonderings. A pity that Adaeze, beautiful and vital as she was, did not quite have the intelligence to match her physical perfection. None of this showed on Jaxon's face as he ran the query in milliseconds.

'No, my lady, indeed you have not,' he said gently. He had found that, overall, an avuncular attitude was the best way to handle this young ruler.

'I thought not. Surely I would have remembered.'

Jaxon inclined his head. 'No doubt,' he agreed. 'Your memory is excellent, my lady. But in fact, there has been very little rain since the last aftershock, the PPA—the post-post-aftershock as we call it.'

He had also learned that, notwithstanding the superior grade of her liveware and software, it was wise to reinforce Adaeze's knowledge of the Pale's history at every opportunity. Her education had been skimped in the rush to replace the former regent, and indeed her attention span was not quite of the quality that previous rulers had enjoyed. Of course, for many matters, that was all to the good. Jaxon outlined the recent history of their weather clearly, in simple terms, reminding her of several other facts as he did so.

'Our rainfall has indeed been scarce, compared to previous decades. And as you, my lady, were no more than an unprogressed embryo at the time of the PPA, you could have no memory of the raging storms that occurred.'

'I have heard that said,' commented Adaeze, her golden brows slanted into a frown. 'That the storms were terrible. My, er, my cousin Élin spoke of those storms more than once.'

There was a short silence. Jaxon imagined that Adaeze, like him, was thinking of how the two of them had combined to bring the last regent's reign to an end, using a plot conceived by Jaxon and put into action by Adaeze. Élin Patraena had fallen to her death from the terrace at the top of the old regent's tower, assisted by a shove in the back from her chosen successor. However, this was a memory on which neither cared to dwell for too long.

'Oh, yes,' Jaxon replied calmly. 'All of us who experienced the PPA have very vivid memories of that time, my lady. Indeed, it was the ferocious and damaging nature of the weather that prompted your predecessor Élin to order the progression of the paramount embryos, including yourself, my lady. This happened long before she might have considered such an arrangement, in the usual way of things.'

'The usual way,' echoed Adaeze. She raised her face to the sky, looking through the curved dome that enclosed her roof garden to the low clouds that seemed to lean down, searching for entry into the policosmos.

Jaxon followed the direction of her gaze and frowned. Crystal beads of rain gathered into strings and chased a steady path south across the plexiglass, showing that the wind had swung around and was now coming from the north. Autumn weather from the north promised cold, and more cold. Likely the rain would soon turn to snow.

'There is nothing usual about any of this, is there?' Adaeze asked solemnly, turning to face him. 'This weather is, well, bizarre. Wrong. It's not normal, is it?'

Once more, Jaxon was jarred out of his own thoughts. He looked into the regent's perfect golden-brown eyes, reflecting that she seemed at last to have realised the gravity of their situation.

'No, my lady. Our policosmos is facing the most desperate crisis of our entire existence. You and I, Adaeze, must ensure that our citizens survive this period. As many of our citizens as can be saved, that is. The Pale must endure, must continue. Save the Pale—it is our first and foremost duty.'

'Yes, I know.' A great gust of wind rattled a handful of hail against the plexiglass roof. Adaeze looked up again, and then away. 'I am ready now. Call the senior officers to the meeting room.' As she spoke, she pointed at the single huddled servant waiting by the door, and the fellow turned immediately to the stairs to carry her message.

Jaxon heard her give a small sound of impatience, no doubt remembering the days, not so long ago, when she had been surrounded by dozens of lackeys, all dedicated to her comfort. Much had changed since Adaeze had ascended the throne.

More had changed since that disastrous crack had opened in the earth beneath the policosmos, splitting the Pale in two.

And Jaxon, for all his centuries of experience and his absolute command of every available data point, was not entirely sure that this was a situation they could overcome without a severe disruption to their comfortable existence. Nevertheless, he was determined that the Pale would survive, no matter the cost.

The cost to everyone but himself, of course.

Chapter 2

Enis saw Hippolyta waiting at the meeting place for the visitors to arrive. Behind her stood the huntmaster of the Storm, Marin, and his partner Willow, along with a handful of other tribesfolk who must have laid down their tasks to greet the visitors. They all stood expectantly, heads high, and Enis read a mix of hope and anxiety in their attitudes. He looked over his shoulder, making sure that the two men following him had found their way successfully through the complicated switchbacks of the thorn forest path. He was certain that Feather of the Storm would be most welcome to the group, but Jarli of the out-clan Owl smelled completely different. Enis was not sure what might happen when separate strands of humans faced each other.

'Leader,' he addressed Hippolyta in formal mindspeech, 'here are two travellers seeking speech with us.'

There was a pause while Hippolyta cocked her head to one side, lowering her nose politely. 'Welcome to our den, travellers,' she said. 'Please come forward where I can scent you.'

Enis looked up in time to see Feather smile broadly. The tribesman stepped close to the pack leader and dropped neatly onto one knee.

'Hippolyta, leader of the canini who guard the ravine,' he mind-spoke with every cadence of respect. 'We thank you for your welcome. I am Feather of the Storm, and I am very pleased to meet you.'

There was some muttering among the tribesfolk, and Enis saw Hippolyta's lip curl in amusement.

She grinned at Feather, motioning him to stand. 'Likewise. You have friends here, as you can see. We are all glad to see you rejoin your tribe. We have heard much about you.'

'Thank you,' said Feather, switching to speak aloud.

Enis saw that he looked briefly over Hippolyta's head, making brief eye contact with someone in the growing crowd, but that he swiftly brought his attention back to the pack leader.

'And your companion?'

'This is Jarli of the outclan Owl,' said Feather, waving Jarli forward to where Hippolyta could ceremoniously sniff him.

The young man stood stiffly. It was clear that he had no notion of what might happen next. Enis hid a smile. The youngster looked as if he thought Hippolyta might take a bite out of him.

'Jarli has no mindspeech?' asked Hippolyta, her mindvoice high with surprise.

'He appears to have no mindspeech,' agreed Feather, still voicing his words so that Jarli could follow. 'His clan, the Owl, is an outlier of the River, and they never had such clear mindspeech as the Storm. Yet I think he may hear an echo of our words.'

'Ah,' said Hippolyta. 'Callan has told me how strong in mindspeech you are, in particular, Feather of the Storm.'

'Callan! You know Callan?' Feather reverted to excited mindspeech, almost, thought Enis, as though it were his native language.

'Oh yes. He too is visiting the ravine. You will find him at the inner den. He will be glad to see you.'

Enis smiled again, knowing that there was more than one joyous reunion in store for Feather. Not only his old friend Callan, the big white canine who had once led the pack that ran for many years with the Storm, but also Feather's daughter Freya would be waiting to greet him. Freya would be impatient, as only humans could be. Callan would be overjoyed, quivering with gladness to see his friend again.

'This is such joy to me,' said Feather, 'to find not only my tribe here, but also my greatest friend.'

Hippolyta inclined her head again. 'I foresee many happy hours.' She raised her snout, her nose twitching again at the unaccustomed scent of Jarli. 'What of your companion?'

Feather changed back to speaking aloud, making sure that every-one would understand his words. Enis noticed that Jarli's shoulders loosened a little at the reversion to ordinary human speech.

'My foster brother Jarli also has hopes of happy news here. Pack leader, we have been told that the ravine canini rescued two human babies from under the very gates of the cursed Pale.'

Silence once more overtook the meeting place. Enis found his heart beating hard and fast. Did this outclansman Jarli have something to do with his own human foster brothers, little Romulo and Remo?

'That is so,' Hippolyta answered cautiously. 'Our scout Mashtuk and our beloved pack member Zélie saved the little humans and have raised them for many months now.'

Enis jumped as Jarli broke into eager speech. 'Is it true? You found them? They are here?'

'They live here in the ravine with us,' Hippolyta confirmed to Feather.

'Yes, my brother, the pack leader tells us that your sons are alive!' said Feather gladly, putting an arm across Jarli's shoulders. The younger man seemed close to collapse.

Enis suppressed a yelp of surprise. All around the meeting place, tribesfolk and canini looked at one another in wonder. Enis caught a thread of distress that matched his own. His eyes met those of Willow across the crowded space. He saw her dream of adopting the twins fall and shatter, and he felt the clenching of his own heart. Those rescued twins, so beloved of his father Mashtuk, so much a part of the pack. Now it seemed that not one but two sets of humans were planning to take them away from the canini.

* * *

'Have we lost any more?' Adaeze asked in a crisp voice, her chin up and her gaze steady.

Jaxon narrowed his eyes in approval. Frightened the regent might be, but here in front of her most important officers she was doing her best to appear serene. Yes, Adaeze was acting perfectly well. A pity, really, that everyone else in the chamber could see the erratic pulsing of the fine biowires in her neck.

'Two more deceased, my lady,' he answered her gently. 'But we are still experiencing an excess of citizens in relation to our biofuel supply. Therefore these demises are not unexpected.'

'Two old service staff,' confirmed Hekili, master of the Wereguard. 'Out of refits, out of date. As the Senior says, no need to waste food on them.'

'And they did, after all, stay upright at their posts for much longer than we had any notion they were capable of,' contributed Hokulani, the Wereguard who currently occupied the post of Head of Service.

'Thank you, Hokulani. That is indeed a boon.' Adaeze cast her gaze along the line of her senior officers gathered in her new meeting room, a space that until recently had been the extensive dormitory of the Pale's trainee forecasters. While every piece of forecasting equipment had been relocated under the porticos of the grander go-ways, out of the weather and easy to access, the forecasters themselves, both the trainees and their seniors, had yet to find any accommodation of their own. Nothing, that is, suited to the importance and gravity of their calling.

That was not the business of today's meeting, of course. Jaxon reflected that of all his guild, he was the only one with a proper roof over his head, the only one not sleeping outside in the wet piazzas of the policosmos. Well, it was only fitting, he supposed. Without him, the Pale would entirely fail. That was the certainty that ruled his long life and underpinned every one of his schemes. Indeed, the weightiest matter of this meeting was the implementation of another such plan. He lifted his chin a little, drawing Adaeze's attention back to himself.

'As you say, my lady. Naturally, to advance the interests of the Pale is the utmost desire of every one of our citizens. I have no doubt that those two service staff were completely content with their lot. They were extremely fortunate. Not every citizen is able to expend their life in so noble and heroic a manner.'

There was, and always had been, only so much information that was suitable for a regent to know, Jaxon reflected. No need to tell her of the contorted, emaciated bodies that had been discovered by the patrol, bodies so plundered and devastated that there was nothing worth the effort of recovery for the biofuel pits or the metal stacks. Of course, if they had more storage at their disposal … Jaxon stopped the thought. Half of the Pale's storage was gone, lost on the other side of the yawning chasm that now divided the policosmos. Until they could successfully build more tanks, their options were limited. Less biofuel dictated that fewer citizens could be fed. Well, those who did not rate a meal could still serve. Hence his proposal, to be finalised at this very meeting. He cleared his throat.

'Now that we are updated on that matter, it is time to move forward with our major project,' he said. 'My lady, Hokulani of the Service will favour us with an overview of the proposed actions.'

Adaeze nodded uncertainly, as if she was expecting to be over-whelmed by military details. Her knowledge of their situation had improved, but her understanding of the geography of Broad Plain was limited. As Hokulani rose ponderously to his feet, his massive bulk dominating the room, Jaxon called up a wall-sized screen. His repeated input of several commands eventually brought to life a map of the area, but he could not resist an irritated sidelong glance at Quauhtli, chief of the teshniks, whose staff had notably failed to stabilise either the com-munications or the visuals across the whole of the Pale. Comms pillars stayed silent or emitted ear-splitting static; screens flickered, jumped, and faded to blackness; and as for the complete failure of the viewfind-ers! Until those could be repaired, the Pale was reduced to using *actual citizens*—service personnel who could be better deployed elsewhere—to watch over Broad Plain and guard the walls. Really, the sooner the teshniks provided some properly functional gear, the better.

Putting aside his annoyance for the moment, Jaxon lifted his hand for attention and indicated the blurry section of the map that repre-sented the agrarian Settlement to their south.

'This,' he said, 'is our goal. We will collect all their technology and as much of their infrastructure as seems useful to us. As much as we can readily transport. We suspect that the settlers may also have fresh food stores that we can acquire, which we can consume readily without the need for storage. For example, they have always kept ovines and fowl, foodstuff that can in effect transport itself, rather conveniently.'

Adaeze nodded. Ailani, the head of recycling, opened her eyes wide. Charged as she was with overseeing both victualling and sanitation, the news of live animals being introduced inside the rigidly cleansed policosmos was not entirely welcome. Jaxon made an internal note to consult with her separately after the meeting. No doubt arrangements would be needed to maximise their use of such primitive foodstuffs. He caught Ailani's eye as he went on, and she gave a small grimace as she settled back into her seat. In truth, her growing reliance on him was gratifying, if a little cloying.

'We will also gather as many humans as we can manage,' Jaxon continued. 'Only those who are strong enough to work for us, of course, so that we can use them for as long as they last. My lady, and respected seniors, Hokulani will now describe our raid.'

'When does the party leave?' interrupted Teiuc, the foremost ingeneer, who was inordinately eager to get his hands on new materials.

'Tomorrow,' Hekili confirmed in response to Jaxon's raised brows. 'Or the next day, depending on this rain. The one after, it may be. But there is no time to be lost. Every day our food supplies dwindle. We need to restock the Pale as soon as possible with as many goods as we can collect.'

'And we also need to reduce our oversupply of hungry citizens,' murmured Jaxon, thinking contentedly about how many advantages there were to the raiding scheme. Aloud he said, 'Hokulani, the board is yours.'

* * *

'I am so glad to see the last of the rain,' said Valkirra. 'There is still much to be done if we are to have any degree of comfort during the winter months.'

'I've been thinking about that,' replied Talis.

He took a place on the bench beside her and watched for a few moments while she finished shelling the last handful of their summer broad bean crop. The beans were shrivelled and brown at the edges, but they would contribute their mite of flavour and bulk to the stew she was preparing for that evening's meal. Talis smiled to himself. There was something very comforting about watching his partner, once the powerful chief of the Settlement, combine the last gleanings of their modest harvest into a palatable supper, just as any goodwife might have done through the ages. As any frugal crofter would have done, even in the long-ago days before the Great Conflagration set them all on their diverse paths to survival. Such a homely action, surely going back to the very beginning of human culture and society.

'Of course you have.' Valkirra's words startled him, dragging him back to the present time.

If Talis had a fault that tripped him up more than once, it was his habit of reverie about the past, over the meanings of words and actions, over the contrasts and continuities of their existence. He shook his head of musings and met Valkirra's rather annoyed gaze with an abashed apology.

'Of course!' he agreed. 'The autumn rains have been the heaviest for many a year, and the elders believe we are in for a hard winter.'

'They say that every autumn,' Valkirra said shortly. 'And in spring they say that the summer will be the hottest, and in winter they say that the coming spring will be the windiest they have ever known. Here, take this.'

She handed him the platter of chopped vegetables, rising to lead the way over to the firepit at one end of the hall. She uncovered the great iron cooking pot, using two hands and a thick cloth to lift the lid. Valkirra gestured with her chin, and Talis carefully tipped the rest of the vegetables into the simmering liquid. At another brief gesture, he took hold of the largest stirring spoon and made sure that all the ingredients were combined to her satisfaction. With a little grunt, Valkirra replaced the lid, put the cloth by the spoon on the nearby table, and wiped her hand across her brow.

'And the more often they say such things,' she complained, 'the more likely they will come to pass. All they need to do is choose the most fitting prediction, and ignore all their other contradictory ones.'

'True,' agreed Talis. 'But this year, I believe they may be right.'

'Oh?' Valkirra straightened and looked him in the eye. Talis was grateful, as ever, for the ready understanding between them. Valkirra knew by the tone of his voice that he had something important to say.

'We have been searching the records. You know that the Temple acolytes who came with us—'

'A handful who no longer believed that the Temple has all the answers,' said Valkirra. 'And who now study philosophy and history with you. What of them?'

'Only when we are not working in the fields and on the walls,' protested Talis. 'But we were able to bring many of the old records with us, mostly the handwritten ones of the early days. Records that had never been sung onto the screens. Records that were considered so out of date as to be worthless.'

Valkirra groaned and linked her arms through his. 'If you're going to give me a long lecture,' she said, 'can we at least walk while we talk? I've been stuck in this room most of the day, dealing with the last of the harvest. The stew can look after itself for a while.'

'Of course. Let's walk the walls.'

'Certainly. The children?'

'With Iver.'

Both Jasper and Cushla, as their parents well knew, grabbed any opportunity to go Outside and could not truly be trusted near the boundary lines of Newkeep. Valkirra preferred them to stay within the walls, flimsy as they were. She nodded her satisfaction and nestled close to her spouse as they continued through the compound toward the gateway.

The walk was a circuit they made daily, sometimes lingering to share a few words with the other members of their new community, and sometimes so deep in discussion that they seemed barely aware of their surroundings. Although there was, by Valkirra's decree, no discrimination of status at Newkeep Port, still Talis was aware that they were treated with a specific respect that bordered on awe. Valkirra never seemed to notice. As he chose the best words to explain his concerns to her, he took pains to make eye contact with his fellow settlers, to smile and nod at the children, to give no sign that he had any particular concern at all. Nevertheless, he also made sure that he kept his voice low.

'Valkirra, my heart, I believe we may indeed be in for a harsh winter. From the early records, we can tell that there has been more autumn rain this year than for several generations. The last time there was so much rain—well before your father's time, indeed even before his father's time—there was flooding in this region as the rain travelled through the Broken Ranges and down into Founders River.'

'Was the Settlement flooded?' asked Valkirra.

'The records say that there was some kind of washout at the river gate. You recall, that gate is set high on steps now—one walks up to it, through it, and then descends into the Settlement. We suspect that the entry was raised after the flood, though there is no mention of such an undertaking.'

'So the records are not complete?'

'Records never are.' Talis shook his head. 'The people writing them leave things out, or forget, or don't even think to mention anything that seems perfectly obvious to them. In any case, that's not all that I wanted you to know.'

'Oh?' Valkirra paused, turning to look at his face.

'The records may not describe alterations to the river gate, but they do mention flood damage,' he said. 'Downriver from the Settlement, it seems the land was impassable for several weeks.'

'Downriver?' repeated Valkirra.

'Yes. Where we now stand. Where we have built Newkeep Port.'

'Ah.' Valkirra started walking again, a little more quickly. 'And you fear we may have floods again?'

Talis shrugged. 'Impossible to say for certain. It is not clear which area downriver from the Settlement was flooded, and it was also a very long time ago. Much may have changed on the land since then. The aftershocks, you understand, especially the most recent one. Rivers have been shaken out of their courses. New heights have sprung up while others have plummeted into new valleys. Broad Plain is very much changed, from what our tribal friends tell us.'

'And who can say what might have happened in the Broken Ranges, or beyond?' mused Valkirra. 'There was no alteration to the Founders River after the most recent aftershock, we know that much. Why should we suspect that anything happened to disrupt its sources? What if the land beyond is just the same as it was all those years ago?'

'That's exactly what has me worried,' confessed Talis. 'If Founders River runs the same as it ever did, will we see flooding again from this prodigious rainfall? I believe it seems likely.'

'I feared that was what you were going to say,' said Valkirra. 'Is there anything we can do?'

'That is what we need to talk about. I wanted to tell you first, but we must discuss this with everyone, I think.'

'Yes, I see. But knowing you, my heart, you have a plan? Or two, perhaps.'

Talis put his arm across her shoulders. 'Are you game for a walk on the Outside, my love? My plan involves a drainage ditch around our boundary, and sand reinforcements to the base of our palisade.'

'If I must,' murmured Valkirra, walking a little closer to her spouse as they exited through the river gate. 'You know I'm still not happy being Outside.'

'Most of us dislike it,' agreed Talis. 'But there are enough of us workers, I believe, to complete the project.'

'Hmm.' Valkirra came to a halt, her gaze running along the length of Newkeep Port's raw enclosure. Large timbers had been sunk into the heavy red dirt at intervals, and woven hurdles of reeds, willow, and thatching stretched between them, reinforced with hand-thrown clay. At each corner, pillars of worked stone, stone reclaimed from the demolition of excess buildings in the Settlement itself, rose like heralds of the sturdy wall that would one day enfold their community in safety. 'Tell me your plan.'

Talis took hold of her hand as he strode around the circumference, one eye on the waning light. No one wanted to be Outside when dusk began to roll into night. He walked a little more quickly.

'Well, say we dig a wide drain, perhaps an arm's length from the base of the wall or more. Whatever measure the builders among us say. We pile the soil against the base of our walls, angling it down in slopes toward the ditch. We should coat the sand with clay to make it stronger, but I fear we have left it a bit late in the year. The clay won't dry.'

'Probably not,' agreed Valkirra. 'But how will a drain serve us? Won't the river flood into the drain as soon as it runs above its banks?'

'Ah, I see what you're thinking. Yes, our drainage from the compound runs down into the river, that is true. I was thinking that this ditch could be dug to drain behind us, sending any excess water back onto Broad Plain. We are after all on something of a rise, and if we provide a route for the rising river to bypass us, then we may escape the worst of any flooding.'

'And the drains in our compound? Won't they allow flood waters in?'

Talis nodded slowly, lifting a hand to his chin as he considered this point. 'A good thought. We need to prepare alternatives. Come, let us bring this to the others. I'm sure they will have good ideas too.'

'I suspect there will be much discussion,' said Valkirra. She tugged on his arm, dragging him back toward the northern gate, closest to where they stood.

Talis quickened his step; night was creeping toward them, and Outside was not the place to meet it.

Chapter 3

Hector had almost completed his turn at watch. Any moment now, Tsendi would come down to relieve him, and one of the Storm's scouts would be with her. Paolo, maybe, or perhaps Freya. There! Something above made a ripple in the rainwater streaming down the incline onto the ruddy soil of Broad Plain. Hector stood and watched as Freya and Tsendi scrambled down to the sentry post.

'All quiet?' asked Freya, looking up as she reached his side, one hand settling the hood on her waxed canvas jacket.

'No problems. Every living thing is staying out of the rain. And above?'

Tsendi arrived in time to answer this. She padded forward to peer over the edge of the post, reassuring herself that nothing was approaching, and then looked back over her shoulder at him.

'Uproar,' she told him airily. 'What did you expect? Freya's father has arrived, and the Storm are behaving like cubs set free from the winter den.'

Freya smiled at Hector's raised brows. 'My father is somewhat special to his tribe, our tribe, I should say. By all rights, he should be the leader, not Marin.'

Hector frowned. 'How is that? And why are you not with him?'

Freya flapped a hand at him. 'We have days and days ahead of us. We will talk when things grow quieter. Besides, he needs food and rest, and I have sentry duty to attend to.'

Hector noticed that she did not answer his question about the tribal leadership, but he did not repeat it. Human conversations were rather more formless than the interchanges between the humachines of the Pale. In general, he liked the eddying range of topics that humans covered, although sometimes—as now—he was left floundering after meanings that eluded him. He tipped his head at Tsendi, and the young canine grinned up at him.

'Go on, you're expected above,' she said. 'And did Enis tell you the best news? Mashtuk has awoken.'

Hector nodded. 'He said so. But not speaking yet.'

Freya, settling into the pinch point, turned at that. 'It seems that he hears the twins, so perhaps his speech may return.'

'Oh! That is good news.'

Tsendi, looking over Freya's shoulder to peer down the entry path, muttered some words that Hector did not catch. It was rare for any of the canini to hide their minds from him. Hector stood still, wondering what had been said, a tingle of unease along his nerves. Just as he was about to leave them to their work, Freya reached out and touched his hand, as if she recognised his disquiet.

'The second man, the other traveller. Jarli of the outclan Owl. It seems that Romulo and Remo are his children. You will find much doubt and confusion above. Nobody knows yet what he intends.'

Hector let out a slow breath. A human with an undeniable claim to the rescued twins. That tinge of genetic connection that he had sensed was no random link.

He looked down at Freya and nodded his thanks. As he climbed up to the entry and made his way carefully through the thorn forest, he realised that the haven of kinship he had found with the ravine canini was about to be disrupted.

* * *

Too many days had passed.

Helm folded his arms across his chest as he looked out of the Newkeep hall, squinting against the watery brightness spilling from the low sun. Hall, they called this half-made, scarcely weatherproof building. He bit his lip. The autumn rains might be coming to an end, but if he was not mistaken, the mean fist of winter was about to close its cold fingers around them. The new settlers had never experienced a winter Outside. Helm frowned. They would have to learn, and he would not be there to aid them. The little rat terrier was right. Too many days had passed.

He bent one knee so he could crouch down beside her. Like him, Rasti was focused on the world beyond rather than the stuffy confines of the hall. She sat erect, her small folded ears pointing forward, a wrinkle of concentration on her forehead as she stared intently at the fence that ran down to the river. That was the gate through which her beloved Feather had gone, too many days ago, promising to return soon. Helm put one hand onto the little dog's back. He could feel the bony points of her spine, the shivery nature of her breathing. Like him, she was finding the wait difficult. Though the injury to her leg had healed well, she was losing condition fast. Only the promise of Feather's return, it seemed, kept her eating at all.

With his palm against her fur, Helm found it easier to hear the little dog's scant and muddled mindspeech. However strong he was in the language that intelligent animals shared with humans, Rasti was weak. Only Feather had the ability for prolonged and detailed conversation with her. Helm took a deep breath, wishing like Rasti that his son would return. But wishing alone would not bring Feather back to them. As Rasti said too often: too many days, too many days. Helm ran his hand caressingly down the little dog's skinny back.

'Too many days indeed, my friend. Shall we go find my son?'

Rasti turned her head to look up at his face. There was a half-moon of white worry around her dark eyes. 'Find?'

Helm nodded, and amplified his idea with hand gestures. 'You, me. We walk. Find Feather.'

That had Rasti on her feet. 'Find Feather!' she agreed. Without looking back, she trotted immediately toward the gate.

Helm stood. 'Wait!' he called aloud. Rasti looked over her shoulder, one front paw raised, all of her scanty weight leaning forward in the direction she wanted to go. 'Wait at the gate,' he said. 'A little. Just wait for me.'

Rasti narrowed her eyes at him. Then she lowered her head in agreement. 'Wait,' she whispered. 'Gate. Walk. Find Feather.'

'That's right. Let me get some gear, let me tell Jana. Maybe she wants to come with us.'

Helm noticed that Rasti trotted to the gate without looking back again. He watched until she sat, obedient but impatient, her whole attention focused on the Outside. Then he turned back into the hall to make the quickest preparations he could. Now that the decision had been made, he realised that in his heart of hearts, he had been planning this for some time. Most of his gear he had already put aside, ready for picking up in an instant. Rasti would not have long to wait.

* * *

'I never thought to belong to such a pack,' said Callan, one paw scratching busily behind his ear.

'Nor I,' commented Feather, cross-legged on the hard floor of the pack's main den. He shifted a little as Callan leaned back against him. On his other side, the half-grown canini cubs Niccolò and Rhosyn were tangled in slumber, their paws occasionally flapping against his leg in a dream run. Feather watched as Callan rose to all four feet, shook himself vigorously, and then settled again by his side with a long, soft exhalation. In the hours since they had rediscovered each other, the big white canine and the tribal envoy had been inseparable.

Freeing one hand to stroke a bit of comfort over Callan's back, Feather looked around the den. From where they sat against the far wall, they had an excellent view of the astonishing company they shared. By the entrance, Hippolyta, the leader of the ravine canini, was engaged in serious conversation with Marin, huntmaster of the Storm tribe, and his partner Willow. Beside Willow, Jarli sat quiet and frowning, listening much more than he spoke. From the way he leaned close every time Willow spoke, Feather guessed that the Storm's foremost couple had recognised the outclansman as the father of the twins, a man whose claim to raise them was greater than Marin and Willow's plan to adopt. The older pair were probably trying to convince Jarli to stay with the tribe rather than taking his infants back to the less safe life of the outclan Owl. Feather was glad to be out of that conversation. The decision was Jarli's, and it would not be easy.

For himself, his only thought was to return as quickly as possible to the new settlement of Newkeep Port, where Jana and little Rasti would be waiting. His father Helm, too. The easy, joyful reunion he had with his own daughter Freya, here in the ravine, had made him think again that he should make more of an effort to bond with his father. He was uncomfortably aware that he had not only failed to mention Helm's return to Freya or to anyone else in the tribe, but also that he had avoided serious discussion with Helm during the weeks they had laboured at the Newkeep site. He swallowed his worries. Problems for another day. It was enough to enjoy the nearness of Callan and the sense of happy community that pervaded the ravine.

In the space between the elders and the den, a handful of tribal children slept among the rest of the canini, human and canini young mingled in attitudes of casual trust while their parents guarded the ravine. He had not seen such a thing since the days when the packs of Callan and Waleen had shared their lives with the Storm. It was a pleasant sight. Lifting his gaze, Feather could see the shadows of equii—Pinto and Violeta, whom he had met within minutes of reaching the ravine. He had been told that the senior equii liked to visit the canini every few days, taking it into their round of the territory as they led the rest of the herd from pasture to pasture. It had given him much joy to find that quite a large herd of equii had found shelter here in the ravine. On their journey, he and Jarli had seen more bones than they cared to study, but Feather was sure that some of them were equii. He had feared that all of them, all the herd who had run from their confined life in the Settlement, had perished on the unforgiving stretches of Broad Plain. That many had found safety, and that at least some of them had once more opened their minds to speech, was an unexpected but joyful discovery.

'That was a good thought of yours, Callan,' he commented, indicating the visitors.

Callan looked away, hiding some emotion. 'For them, I daresay. There was no future for them out on Broad Plain. I don't know that they've added much to our comfort, though.'

Feather smiled at the back of Callan's head. 'They have rediscovered their language, and they are safe. Knowing that must be counted as a benefit to all of us as well. Their lives are precious, and worth saving.'

'Hmm.' Callan sent a look back over his shoulder, his face creased in the semblance of a grin. 'Trust you to find some good in that. As long as they don't completely strip the ravine, I suppose there will still be food for all.'

'Undoubtedly.'

They stayed silent for a while, enjoying the contentment of their reunion. The afternoon was fading, and Feather noticed a ripple of movement as the next detail of lookouts left to take up position at the pinch point of the trail. A good sentry post, but also a death trap, by everything Callan had told him. He waved back at Freya as she returned from her stint on guard, glad that he had seen no sign of the giant vulpini horde as he and Jarli had crossed Broad Plain. They had encountered only carcasses. In fact, it looked as if the vulpini had grown to excessive size and then suddenly died, all their life-force sucked out of them by the freakish growth spurt. Interesting.

Just as the thought stuck him, he saw the humachine Hector join the group by Hippolyta. The big silvery creature sat at the leader's feet, accepting a bowl of stew that one of the Storm youngsters handed him.

Feather stilled his hand on Callan's back. 'And that one,' he said softly. 'What is he? Who is he? Can we trust him, Callan?'

'Ah!' answered Callan. 'That is Hector of the Ravine. Mashtuk adopted him. He is to be trusted, yes.'

'He's from the Pale,' murmured Feather, frowning, although he heard the faith and affection in his friend's voice.

'Let me tell you his story,' offered Callan.

* * *

Brettin, Lady of the Temple and now leader of the diminished Settlement, sat with her usual feeling of faint distaste as she listened to the ill-considered speeches of various members of the Settlement's Assembly. Though she would never admit it, the task of managing the discussions at Assembly was more difficult than she expected. Every now and then she recalled with envy the power of Valkirra's voice and the calming gaze of her spouse Talis. A single word from Valkirra, or a direct look from Talis, had generally reminded any wayward speaker that he or she was in a formal meeting with a defined set of rules.

Assemblies in Valkirra's time had rarely descended to the pointless, vapid repetitions that passed for engaged debate under the current arrangements. Sadly, Brettin reflected, it was the new-found eminence of the Temple officers that she found most annoying. None of them had much experience in the formalities of the Settlement's political systems, and they behaved as if the Assembly delegates were nothing more than a congregation of Temple worshippers, hanging on their every sacred word. Esteri, the ageing son of the previous Lady of the Temple, had an especially overblown appreciation of the importance of his opinion.

'But we cannot return to our former ways!' he was saying. 'Our renewed Settlement must run along more traditional lines, with due reverence and proper observances. The importance of markets cannot compare with our duties of daily contemplation and worship.'

'Much you know!'

Anielka's words were laced with a contempt that surprised Brettin. She had always counted Anielka as one of her staunchest supporters, a woman with marked—if not strongly felt—reverence for the rites of the Temple. Brettin made an open gesture with her hands, preparing to speak, but the discussion continued around her and over her with no sign that anyone even recognised that she was in the room.

'And what do you suggest we should live on?' Olinna was asking. 'The tribes have abandoned us. Why should they make the effort to deal with us when the Temple orders their traders away from our walls? The tribes no longer bother to come anywhere near us. Of course they don't! They never get further than the gate guards. All because you force us to stay indoors and meditate every morning, and to gather in the Temple compounds at sunset to pay reverence to the Power of Light!'

'Making a show of asking it to come back the next day,' came a muttering from the far end of the table.

'Pretending that the sun won't rise unless the Temple makes a special request,' someone else added in a tone even more tinged with scorn.

'Blasphemy!' Esteri got to his feet, trying to see who had spoken. He was not a tall man, and as the district delegates shifted in their chairs, leaning forward to hide their smiles in their hands or deliberately to prevent him seeing which of them had voiced the comments, he wrung his hands in frustration.

'The Temple leaves us no trading hours worth the mention. Lady? Do you have aught to say of this?' Anielka at last turned her attention to Brettin, not entirely to the Lady's comfort.

Brettin drew in a breath, and around her, finally, the members of the Assembly grew silent to hear her words. Relishing the pause, she lifted her chin as if she had merely been waiting for proper order to be restored before she deigned to speak. Esteri was still on his feet, looking like an undersized and befuddled rooster. Brettin raised her brows at him, and he straightened his robes and sat down again, a hectic colour staining his wrinkled cheeks. Brettin took her time, meeting the eyes of those gathered about the table.

'I hear what you say,' she said as calmly as she could. 'And I understand something of your distress, district delegates. But I thought we had all agreed, when the split in our community occurred, that we would return to our traditional ways.'

Anielka sat forward, one hand raised in a commanding gesture. 'Much as I dislike to disagree with you, Lady, that was not our agreement.'

'It was!' Esteri piped up. 'It was! The Settlement was to revert to its traditions. To have proper respect for the Temple.'

'Not so,' said Olinna, her enormous headdress quivering with the contained passion of her anger. 'I for one voted for no change. No change in Assessment, and no change to our usual round of business.'

'That's right!' said another delegate. 'None of us here wanted to go with Valkirra and return to the starveling days. We voted to remain as we are.'

'We did.' Anielka was adamant. 'What we voted for was to maintain Assessment. To keep the low-Assessed at their work, and allow the high-Assessed freedom to attend to their responsibilities. Their positions of power.'

'We certainly didn't agree to restricting trade and giving the Temple the last say in how we order our days. Our split was about Assessment, and nothing else.'

Brettin stood, and a shocked silence fell in the meeting room. As she drew her robes close about her throat, the Lady looked down her perfect little nose, her flawless white skin somewhat marred by a mottling of anger.

'I hear you, delegates,' she said softly. 'And I do not like what I hear. Do none of you have any reverence for the Temple? Respect for us who have shielded you from the worst excesses of your own natures? Is it not the Temple that has overseen Settlement partnering for generations? Who else will keep the stain of genetic modification out of our community? Well?'

Anielka flapped her hands in something close to contempt, waving the Lady's words away. At least twice Brettin's age and with a lengthy record of active delegation and debate, she had never been cowed by Valkirra's haughty ways and Brettin could see that she had a very low opinion of her own shaky grasp of the leadership. Her cheeks flaming, Brettin spoke in words of ice.

'When any of you has recovered your temper sufficiently to speak to me with proper civility, you may request admittance to my office. Until then, I suggest you attend to your own districts and to your own business. I will not have Temple matters bandied about in such a way. Temple business, let me remind you, is not for your discussion or your criticism. I advise you to focus on your own meagre concerns. I say it now and I say it for good: we will go on with proper observances. We will not fall back into the irreverent, heedless ways that almost brought about our downfall.'

Pretending not to hear the angry muttering behind her, Brettin swept from the room, Esteri and Blazej hurrying to catch up with her. She was horrified to find that her hands were shaking, and quickened her steps. The words 'damned Temple interference' and 'that woman's stupidity' reached after her, doing nothing to soften her determination to exercise Temple control to its fullest extent.

CHAPTER 4

'But we thought you would spend the winter with us!' cried Valkirra.

Helm blinked. This was not the reaction he expected to the news that he was leaving Newkeep to seek out his son. Instinctively he looked across at Talis Jarisson, Valkirra's partner, to get an idea of how to respond to her protest. Talis was an expert in managing his partner's moods and in assisting others to deal with her. Although she was not especially moody, Valkirra was accustomed to command and Helm knew that she had somewhat limited insight into the needs of others. On this occasion, though, Helm found that Talis looked every bit as dumbfounded and affronted as Valkirra. He took a deep breath.

'I must find my son,' he told them. 'He has been gone too long. You know this is so. An exploration of some few days, to try to discover some trace of Jarli's twins, was what he said. That was all he set out to do.'

'And it has been weeks.' Talis spoke with a heavy heart. If Valkirra did not know it, at least her partner recognised that they had no hold over the tribesman.

'Yes,' agreed Helm. 'Perhaps they found trouble. Perhaps they had to journey further. Perhaps they need help.'

Valkirra sat on the long bench and put her elbows on the table, her head in her hands. 'I am sorry,' she mumbled. 'Forgive me. I thought—I thought you were settled here with us.'

'I too,' put in Talis. He sat beside his wife, and indicated that Helm should take a seat opposite. 'I had hoped for more of your help, I confess. You have been so much a part of all we have achieved this summer. Without you, we would have no hope of surviving the winter in our new home.'

Helm sat reluctantly. Everything was taking so long. His heart was protesting just like Feather's little dog Rasti—all he wanted was to go, go and find Feather. Sometimes the need was so urgent that his heart clenched like a fist in his chest. He leaned a little forward and clasped his hands between his knees. He couldn't spare the time to begin a long conversation about whatever new project Talis had in mind, or how the little community could best live through the cold months, even though a part of him wanted to give them warnings, wanted to impart advice. He looked down, unwilling to let them see the doubt in his eyes, bidding the impatient fluttering of his heart to calm.

'My friends, I am sorry if I have not been clear about myself. I am a tribesman. I do not stay long inside walls if I can help it.'

'Like your son,' Talis said, nodding.

'But you seemed so at home with us!' protested Valkirra. 'You are always—you were always so happy in our hall. I thought you liked the talk, the company.'

Helm inclined his head. 'I am happier in company than Feather is, that is true. Perhaps a little more comfortable with walls, but then again, there is much I have learned to tolerate on my journey that I would not choose. If I had a choice.'

'You chose to help us build those walls,' said Talis. 'You chose to stay inside them, flimsy as they are.'

Helm got to his feet slowly, making sure that his whole body confirmed his intent. 'That is true, Talis, my friend. I chose to assist. I wanted to put what little knowledge I have to use. I wanted to help you, but in truth I know more of camps than of permanent walls. And my time and strength—of course, while I stayed with you, you were more than welcome to my work. But now I must go, truly.'

'Now? Tomorrow morning, surely, would be better?'

'I am sorry, Talis,' answered Helm. 'I cannot stay longer. Morning, noon, night: I can travel at any time.'

'Does Jana go with you?' asked Valkirra, a frown between her brows. The idea of losing another member of their group was obviously not welcome.

Helm was able to reassure her. 'No, Jana will stay here. She has every confidence that Feather will return to her here. He always has, in truth.'

'You have your doubts about that?' Talis asked, rising to his feet too.

Helm tilted his head again. 'I do not know. I feel I must find him first. It may well be that he is even now on his way back to her.'

Valkirra stood too, a smile of resignation on her pale face. 'We are sorry to see you leave,' she said simply. 'We hope you will one day visit us again.'

'That may well happen,' agreed Helm, touched by their evident feeling for him. He shrugged his jacket over his shoulders and went to retrieve the neat pack he had left at the entry to the hall. He settled his bow over one shoulder; the thin, sharp knife he had carried for many winters rested in its sheath on his belt.

Valkirra and Talis walked with him toward the river gate, and Helm noticed several heads turn to watch them pass. Despite the months he had spent among these people, helping them to build a home here on the banks of the wide Founders River, Helm felt no desire to share farewells with any others, just as Rasti had never joined the cheerful troupe of rat terriers who lived here with the pilgrims. All their focus was on finding his son.

The little rat terrier was waiting, looking out of the gate toward the dull red expanse of Broad Plain. She jumped up as they approached and gave one excited yap. Then she turned immediately and trotted away without looking back.

'Somebody's trying to make a head start on you,' commented Talis.

'She's impatient,' said Helm. 'She would have gone days ago had I not dissuaded her.'

'I keep forgetting,' Valkirra murmured, 'that you can speak with her.'

'Feather has more skill than I in mindspeech,' said Helm. 'But we understand each other well enough, that little creature and I.'

Talis looked puzzled. 'That's not the way they went,' he said. He pointed to where Rasti was heading diagonally north-east across the plain. 'Feather and Jarli went directly north toward the Pale.'

Helm hefted his pack. 'Tracking them now would be impossible, after all that rain. I'm content to let Rasti lead. She'll follow her heart.' He looked up to find Talis and Valkirra glancing at each other, and gave a soft laugh. 'Rat terriers as well as canini,' he said, 'generally know where to find the others of their pack. I don't know how they do it exactly. But I trust her to find Feather.'

'I am sure you will find him,' Valkirra said formally. 'And we wish you success in your search.'

'Indeed,' Talis echoed. 'Fare you well, Helm of the Storm. May your search succeed, and your journey be safe.'

Helm bowed his head in salute and followed in the wake of the terrier. Already he was calculating how far they could walk before they sought shelter for the night. They could keep going for two or three hours, he reckoned, before they would need to find a safe place. Every living creature knew that the open expanse of Broad Plain was no place to be trapped in the darkness.

* * *

A day after the rain stopped, Adaeze stood on her domed terrace, her eyes narrowed as the sodden expanse of Broad Plain glistened in a watery sunlight.

'How soon until the troops can leave?'

'A day or two yet, my lady,' replied Jaxon. 'There is little to be gained by marching while the ground is still saturated. We will wait until the plain dries out somewhat. That will allow us to make full use of wheels and wagons. We will therefore travel more quickly, and arrive not many hours later than if we set out this minute and tramped our way through the mud.'

'I see. Are we so ill-suited for marching across Broad Plain?'

'My lady.' Jaxon stepped forward, joining the regent in her study of the rather dismal view. 'We humachines have been designed and perfected over several generations to live inside the ordered policosmos. As the Pale was built to suit our needs, so we have gradually adapted ourselves to match it.'

'But service patrols regularly go Outside! They clean up the debris around the walls, and collect material for the stacks and the tanks. Why can they not march further through the Outside to reach the Settlement?'

'We built go-ways around the Pale,' Jaxon reminded her, 'many decades ago. Once we had become self-sustaining, there was no need for us to travel any further into dangerous territory. We developed better methods of covering the ground. Any ground we needed to cover, that is.'

'You mean the wheels that the service personnel wear?'

'Wear is not quite the word. The wheels that are embedded into service liveware, yes. These were designed for smooth go-ways, not for the degenerate landscape of the Outside.'

'Our citizens did not always have this hardware?'

'No, my lady. In the early years, we had much occasion to venture Outside. Our aim then was to collect as many resources of value as we could. We harvested what we could from every available source and worked our way through extremely difficult terrain. The go-ways were not laid until much later.'

Adaeze nodded. 'And using those recovered resources, we created the richest, safest haven in the land.'

Jaxon opened his mouth to murmur a comfortable agreement, and then said nothing, leaving the regent's words to close the discussion. He was well aware that the magnificent policosmos, his home for over two hundred years, was facing its most dangerous challenge yet. Unless they could capture enough materials to repair the gaping chasm that had opened beneath their feet, they too would be homeless in the ruined land of the Outside.

* * *

Brettin had always loved this room. Previously the private study of the Settlement's chief, it had a large glazed window that looked over the chief's private garden and beyond, offering a view of the town below. The four plazas, one near each of the main gates, were surrounded by the stately manses of the richer merchants, and connected by a network of neat cobbled laneways, wide enough for the passing of a cart drawn by two equii. Brettin huffed, a short sound of annoyance. Most of the equii had left the Settlement soon after Valkirra and her ragtag runaways had made their noisy and foolish exodus. No matter.

Luckily, enough breeding stock remained to begin a new herd, and the lack would soon be mended. In the meantime, smaller carts and hand trolleys would suffice.

Brettin frowned, looking beyond the four major entryways to the lowest gate of all, the river gate situated between the furthest reaches of the Lower Town and the banks of the wide Founders River. There was now a sizeable expanse of empty ground stretching from the last of the workers' dwellings to the wooden palisade that ran along the river. Since the runaways had left, the settlers had dismantled as many buildings as they could conveniently live without, happily gifting the materials to the creation of the new site downriver. The new site, the new settlement—Newkeep Port, she should call it, she supposed. That was the name they had chosen.

Brettin pursed her lips to prevent the escape of another breath of derision. An over-large name for a muddled heap of half-built shedding perched beside a flimsy pier on a riverbank, a place that had neither keep nor port. Nothing new about it, either, she reminded herself with a firm nod of her head. A patchwork of recycled boards and tiles and cut stones, no doubt, ill-made and unconvincing. Not that she had ever seen it. In fact, she had no intention of visiting the place. In her vision of the future, the community of Newkeep would depend wholly on the Settlement, bringing their wares to market and widening trade. Now that they lived on the Outside, they would be able to provide many of the goods that the tribes had brought to trade in former times. If Brettin had her way, the Settlement would never again deal with any tribesfolk. Better to transact their business with the runaways, who, despite their foolish decision to leave, still understood Settlement ways. It was despicable that they had decided to abandon their homes and responsibilities, but then discontent and a hunger for change at any cost was always present in any group, no matter how well-off. How fortunate that enough settlers preferred safety, tradition, and certainty. The Settlement would not suffer from their cowardly escape. However, that vacant land …

'Esteri,' Brettin called, startling her notary from his task of recording the latest offerings to the Temple. 'Tell me, have we finalised plans for the fallow fields by the river gate?'

He blinked at her rather stupidly, and once more Brettin had to swallow a feeling of annoyance. 'The … the fallow fields, my lady?'

'Yes, Esteri, the fallow fields. The land where the cottages of the helots formerly stood. Where the workers who failed Assessment once lived. You must know the place. Why has nothing been done to put that area to productive use?'

Esteri stood and gave her a bow indicating his comprehension. He looked at her uncertainly. Brettin tapped one finger on the windowsill.

'I am waiting,' she said when he made no further effort to speak.

'My lady. There is, that is, we do not—my lady, we do not at the moment have sufficient workers to plough those fields. Or to plant the seeds, or tend a crop, or manage a harvest, or …'

Brettin shook her head. 'Then those workers who remain must work longer hours. We simply cannot leave that land empty. Why, anyone looking at that space could well imagine that houses could be built there. Esteri, hear me. We must put that land to use. There must be no option available to the runaways within these walls. See to it.'

Esteri opened his mouth and shut it again. Brettin heard him swallow and saw how his eyes flickered from hers.

'My lady,' he faltered, 'the winter comes on. It is not the time for planting.'

Brettin laughed. 'This is not the time to be timid, you foolish man. We must make ourselves strong and independent. The river of life runs only in one direction: into the future. Nothing from Outside will ever live in here, let me tell you. Those who abandoned us will never return to our community.'

'But, my lady, but, the Assembly—'

'Will follow my orders. Am I not the Lady? Am I not the new chief of our Settlement?'

'I … I mean, yes, my lady, of course.'

'Then see that my orders are carried out.'

'Yes, my lady.'

Brettin watched him as he sketched a clumsy reverence and left her. She let out a long breath. If endless discussion was what the Assembly preferred, let them have it. Let them enjoy it! In the meantime, she would proceed with the business of running the Settlement, relying on her own judgement without the need for their interference and complaints. After all, the muddled combination of multiple viewpoints—democracy—was something they had recognised many generations before as stupidly dangerous. If the rule of the educated aristocracy had become just as muddled, she really had no choice. As Lady of the Temple, Brettin was almost forced to use her own wisdom as the sole guide to their prosperous future.

Feeling rather satisfied, she turned back to the window, confident that soon there would be no chance of any vacant ground tempting the return of the runaways.

* * *

Mashtuk liked the scent of the newcomer.

Not so new, now, he realised. Jarli had been part of the ravine community for some weeks. Mashtuk, only now beginning to work his way back onto all four feet, had grown very accustomed to Jarli's presence. He knew to his bones—every sense told him—that Jarli was pack with the human babies. Wherever Romulo and Remo were, there Jarli could be found. And that meant that wherever Mashtuk lay or sat, Jarli would be nearby.

'Walk,' he said to the two little ones, knowing they could understand his weak and muddled mindspeech better than the rest of the canini seemed to. In fairness, he found he understood the chatter of the human twins and the pack's cubs better than all the careful attempts of the adult canini. Something had shifted in his head after the severe wounds he had suffered during the disastrous attack of the vulpini.

That day was the worst of his life, worse even than the time of the dreadful post-post aftershock that had seen so many elderly, infirm, and juveniles die. He had been young and full of courage at that terrible time, and quivering with a fervour to live. Now, though—now was different. The vulpini had murdered his beloved Zélie and left him maimed and diminished. Mashtuk knew that his store of hope, his heart-deep eagerness for life and all it entailed, had deserted him. He knew he would live, that was true. If in early days it seemed that he was going to die of his wounds, those days were over. Life was his, and despite the gaping emptiness of Zélie's place and his own crippled being, he retained an irresistible need to keep breathing, to keep trying, to keep serving his pack in any and every way he could.

With Romulo at one shoulder and Remo on his other side, Mashtuk slowly raised himself to all fours. His balance was poor, but then his ears were all wrong. One was half-torn from his head, he knew, and despite the careful sewing efforts of Willow of the Storm, it didn't feel right. It felt lifeless, a burden. Like something stuck on his fur that he would prefer to fling off. Mashtuk panted with the effort of standing and resisted the instinct to shake. He had tried that before with no better result than an uncontrolled fall and a throbbing pain in his head. Damaged he might be, useless for the hunt and stupidly smudged in mindspeech, but he could still learn. So, don't shake. Let the little ones help with balance, speak to them in single words. Keep listening. Surely, surely his mind would soon clear enough for him to hear the others.

He was about to try walking forward when he noticed that Jarli had risen from his place by the wall and approached them. Mashtuk was surprised when the outclansman came and stood in front of him, and even more surprised when Jarli dropped onto one knee and spoke. His words were aloud, true, but Mashtuk began to suspect that a little of the mindspeech he shared with the twins was starting to mean something to their kinsman.

'Mashtuk,' Jarli said simply, 'I give you my thanks. But for you, my boys here would have died out there by the Pale.'

Mashtuk lowered his snout, looking up through his lashes at the young man. He could not find the words, but he blinked deliberately, saying as well as he could that no thanks were necessary. Then some words came.

'It is what I do.' Mashtuk pulled his head back, surprising himself at the clarity of his own mindspeech.

Jarli nodded as though he could hear the words. 'You are a beacon of hope, Feather tells me. He and Callan speak much of you and your knowledge. I can never thank you enough for your kindness.'

Mashtuk tilted his head to one side, letting the ugly torn ear dangle toward the ground. Romulo, feeling the unsteadiness of the moment, patted the ear encouragingly. It was such a strange but well-meaning little gesture that Mashtuk could not help but grin. Jarli smiled back.

Mashtuk felt his heart shift and boom. 'Pack,' he mindspoke, suddenly very sure of how he felt about this stranger. 'We are pack.'

'We are pack,' Jarli echoed aloud.

'Pack,' said Remo on Mashtuk's good side.

'Of course we are pack,' Romulo mindspoke. 'Come, Papa, walk.' Looking up, he reached one hand to Jarli and left the other resting on Mashtuk's back. Together they took a few faltering steps around the den. When they reached the resting place again, Mashtuk felt a sharp-edged gladness as Jarli sat much closer to him. He let out a long breath. In his heart he knew that Jarli was staking a claim to his sons, but he also knew that Jarli accepted him as part of their family. He felt the hurt and the warmth of that.

It was life.

It was enough.

Chapter 5

'Are you sure?'

Rasti whined in reply.

Helm squatted beside her. The terrier had her pointy black nose lifted as high as it could be—somewhere about the level of Helm's knee—and was sniffing industriously. She had been doing that for a long minute and had finally raised one front paw, indicating east. Helm squinted into the rising sun. They had spent the night hours huddled close together in the lee of a blasted tree, out of the chill wind but all too close to the hunting grounds of the panthera, to judge by the sounds that cascaded around them. Sleep had been impossible, and now at first light, Rasti seemed determined to lead them across the worst of the terrain. Impossible country, Helm would have said in his days as a tribesman. Now with many years' wandering behind him, he knew the seemingly impossible was not always so. He gave a nod. If this was the quickest way to find his son, then this was the way they would go.

'If you say so,' he muttered, shouldering his pack and patting his hands over the straps and buckles of his gear, checking and rechecking his preparations from long habit.

He knew Rasti preferred not to share her mind thoughts with him, if she could help it, and he respected that. Her mind partner was Feather. In the meantime, the two of them managed well enough with his words and her gestures. Helm considered himself somewhat of an expert at reading canini body shapes, vocalisations and expressions. If he was sometimes slow to observe, Rasti was quick to demand his attention with a yap or whimper.

Satisfied that she had his interest and agreement, the rat terrier set off at a steady pace, heading toward a flat-topped ridge that appeared to be completely covered in bindvine and thornbush. Helm compressed his lips. No doubt he would be required to carry his small companion through the worst of the scrub. Then he smiled. She was a determined traveller and set a steady pace despite her size, and in defiance of the heavy, sliding red sand that made each of her steps such an effort. Rasti would only ask for help as a last resort.

As they drew closer to the rising ground, Helm became a little more cautious. He could see that the scrubby vegetation covered a great many folds and dips in the rocky base of the ridge. The shadows among the trees were too dense; there would be pits and gulches, crests and knolls. There would be, perhaps, lairs of pantheras, or the warrens of vulpini. Maybe a strikebeast den. There would definitely be wood-adders. Helm loosened his long knife in its sheath and shifted his bow onto his right shoulder. A feeling of danger prickled his skin as Rasti went ahead of him up the shallow slope and into a thicket of thorn. The unstable sand around the base of the rock slid and eddied under his boots like a grainy stream, and he bent low to keep his weight balanced, doing his best to avoid the clutches of the thornbush. Rasti looked over her shoulder, grinning. For once she had the advantage. Four feet, weighing next to nothing, perfect balance.

'I'm coming,' he told her.

He trudged in her wake, rarely able to use the low, narrow trails she favoured, but following her general direction. At the height of the ridge, a barren rock face resisted all the advances of thorn and bindvine.

Rasti stood perfectly still on the edge of a clearing. Helm came up beside her and gratefully stretched himself back up to his full height. The feeling of danger was like a blast of wind in his face. Looking down, he saw that Rasti was wrinkling her nose. At the same moment, a foul stench of unwashed humanity descended on him.

Helm mindspoke instinctively: 'Hide!'

Rasti melted backward into the underbrush. Helm let out a breath, fitting an arrow to his bow with all the appearance of calm. His heart was thudding painfully, a series of hard blows against the inside of his ribs. He set his feet a little wider apart, careful to show no surprise when two wild men appeared on the far side of the clearing. He was gratified to see that they pulled up short, amazed to see him. He decided that a mild approach would be best.

'Greetings, travellers on the land.' His words were quiet, but his stance made it clear that he was ready to defend himself if necessary.

As a couple more young fellows joined the pair already in the clearing, Helm realised that he was far outnumbered. Not only that; it was evident from the look of these youngsters that they were barely surviving. The modest pack of food and supplies Helm had strapped to his back probably looked like luxury to the half-starved group. He suppressed a shiver as the leader, a bulky youth with a wild mane of tangled brown hair, began to laugh.

'Greetings yourself, old man.' Someone behind him let out a snicker. 'Good of you to bring us some breakfast.' He took a step forward, and Helm lifted the bow, sighting along the arrow.

'Young fellows like you,' he said calmly, 'can no doubt fend for yourselves. I have a long journey ahead of me and little enough to last me.' Somehow he felt that tribal norms of hospitality and sharing would be unknown to these wildlings.

'Stupid,' the leader said, shaking his head. 'We *are* fending for ourselves, old goat. We're gathering from you.'

'I think not.' Helm's voice was steady and his aim unwavering. 'That would be very costly. I can take down one, probably two of you. Is that fair exchange for a couple of hard biscuits?'

The leader stood quite still. Behind him, a taller youth spoke. 'He's bluffing. Old dodderer like him, bet he can't even pull the string.'

Helm smiled. 'I'm happy to demonstrate, but only on a living target.'

They stared back at him a long minute, every one of them unmoving. Then Helm made a sound of exasperation. He narrowed his eyes and lowered his weapon.

'Ah,' he said. 'Peace, my friends. I know you. You are of the outclan Owl, though you seem to have forgotten your manners. I am Helm, son of Kestrel of the Storm, and related to the River tribe through my father's mother. I claim a kinship.'

The young men gasped and stepped back, drawing apart and then together. The tall youth stepped forward. Helm could see no threat in him. On the contrary, the youngster looked shocked.

'What do you mean?' he demanded. 'How could you know such a thing? Why should we listen to you, old man?'

Helm shouldered his bow and replaced his arrow in the quiver on his back, all his actions smooth and unhurried. He hardly glanced at the anxious group in front of him, muttering among themselves and fidgeting with their weapons. Ready to continue his own journey, he mindspoke to Rasti. The young men gasped again as the little terrier scurried out of the underbrush and stood with both front paws on Helm's leg. He bent and lifted her, cradling her in the crook of one arm, hushing her confused growls. Then he began to walk toward the ragged group.

They stepped back, uncertain. 'Who are you? How do you know us?'

Helm stood among them at his ease. 'I have said. I am Helm of the Storm. As for you, I don't know you, but I do know Jarli. He and I have spent several weeks together over the summer.'

'Jarli! That's nonsense. You're telling lies, oldster. Jarli is gone. He walked away from us, months ago,' protested one.

'He must be dead by now,' another said. 'Nobody can survive on Broad Plain alone for so long.'

Helm shrugged. 'Jarli did.' He began to walk away from them.

One of the young men, shorter and slighter than his companions, plucked at his sleeve. 'Please,' said the youth. 'Tell us of Jarli.'

Helm turned to look him in the face. 'You must be a brother, or maybe a cousin. You all have the same look. Jarli was well, last time I saw him. He is travelling across Broad Plain with my son. My companion and I go now to join them.'

The young men, looking rather crestfallen, gathered around him. 'We thought him dead,' one confessed. 'We were angry. The elders threw him out. Nobody would go to look for him, so we came ourselves.'

Helm cocked his head. 'None of outclan Owl searched for him?'

'Only the four of us.'

'And we haven't done it very well,' mumbled the smallest of them.

'You are right. I am sorry for our rudeness, Helm of the Storm. I am Jarli's brother. My name is Daku.'

'Jarli was made outcast,' clarified the leader. 'The elders didn't like his choice of partner.'

'Ha!' said Helm. 'What a thing to say. The Settlement didn't like it either.'

'But—that's where Jarli went, isn't it? That's what we're trying to find. The Settlement, so we can join Jarli,' Daku protested.

Helm frowned, wondering what kind of lore these youngsters had been taught. They seemed to have only rudimentary weapons, and to have made heavy work of their journey across Broad Plain. Surely even an outclan—even though they preferred to roam only a small area— had better travelling skills. None of this made sense.

'Don't bother going to the Settlement,' he advised. 'You won't find Jarli, and you won't be welcomed. The Settlement rejected Jarli's children, and his partner too. Jarli is bereaved. He is with my son Feather, trying to discover any traces of his little family out here on Broad Plain.'

'No, that can't be right. Jarli said he would be safe in the Settlement. He said!'

Helm shook his head. 'He was mistaken. You won't find him there. You had better go back to your clan.'

Rasti whined, reminding Helm that she wanted to be moving on and prodding his thoughts with her wordless feelings of impatience. Helm set her down on the ground and she immediately turned directly east again, scampering over the bare rock face of the clearing and disappearing all too quickly into the next patch of tangled bush.

'I must get on. Go back to your clan. You can't stay Outside like this.'

'Like what, old man?' asked the leader with a burst of bravado. 'We can look after ourselves.'

'I would be glad to think so,' replied Helm, turning away. He felt a twinge in his heart—was it regret that he couldn't help them? They seemed so incompetent. Yet they were young and fit, and could surely find their way back to the Owl. Surely. They were not his responsibility.

His heart thudded strangely as he bent again to make his way through the undergrowth in Rasti's wake. Was it anxiety to get on and find Feather? Probably. Possibly. Nothing more than that. He was experienced and strong. He could make this journey. He would find Feather and speak with him. He would tell Feather everything he wanted him to know.

He laboured after the little terrier, trying to ignore the confused arguments of the group in the clearing.

* * *

The day had arrived. Jaxon, the deep silky purple of his formal robes making him look like a dark shadow in the dull light of the morning, stood beside the regent Adaeze and looked over the Capitoline Plaza where the raiding party had gathered. Few enough: three dozen service staff; an equal number of recyclers, reprocessed for the purpose; and a dozen of the strongest sanitariat workers, who needed no reprocessing as their only role was to do whatever task they were set. Plus eight of the nameless Wereguard, the tireless, invincible original humachines of the Pale. They were, unlike their fellows Hokulani and Hekili, almost completely non-verbal.

Adaeze touched his sleeve. 'Tell me, Senior, who will command this party?'

Jaxon hemmed. 'My lady, the Wereguard have all the instructions they need.'

'I see. But how can they convey these instructions to the rest of the force?'

'A good question, my lady. As you know, these fellows have a limited command of language. They do not require it, indeed. However, they are closely connected to Hekili and Hokulani.'

'Oh! And Hekili and Hokulani can command them from a distance?'

'Oh yes! It is something that has not been done for many, many years, but quite common practice in the early days of the Pale.'

Adaeze appeared to consider this, tilting her head to one side. Then she descended the few steps to the level plaza and started to walk along the ranks of her forces, looking for long moments into some silvery faces, skimming quickly past others.

Jaxon followed, wondering what she was thinking, why she some-times paused and sometimes hurried. As they commenced their inspection of the second row of troops, he began to inspect them more closely himself. Ah. Some of the service personnel had features that were scarred and battered, lumpy or sunken, the silvery planes of their faces no longer the perfect model of strength and duty. How had he not foreseen that this would bother the regent? Because it made no difference to him, he decided. He knew that many of these service personnel were nearing the end of their allotted upgrades, the end of their share of biofuel, software, and hardware. The end of their usefulness, if truth be told. He expected them to appear worn. He had forgotten that the regent was so young that she was struck by any show of age and decay. He decided it was well to remind her of their purposes, of the nobility of their cause.

'Observe, my lady, how dedicated are our service staff. Some here, my lady, are determined to use the very last weeks of their allotment in this task.'

Adaeze stopped still and turned to look at him. 'Their last weeks?'

'Why yes, my lady!' Jaxon walked on, giving only a cursory glance to the troops he passed. Adaeze now kept pace with him, as he expected, pulled along by his energy. 'We have spoken of this. You remember. The Service has been most generous in gifting us, and all the other citizens of our great policosmos, with the self-sacrifice of their earliest model staff. You will remember what Hekili told us of this. They will continue to serve as long as they stand.'

Adaeze nodded. 'Yes. I remember that some have already made the sacrifice, guarding the gates in the outer Pale.' This was the name they had agreed to use for the stricken districts, now empty, separated from the rest of the policosmos by the ever-growing chasm that had opened through the fabric of the city.

'Correct, my lady. A handful have already had the honour of serv-ing their last moments with that valour.'

They came to the end of the rows of service personnel and began a stately progress past the dozens of lesser troops—the altered recy-clers, the clumsy sanitariat. These citizens had at least their typical appearance of health, as they had always operated on a lesser diet of biofuel, a lower allotment of upgrades, a more meagre original portion in both liveware and hardware. The reduction in food had made less of a change for these than for the Service. Well, Jaxon corrected himself, less of a change than for the service personnel who had been designated to receive no further biofuel at all. Those would simply operate on their inner reserves for as long as they could. After all, with the tanks of the outer Pale quite unreachable, and the slowness of the ingeneers in building new ones, the food supply of the policosmos was greatly diminished. Some citizens simply had to be culled. As well to make them useful while they deteriorated.

At last the regent and her senior forecaster came to the far side of the plaza, where Hekili and Hokulani waited with their fellow Wereguard. It was perhaps extravagant to use eight of the Wereguard on this mission, but Jaxon and Hekili had considered the matter carefully. More Wereguard meant a swifter, more complete raid. A quicker return too. More ridiculous settlers captured and killed, more resources rescued and returned within the walls of the Pale.

Jaxon suppressed a surge of annoyance. The walls of the Pale. The very words brought to mind the catastrophic failure of Alpha Gate, the disastrous cracks and the leaning panels of the entire perimeter in that section. He calmed himself with his most recent mantra: the fault will be repaired. The walls will be made good. The Pale will survive this peril.

Then he blinked, brought back to the present by a low, resounding voice.

'My lady,' Hekili was saying. 'Our force is ready to depart. We thank you for the opportunity to serve.'

'The Service exists to serve the Pale,' intoned Hokulani, as if this were not self-evident. Sometimes Jaxon wondered whether any of the Wereguard was truly capable of conversation.

'We exist to serve,' said the troops, confirming the vacuous statement.

Jaxon lowered his head and clasped his hands together under his gleaming robe. The sooner this little army left the confines of the Pale, the better pleased he would be. However, there was a small delay in which nobody moved or spoke. Ah. Jaxon lifted his head and leaned a little closer to Adaeze.

'My lady,' he whispered, 'they await your words of farewell.'

Adaeze breathed out in relief. Truly, she had so little notion of how to go on. Never again, Jaxon reminded himself, never again would he promote so young and ignorant a regent. No matter. There would be time to amend this one's ways, he was sure. Time to progress and grow and educate more paramounts, time to nurture and choose a new ruler as soon as he needed one. First, to secure the city itself. First to save the Pale.

As Adaeze spoke words of gratitude and encouragement to the assembled citizens, Jaxon nodded slowly, a grave expression on his silvered face. Her words were more true than the general run of platitudes, he realised with a degree of discomfort. The Pale *was* relying wholly on these troops; their future *did* rest in their hands. Everything *did* depend on their successful return.

Never had platitudes made him more uncomfortable.

* * *

'I wish Jarli could be more at ease with me.'

Callan looked up at Hector. He had observed that some members of the Storm still jumped with fright whenever they came upon Hector unexpectedly, and it was clear to him that Jarli had never been so close to anything from the Pale.

'Jarli is an outclansman,' Callan explained. 'The outclans are less organised than the tribes.'

'Organised?'

Callan scratched behind his ear. He wished, not for the first time, that Mashtuk could speak. It was Mashtuk who always had the right words, and the right knowledge of what had gone on, back in the before-times, that made the tribes and the outclans, and the settlers and the humachines of the Pale, what they were. But Mashtuk's words were locked inside his head. Callan had often discussed such matters with Kilimanjara, though, so he tried to make sense of the situation for Hector. Although he had accepted that Hector was pack with the canini of the ravine, he admitted to himself that he harboured a shiver of fear, of doubt, about him. Just his size, perhaps, and the metallic gleam that shone from under his skin. He looked up to find Hector waiting politely for his response, and grinned. One thing he did appreciate about the enormous human-humachine was his excellent command of mindspeech. Hector was stronger and at the same time more subtle in his speech than any human Callan had ever spoken with. Feather included, which was surprising.

'Sorry, my friend, I am trying to find the right words.'

Hector hunkered down beside him. From where they sat, on the edge of the main clearing by Hippolyta the leader's den, they could watch the comings and goings of the pack: sentry changes to the guard post, scouts and hunters into the deep ravine, den-wardens checking on the young and the elders. The tribesfolk were busy about the clearing too, though their main camp was some way further inside the ravine, closer to the wide meadow where the equii based themselves.

'I wish I could ask Mashtuk.'

'I wish that too.' Callan's mindvoice was taut with pain.

'I didn't mean that I don't like speaking with you,' Hector hurried to explain. 'It's just that, that ... Huh. I don't know what it is exactly.'

'Yes you do,' Callan said with decision. 'We both know. You love Mashtuk and you trust him. As do I.'

Hector looked aside. Strange, thought Callan, he has even adopted the ways of the canini in his gestures. Hector's love was deep, and he preferred not to speak of it. Callan understood. Some words brought grief to mind too sharply to be borne. The wise canine did not court such pain.

'The outclans,' Callan said, as if there had been no words between Hector's question and now, 'are humans who decided not to live under the rule of authority. Most of them were once members of a tribe, but some, Feather says, once lived in the Settlement, or ran free.'

'And they are not organised?'

'Ah. Not the best word perhaps.' Callan scratched his ear again, thinking. He knew that on occasions, he and the tribe used the same word but meant something different. What meaning a humachine might put on any particular word, he did not know. Well, it would not hurt to say so. 'I am not sure, Hector, what you would think of as "organised". For the outclans, this is what I know. They choose not to have a leader or to listen to the decisions of elders. They move in family groups, sometimes together, sometimes separately. They do not wish to be told what to do.'

'Huh.' Hector rubbed his chin. Callan noticed for the first time that there was the beginning of a beard there, some dark bristles just starting to grow through Hector's smooth skin. He narrowed his eyes, confirming the impression that had just touched his mind. Hector, for all his great size and the machine additions that the Pale had made to him, was looking more and more human by the day.

'I don't much like being told what to do.'

Callan tipped back his head and laughed.

'What is it?' asked Hector, a smile creasing the perfect planes of his face as he looked at the big white canine.

'I was just thinking, my friend, that you are looking more and more human. Now you are sounding more and more human.'

Hector tilted his head to one side, in the way that the canini did to show that they appreciated something humorous. He smiled again. 'Thank you, Callan.'

Chapter 6

The time had come for the Storm to make their way south, back to their usual tribal circuit before the worst of the winter caught them still journeying along the edges of Broad Plain. Marin the huntmaster knew this, and so did all the other tribesfolk. Yet still they delayed. Callan realised that something had to be said. The tribe could not over-winter in the ravine. There was simply not enough food to support them. With two packs and the herd of equii, resources would be stretched enough, and anything they hunted or gathered had to be contested with every other living creature that called the ravine home. In the general way of things, the lizards and avians, patchwork hares and sandgrubs, hop rabbits and skinks, lived in a goodly equilibrium with the canini. They provided both competition for food and also prey, a neat balance that ensured they were never hunted to nothing and always had a fair chance to survive. Although, truth to tell, the rabbits and hares had now to take their chances with whatever areas the equii had not grazed to bare soil. Hungry things, those equii, though they looked like nothing but serried ribs on four over-long legs. Still, Callan thought, better that they have the prospect of life here in the ravine than simply run themselves to death on Broad Plain, easy prey for the vulpini and pantheras that hunted there.

He was making his way back from a turn at sentry duty down at the pinch point. It was a place he both despised and admired. There were excellent views over the base of the escarpment, indeed right across Broad Plain toward the hulking Pale in the west. There was also nowhere to hide or to run should a mob attack. Ah well. Life was danger, and he would always choose it. He shouldered his way through the last of the thornbush forest and came into the clearing. As he had hoped, Hippolyta and Thestia, the other senior canini, were seated at the entrance to Hippolyta's den.

'Greetings, pack leaders,' he began, drawing close and dipping his nose in respect.

Hippolyta wrinkled her snout to wave away the reverence. 'Pack leader,' she replied. 'Come speak with us. We have worries.'

'Ah. Perhaps the same as mine.' Callan stepped close and then stretched and shook himself before settling in a lopsided sit by the entrance to the den.

Their eyes met, and all three tightened their mindvoices to speak privately. None of them wanted any of the tribe to overhear their concerns, and too many of the Storm had some sort of mindspeech. Perhaps they should not have been surprised that living together had reawoken some of the old communion between the humans of the tribe and the canini. The only truly surprising outcome had been that Jarli, the half-wild outclansman, had developed the best mindspeech of all the newcomers. But then, his twin sons were gifted—Callan shook his head, bringing his thoughts back to the matter at hand.

'Pack leaders, winter comes,' he began.

The other two nodded, Thestia's eyes sliding sideways to check that no tribesfolk were near. 'Greenstuff grows ever more scarce.'

'When the weather closes in, hunting will be more difficult,' added Hippolyta.

'And the equii have increased our numbers,' Callan said with some diffidence. He was the one who had invited the beleaguered equii to share the ravine, so he knew himself largely responsible for the way they stripped the young trees bare of growth and trimmed the grasses down to the ground.

'And although we ourselves have lost pack members,' Hippolyta said with a delicate edge to her voice, 'our cubs are growing and need more food.'

'And we are not sure how many of our visitors will remain with us.' Thestia spoke with a sharpness Callan had not quite expected.

It was the way of the canini, whenever something difficult was to be discussed, to first lay out in simple terms all the points that needed to be considered. Usually this was done without any heat, at least until they began to debate their options.

He looked away briefly, over the heads of the other two. Thestia lowered her nose and blinked in apology. Although Callan had renounced the leadership of his own pack some months earlier, he would always retain his seniority. He was glad that Thestia had accepted his silent rebuke in good heart. He had no wish to quarrel with her, prickly as she was.

'So, we have too many souls to support.' Hippolyta relaxed and the other two followed her example so that they lay with their heads close together, looking out over the cleared space in front of the den.

'The solution is clear,' said Thestia. 'The tribe must move on.'

They sat and thought about this for a long minute.

Callan said mildly, 'There is confusion over who is tribe and who is not.'

'Their pack boundaries are weak.' Thestia was rather scornful of the eddying of human companionship. They went about in mixed groups, and sometimes shouted at each other and did not immediately apologise. They turned their backs or clasped each other close, hugged or traded blows with equal energy. There was no understanding them.

'To be fair,' said Hippolyta, 'I am confused about who is pack with the tribe and who is not. How could they possibly know, with their weaker senses? Callan, you lived with humans a good while. Do you understand how they manage these things?'

'They are not good at accepting what they do not like,' Callan told them. 'Often we have noticed this. A canine could easily see that all the game is fled, but a human will keep looking. They hope that something will change.'

'They imagine that hoping will make it so,' said Thestia with a snort.

'Yes.' Callan tilted his head. He had seen humans in the grip of both hope and despair. Of the two, he preferred them to live in hope. The same with canini. Hope could bite, but despair could kill.

'And they do not want to think that the human twins will not join their pack.' Hippolyta ran one paw over her snout. 'When will they accept this?'

'It is another thing they hope will change,' said Thestia. 'Foolish.

Romulo and Remo are pack with Jarli. Jarli is not pack with the Storm.'

Callan sat up, Thestia's brisk words striking home. He chastised himself for not perceiving this before. 'You are right, Thestia. I should have seen this. Ai, I have spent too many summers with the humans and allowed myself to be deluded by their hopes.'

'You have much love for the humans of the Storm,' Hippolyta told him. 'To love greatly is not always to see most clearly.'

'True.' They stayed silent for a long while, pursuing their own thoughts. Callan rather hoped that the two females did not despise him too much. He could not deny that the years he had spent living with the Storm had changed him, changed how he looked at the world, how he looked at life. Yet he did not rush himself. It was important to take time considering with all his senses the relationships that were developing around him. He had made quite enough observations for that. He appreciated the fact that Hippolyta and Thestia waited for him, though he supposed that to them the solution may well have been obvious for quite some time. Thestia was right: Jarli and the twins were pack with each other, but Jarli was not pack with the Storm. Jarli was pack with Mashtuk. Jarli was pack with the canini.

'Will you speak to them?' Hippolyta asked at last.

With no further discussion, it was clear that they had come to a decision about what had to happen, what must happen for the good of all. Sooner, rather than later, the Storm had to leave the ravine. There was no happiness to be gained from further waiting. The human twins were never going to live with the tribe. Whatever Marin and his partner Willow had hoped, those dreams would never come true.

Callan lowered his snout in agreement. 'I will tell them,' he said. 'I will tell them now.'

* * *

Brettin looked up at Olinna. The older woman, her elaborate green-and-yellow turban shaking as she quivered with strong emotion, stood on the other side of the Lady's wide desk. She was in severe agitation, wringing her hands and moaning under her breath.

'I do not see the need for such distress,' Brettin said. Her manner was chilly, as usual, but underneath that she was very angry. The sense of betrayal was almost overwhelming. After all she had done for the settlers! The evil ideas she had rooted out, even to the extent of ensuring that anyone with those wild notions of 'self-determination of standards' and 'freedom from the rule of the Temple' left with Valkirra—the onerous management of the day-to-day organisation of an entire community—the introduction of new and better procedures for prayer and meditation that would benefit all—the complete restructuring of the markets to ensure the Temple would always be strong enough to care for the community—after all she had done, this was how she was repaid! She took a deep breath, shutting the lid on her anger before it escaped in an untimely manner.

'The matter is simple. This young woman has forfeited her right to live with us here at the Temple Settlement.'

Olinna moaned again. 'Truly I do not see how it can have happened. Pirinna has one older child, and there is nothing strange about her. She is not of Assessment age yet. The daughter, I mean.' Olinna shook her head in sadness. 'I never once thought that the children of Pirinna and Denn would fail Assessment. They were both very highly assessed.'

Brettin opened her hands in a gesture that was meant to show her calm, her reasonable approach to a very difficult matter. 'It is shocking, I agree, Olinna. You must feel it, indeed. I am sorry for you.'

Olinna compressed her lips, her face stained an ugly dark red that contrasted in a most unflattering way with the bright yellows and greens of her robes. 'The standard-resisting runaways have been gone for months. The tribes have not visited. You promised that we would eliminate every wild strain from our community!'

Brettin raised her brows. 'My dear Olinna, neither you nor I can be responsible for poor decisions made by any one person in our community. If this young woman chose to make an unwise liaison elsewhere than in her partnership with Denn—an excellent fellow, he works in the clothing trade like my own dear father—well then, if this girl chooses a casual partner who is non-standard, what could you, or I, or poor Denn do about it?'

Olinna sank into the chair that Blazej, now always at Brettin's side, had provided for her some long minutes since. 'I hear you, Lady of the Temple,' she said. 'They swear, of course, that it was not so. Both of them, Pirinna and Denn, that they have never had relationships beyond their own partnership. And yet …'

'And yet she has borne a child with a cleft in its lip.'

Olinna sighed. 'I do not suppose the boy will survive. He cannot feed properly. It is an ugly sight, indeed. I don't see how he could live many more days.'

'Just as well.'

They sat in silence, considering.

Eventually Olinna said, 'I do not see how such a flaw can have occurred. You promised us we would have no more freaks.'

Brettin motioned to Blazej to return to his desk. 'That is why I say that she has made her own disaster. The tribes have not visited us since the Settlement split, so we cannot suspect any relationship there. We have kept our gates tightly closed against the outclans too, since that ridiculous business with Magda Gawelsdottir and her repulsive twins.' Brettin shivered, a subtle movement, and then visibly straightened herself, very much the Lady of the Temple, the decision maker, the pattern of correct behaviour and beliefs. 'Olinna, I would advise you to look first at any servants they have in their household. Pirinna is high-assessed herself. This thing's father must be non-standard, so it is not Denn.'

Olinna shook her head, the massive turban slipping a bit sideways with her movement. Reaching distractedly to right it, she said, 'They have only female servants, from their housekeeper to their stock hands. This crime did not occur in their household.'

'Worse and worse,' spluttered Brettin, feeling the warmth of anger flush her cheeks. 'How dare she pollute us like this! She must have associated with some man from the Lower Town, some non-assessed villein or helot perhaps.' A thought struck her, holding her motionless a moment. Were they wise to allow such people to continue to live inside the Settlement? Villeins and helots were in general refugees of some sort—folk who had once been in a tribe, or run wild on the Outside alone or with an outclan. They were miserable, needy people who sought sanctuary inside the safety of the Settlement's palisade. They were, she had always understood, so grateful to be safe from the Outside that they worked long and hard and for nothing more than their keep. The villeins and helots had always been a valuable source of cheap labour for the settlers. Many of the lesser jobs were now solely the preserve of such lowly types. Yet if they posed a danger to the settler community by introducing non-standard genes? How any assessed settler could even look upon such paltry creatures as possible partners! Brettin shook her head, belatedly seeing that both Olinna and Blazej were regarding her with concern. Well, she thought, that must be a matter for later consideration. First deal with this unfortunate matter.

She regarded Olinna with a sadness that was not completely assumed. Pirinna's error could well cause dire ripples through the entire community. 'My dear Olinna, we are at least fortunate that the flaw is clearly visible and not a hidden genetic anomaly, one of those cursed internal modifications.' She had no need to feign the shiver that ran over her. 'I feel ill, just thinking about it.'

'What do you suggest, my lady?' Olinna waited for her instructions.

'I suggest that we do not record the birth in the records. Blazej, do you hear me? Nothing is to be mentioned of a child born to Pirinna at this time. This discussion between myself and District Representative Olinna did not occur. We did not have this meeting today.'

Blazej nodded. 'Of course, my lady.'

Brettin kept her eye on him a moment longer, watching as he began to delete the notes he had made on the singing screen. Then she looked Olinna in the eye.

'Let me know, as soon as this—as soon as it dies. If there is any way to hasten that, please arrange it. Nothing crude, though. We do not wish to cause undue suffering. The Temple always shows a kind face to the unfortunates among us.'

Olinna nodded slowly, one hand keeping her turban in place. 'I will not make a fuss about it. I will let the child die and convey my regrets. I have placed a woman in the household, as an offer of help, you understand, in this misfortune.'

Brettin raised her eyebrows. 'An excellent notion, Olinna. Well done. Perhaps your servant could assist with the sad end that must come.' Brettin looked down, studying her simple Temple rings, one on each slender white finger. The light coming over her shoulder from Valkirra's big window produced a lustre that was quite soothing. Valkirra had worn one large, chunky gold ring set with an enormous golden topaz. A symbol of power and strength. Well, the Temple ruled here now, with quieter and altogether much more efficient and respectful methods. She looked up as Olinna spoke again.

'Brettin, they will wish to register the birth—and I suppose the death in its turn—at the Temple. I understand that it is wiser to have no mention made at all of this child, as you say. What do you suggest? What happens when the parents present themselves at the Temple?'

Brettin briefly met Blazej's eyes, and the man nodded in agreement. He would manage whatever needed managing in order to have the records exactly as Brettin wished them.

'Olinna, I think you should offer to register this yourself—or at least to go with them to the Temple when the time comes. Say to whichever acolyte greets you that you would like the event recorded by Blazej here. Is that clear? He will be called and ensure that the records say only what we wish them to say.'

'I will do that.' Olinna rose to leave, giving a long breath of relief. Clearly, thought Brettin, she is glad to have me make these difficult decisions for her. She held up a hand, though, to indicate that she yet had more to say. Olinna stood and waited, her fleshy face looking entirely miserable.

'That deals with the infant individual,' said Brettin. 'But there is still the matter of its mother. You must encourage—no, you must direct—this Pirinna to leave the Temple Settlement. She would be much better placed down with the runaways. With the makers of Newkeep, as they now call themselves. They are happy to overlook such indiscretions. They do not even consider them as such. She may do whatever evil she likes in that community. But not here, do you understand?'

Olinna made a small reverence, marred in its grace only by her need to keep her head straight under the towering turban. 'I hear you, Lady,' she said formally. 'I will find a way. None of us ever wishes to see such freakish persons inside the Settlement.'

'Indeed. Denn is high-assessed and may take another partner. The Temple will happily dissolve the current arrangement.'

Olinna blinked, looking a little uncertain. 'In time, I am sure he will do so.'

'I am glad to hear it. Enough of this matter. Thank you for bringing it to me.'

Blazej opened the door for the district representative. As he closed it behind her, he gestured at the singing screen he used to take notes of every one of Brettin's meetings. 'My lady, much time has just been spent on a meeting that never happened. May I bring you some refreshment?'

Brettin narrowed her eyes at him. She did not, in the usual way of things, approve of levity. However, his suggestion was welcome.

'Please do, Blazej.' He bowed, and Brettin added, 'But never mention this morning's matter again. Not to me, certainly not to anyone else. The Temple's business is for the Temple alone.'

Blazej bowed once more and left the room. Brettin rose and looked through the wide window over the chief's garden toward the gate that led to the Lower Town. Her mind ran with ideas and plans. There must be a way, she thought, to reduce the danger of the Lower Town folk mixing too freely with high-assessed settlers. There must be a way, and she would find it. Another tax, perhaps, or a restriction on the hours that the Lower Town folk could enter the High Town.

No, thought Brettin; that would not serve. Too many of the Settlement's servants were needed at all hours of the day. Perhaps the Temple could institute a restriction on the numbers allowed in the upper districts at any one time. Oh, and a permit from the Temple would be needed for entry.

Yes, that would do it, she decided. Anyone residing in the Lower Town—whether a villein or a helot or an elder or just one of the non-standard working settlers—any one of these folk requiring entrance to the upper levels must have a current, valid permit that stated where they were allowed to go and between what hours. In that way, the Temple could ensure that Lower Town inhabitants of breeding age could be kept in their places overnight. Permission for evening and overnight work would only be granted to the elderly, or to those so vile that no high-assessed settler would ever think to lie with such a creature.

Brettin turned with a smile as Blazej re-entered the room, carrying a tray of refreshments. She could smell the spicy scent of cinnamon tea and the burnt-sugar tang of custard tarts.

'Blazej, put that down. I can pour for myself. I need you to take notes, quickly, while I have all this fresh in my mind.'

'Yes, my lady,' said Blazej, seating himself at the singing screen. Brettin liked the way that he nodded enthusiastically as she dictated her—she should say, the Temple's—new arrangements for dealing with the Lower Town.

Chapter 7

Hector stood to one side of the clearing, watching as Mashtuk walked a slow circle of the swale. Alongside the injured canine, a rabble of young things kept pace. Mashtuk's own cubs, Niccolò and Rhosyn, stepped along with him, one on either side. They were close enough to steady him if he needed it, but were also giving him the space to grow back into his own strength. Hector approved their care and the way they allowed their half-crippled father his dignity. Around them, the human twins gambolled in a most ineffective manner, sometimes crawling, sometimes staggering a few steps before falling either on their faces or on their swaddled behinds. A good notion, that was, of the tribesfolk—to clothe the infants in washable linen until they learned better how to relieve themselves efficiently. He wondered whether the same had been done for him, all those years ago. Of his infancy and childhood, he remembered nothing. As far as he could recall, his life began at the gates of the Pale.

Hector shrugged his shoulders and resettled himself. He was a long way from the Pale. Where he would go next, he had no idea. He wished he could talk it over with Tad, the humachine who had acted almost as a father to him, but Tad had been dead many months. That his metallic skeleton, now stripped of any liveware, was suspended in the resting place of the canini, was a kind of comfort. Sometimes Hector went to the place to look at Tad's silver bones, and at Zélie. Among the other carcasses and skeletons that hung there, Zélie was still recognisable by her slight shape and the remnants of her hide, once a glossy pale grey with darker stripes. She was dull and diminished now; the vulpini horde had torn her mercilessly. Hector shook his head. If only he had been in the ravine at the time of the attack, he thought again as he had thought many times, if only. Zélie would be alive. Mashtuk would be whole and hale.

The Storm, the tribe that he with Enis and Tsendi had brought back to the ravine, they would not be here. They would not be making plans to take Romulo and Remo away. They would not—

Hector saw that Mashtuk had paused in his round, as if to regather his strength. Niccolò waited beside him, while Rhosyn walked a little ahead. Her eyes met Hector's and he understood her message. He strode across the sward and went down on one knee beside the injured canine.

'How is it with you, my friend?' he asked. 'Have you walked far enough for the moment?'

None of the pack was sure exactly how much Mashtuk understood of their mindspeech. They only knew that they could not get much in the way of clear thoughts from him. His mind looked cloudy to them. Words and senses shifted like leaves in the wind, turning first this way and then that, never still, never certain. To try catching Mashtuk's thoughts was like trying to catch a slice of flowing river. Hector had a little less trouble, perhaps because his mindspeech was marginally less subtle, less agile, than that of the canini. Hector mindspoke strongly and well, but he mindspoke like a human. Like the best of humans, Enis had told him, better than any of the others, but without every nuance of the canini. Hector knew that was to his advantage in dealing with Mashtuk. He could read the bigger message where the rest of the pack looked for something more delicate.

Hector also had the use of his Pale-adapted sensors, fading with time as he no longer had access to the policosmos biofuel and energy sources, but functioning and useful. His sensors told him that Mashtuk was exhausted now, that he had pushed himself a little too far. Ready to fall down, said Hector's sensors. Huh. Not if Hector had anything to say about it.

With a nod to Niccolò and Rhosyn, Hector reached out and gently gathered Mashtuk close. He was careful to carry him in the most supportive way, the manner that hurt him least: one arm scooped under his back legs, one under the front of his chest. Mashtuk breathed out noisily, settling his head against Hector's shoulder.

Hector had the sense that he was annoyed with himself, frustrated by his weakness. 'Time, my friend,' he said. 'You are growing stronger. Now you must rest a while. That was a good morning's walk.'

With the youngsters following behind, they made quite a parade heading for the depths of the den that Mashtuk had shared with his partner Zélie for so many seasons. As he set the old canine down, Hector heard a commotion behind him—the twins. Romulo and Remo were squealing with delight. That could only mean one thing—Jarli.

Hector turned to discover that both Jarli and Feather had entered the clearing. The human twins scrambled to pull their father—their human father—inside, clambering over him and tugging at his clothing as if they wanted to show him something. But Hector knew it was no such thing. Romulo and Remo just liked to pull Jarli into the den. It was their way, he thought, of telling him they were pack with Mashtuk. How that would play out with the folk of the Storm, Hector had no idea. He looked up to meet Feather's steady gaze and stepped back into the clearing. It seemed there was something the tribesman wished to discuss.

Hector liked Feather, knew him for a good man. Whether Feather had quite gotten over his surprise and distrust of Hector was another matter. But then, Hector was accustomed to the suspicion of humans. Not every member of the Storm was comfortable around him; not everyone cared to be too close to his metallic bulk. He had good friends among them, it was true, but he knew he could never join them as a permanent member. He was not pack with them, as the canini would say.

Nobody knew what pack Hector had sprung from, least of all himself.

He narrowed his eyes questioningly at Feather, who motioned with his head. They walked a little way over the sward, and Feather folded down easily to sit cross-legged in the lee of a straggling sour pear tree that kept off the worst of the cold wind. Hector lowered himself beside the tribesman, not quite as agile, but neatly and easily considering his size. He sat with his legs bent up in front of him, his elbows resting on his knees. Even so, he towered over the tribesman, who was not as tall as most of his fellows. Like him, though, Hector faced the den where the little family of humans and canines were gathered. Like Feather, he looked straight ahead.

'I wished to speak with you,' Feather said, his voice low so as not to carry to the den. 'The tribe are preparing to leave.'

'Oh.' Hector was not sure what to say: so soon? now? sorry to hear that? He would miss them. Romulo and Remo, the babies he had protected and carried; Freya, as much a friend as any human could be to a humachine; Willow, who always had a kind word for him; Marin, who called him 'son', though Hector knew this was just a habit and had no true meaning. He had enjoyed hearing the tribesfolk speaking aloud. Their ways were so noisy, their conversations so complicated. He rarely posed them any questions, being careful not to startle them—many of them looked on him as nothing more than a huge, mindless machine—but he had learned much from listening.

'You do not ask when,' Feather said. 'You do not ask who goes.'

Hector chanced a sideways glance at the rather severe face beside him. In the manner of humans, Feather was, he supposed, a good-looking man. His daughter Freya was like him in many ways, though she had told Hector that she resembled her mother more closely. Hector thought that Freya was very fine to look upon. He would miss her when the Storm returned to their circuit.

But Feather had made a comment, and was waiting for a reply.

'I do not have any such questions,' Hector told him. 'It is not for me to ask who goes.'

Feather looked up at him, a slight smile on his face. Hector read this as an encouragement to go on.

'Are you saying,' he asked carefully, 'that not all of the tribesfolk are leaving the ravine?'

'That's right. Some are considering asking the canini if they can stay. Marin wanted me to ask you, though, what it was that you wanted. To stay here in the ravine with Mashtuk and the rest of the pack who adopted you, or to join the tribe?'

'Marin said I could join the tribe?' This was news to Hector.

Feather put out his hand, flattened, and moved it up and down, as if to say that the matter was not settled. 'Marin wishes to keep the tribe together. He and Willow would gladly welcome you, treat you as a son of the family. I should tell you that not everyone is happy with the events of these last few weeks, though. This matter of the twins, you must know, has created some discontent.'

'The Storm want to take them away from the ravine.'

'Yes. True. Some of them think that it would be best, best for the babies, you see, if Marin and Willow adopted them. Others think that Jarli must be allowed to make the decision, because he is blood kin, and also because he is younger than Marin and Willow. Most of them want all three to join the Storm. Every one of them fears that if Jarli returns to his outclan, the twins will have a lesser life than the Storm could give them.'

'I see. I think I see. You all want what is best, but you do not really know what is best. Also, you do not know who has the right to choose.'

Feather nodded. Hector liked the tone of approval in his voice as he continued.

'The canini, now—they believe that it is Mashtuk who should decide the fate of Romulo and Remo. It was his actions that saved them from certain death, when all is said. The canini believe that his right of choice is greater than the blood tie of Jarli. Yet some of the canini, too, wonder if the twins would be better cared for among humans.'

Hector felt a strange shudder in his chest, as if the hardware there had lost its perfect timing. The moment passed and he frowned at Feather.

'Those twins are pack with Mashtuk. You can see that, I know.'

'I do know it. Not all of my fellow tribesmen understand it. And even those who are pack with each other are not always able to live together.'

'Huh.' Hector looked away, replaying in his mind the words that he and Feather had exchanged. The tribesman waited patiently, still and silent beside him. Hector realised that Feather was a very restful person to be around. He crossed one leg under himself so that he could turn and look Feather in the eye more easily.

'I have questions now.'

'I am listening.'

Hector could not help but grin. 'In the Pale, you know, I wasn't permitted to ask questions.'

'I wonder if you asked them anyway.'

'I did, until I learned better. You can pick up a lot of knowledge from a few smacks across the ear.'

Feather shook his head, a sad look in his eyes at odds with his rueful grin. 'What a life you have had, my young friend. Well, ask your questions.'

'This is what I want to know.' Hector began to number them off on his fingers. 'Are the Storm taking the twins? Are you going with the Storm? What are Jarli's plans? Will Callan stay in the ravine, or go with you?'

'Good questions,' Feather said. 'Not everything is quite certain, but Jarli wants to stay in the ravine with the twins. He says it is safer and more like home than anything he has ever known. He wants to be accepted as pack with the ravine canini.'

'Huh.' Hector looked down. 'That is good. I think they should stay. There is nothing now they need that the canini cannot provide.' He met Feather's eyes again. 'Maybe clothes. They are better with clothes.'

Feather laughed. 'I agree. Callan also will stay. He has decided to remain as a member of the ravine canini. He and Mashtuk are old friends, and he believes that the ravine pack has need of him.'

'That is good,' said Hector again. 'I have noticed that Mashtuk likes to have Callan nearby.'

'As for your other questions, there is one last chance to decide. Some of the tribe have enjoyed our stay in the ravine. They have found a sort of peace they have never known on the circuit. Will they continue to travel with the Storm, or try to find their own place to stay, their own ravine-type home? Their choices must be made soon, though. The Storm will leave in a couple of hours, and without the twins. Marin and Willow are rather sad.' Feather paused. 'If you do not mind, Hector, I would ask you to speak with them. Reassure them about Romulo and Remo.'

'I will do that. I like Willow and Marin.'

'I also.'

They sat in silence for some time. From within the den, the cheerful squealing of the babies intensified as they began some sort of wrestling game with the cubs. Hector could see that Jarli sat with his back against the far wall, Mashtuk nestled beside him. The youngsters mingled as if they had sprung from the same birthing, in a comfortable tangle of limbs, some furred, some bare. Hector found it a pleasant sight. He would miss the company of the canini, if ever he decided—oh. The choice was easy, when it came down to it.

'Feather,' he said at last. 'I don't think I can leave the ravine. I am pack with these creatures. They saved me from Broad Plain. I never knew that anything that lived in the Outside could be so kind. I owe them so much.'

Feather nodded. More, he put a hand on Hector's shoulder. 'I understand. Could you explain that to Willow? To Marin?'

'I will.'

'Good.'

'What about you? What will you do?'

'Ai,' said Feather. 'I have many tasks ahead of me. I must return across Broad Plain, back to Newkeep. My partner Jana—Freya's mother, you understand—is waiting on my return. There is also the matter of making sure they are prepared for the winter. I have a new friend there too—a rat terrier from the Settlement. Rasti. When we are reunited, she will join me in my travels.'

'I see. You travel a great deal, it would seem.' He paused, choosing his words. He had noticed that it was not always prudent to speak exactly what was in his mind, where humans were concerned. 'Freya said that the Storm want more of you. That they want you to be their leader.'

'They want what they cannot have.'

Hector nodded. He was right; this was not something that Feather wished to discuss. 'So you mostly travel all around, but spend some of your time with Freya's mother. After winter, it may be, you will come back to the Storm?'

Feather made that maybe-maybe not gesture with his hand again. 'Perhaps. There is another matter I must attend to.'

Hector looked at him and noted that the tribesman's mouth was set in a grim line. He had grown more adept at reading human expressions, and he somewhat regretted the turn that their conversation had now taken. 'Something difficult? Something bad?'

Feather shook his head. 'In truth, no. Something I have been avoiding.'

Hector was surprised. Feather, among all the tribesfolk he had met, seemed to him the last one to shirk any duty that needed doing. It shocked him so much that he felt he had to offer his support.

'Is it something I can help you with, Feather? I am very strong, and I have good endurance for any journey or any burden.'

Feather laughed aloud. 'My friend Callan is right! You may be half-way to a humachine, but you have the best of human hearts. Thank you, my friend, but no. It is a family matter, one that only I can attend to.'

'So you are leaving us too?'

'I am. Tomorrow. It may be that Freya travels with me; I am planning to ask her now. In fact, there is quite a gathering down at the leaders' den, where the tribesfolk are preparing to start their journey. They have tarried long enough, and now they wish to be out of the ravine and some way across Broad Plain before night falls. Anyone who does not wish to go must make that choice now.'

Hector stood. 'We had better join them. I don't want to miss Willow or Marin. And I need to explain—'

'You do,' Feather agreed. 'There is some hard news for them this day.'

* * *

The rains had stopped days before and showed no sign of returning, but the Founders River was running higher every hour. Talis did not think he had ever seen such a surge of water flow through it. Both banks had disappeared into a grave of liquid mud. Here on the Newkeep side, water was spreading into the long grass along the riverside path, a path that was usually more than ten feet about the water level. Would the river rise further? Talis feared rather than knew that it had not yet peaked. Standing with Iver behind the lateral drain they had recently completed, he watched the slow purling of the wide water. Strange that, with so much water in it, the river appeared to flow less quickly. But for the mysterious swirls and eddies on the surface, they could have been standing beside a lake. A lake full to the brim with thick, reddish-brown water and studded with floating branches and the sorry shapes of small drowned creatures.

'Never seen it so high,' Iver commented. 'And I've lived beside this river a good many years.'

'I believe it happened once before, but many generations ago,' Talis told him. 'Before the river gate was built at the Settlement.'

'Is that so?' Iver considered. 'I never heard that.'

'There's mention of it in the archives. Not much detail, though.'

The two men watched the water lapping lowly toward them. Talis put a hand on Iver's shoulder, and the old man turned to face him. 'More digging, I think.'

'Surely it's close to its height? It couldn't rise much more, could it?'

'Better to be safe is what I think. Iver, would you tell Valkirra what I'm about? I'll gather a couple of the younger men to help. If we can just divert some of this flow ...'

'I'll tell her,' said Iver, though he sounded doubtful. 'Talis, where would you divert it to?'

'I thought—no, you're right, Iver. Every drain we have dug is breaking its banks. We've directed a riverful past our walls and back onto Broad Plain as it is.' Talis rubbed his hands over his face as if he could scrub away his worry and uncertainty.

Iver patted his shoulder. 'We can't dig these drains any lower now. They're man-height deep as it is, so nobody can get into them to dig. Talis, lad, we've done all we can.'

It was many years since anyone had called Talis 'lad', but if anyone had the right it was Iver, who had given up so much to join them at Newkeep. At this very moment, he could have been sitting comfortably in his solid home up in the Settlement, Talis supposed as he nodded his agreement. Iver, and old Ahrenkild too, could have stayed safe, enjoying their last years in their respected roles as district representatives. Instead they were offering their wisdom, their knowledge, their skills, and whatever strength they had to the building of a new type of settlement. A reimagined settlement, where merit counted for more than a strict adherence to a standard shape, size, and metabolism.

As both men turned back into the enclosure that was their new home, Talis shook his head. So many people had joined the dream that he and Valkirra had put into action, so many of the old, the young, the hopeful and the hopeless, those who had been judged by the

Settlement as unfit to breed, and those who no longer wanted their community ruled by such arbitrary Assessment standards. All of these folk had put their lives into the hands of Valkirra and Talis. Every one of them was precious.

Inside their new walls, Talis saw that Valkirra was already giving directions to save as much as possible from the rising floodwaters.

'There you are! Can you help the children with some of the bigger pots?' she called, sending him just one look of welcome and relief, as if for a moment she had imagined him swept away by the river. Talis sent her a reassuring grin in return and looked about for where he would be of most use.

He might have known that his partner would leap straight into action while he pondered what they should do. Valkirra had a strong, practical streak, one that had proven especially valuable in the past. He expected she would do the same again many times in the future, now that they lived in much closer connection to the Outside. So much closer to danger.

Whatever could be lifted and stored on tables and benches, or hung from beams or hefted into slings, was in the process of being moved. Talis went quickly to help with a heavy basket of whole grain, and Iver stepped over to one of the storage huts, pointing out the woven tubs that must be moved and explaining that the foodstuff stored in pottery could take its chances. The water would have to rise very high to get into the necks of those large storage jars, and if it did, they would have more to worry about than a few gallons of oil. Talis retained some hope that the flood would soon reach its peak and then start to recede. But for now, everything that could be moved must be moved.

As water began to ooze across the ground, sloshing about with their every step, Talis paused to look for the next armful to be shifted to a higher position. There was nothing. They had done as much as they could to deal with the threat the Founders River posed. Until the peak passed, they could do nothing but wait.

Valkirra obviously thought the same. She came to stand beside him at the entrance to their hall, looking out over the saturated ground, her youngest child Cushla in her arms. Behind them, Iver and Ahrenkild also stood in silence. Eventually Iver tapped Talis on the shoulder.

'I doubt that Founders River has ever thundered along quite like this, no matter what your records say, Talis. I wonder how they are faring at the Settlement.'

'I wonder that too,' said Valkirra.

Talis watched the advance of the water and did not reply. His thoughts were grim, and not to be shared in this time of danger.

CHAPTER 8

Helm worried about the young men he had left behind on the staggered ridge of thornbush. They had been arguing as he followed Rasti down through the tangled growth of the eastern flank, and he did not like the tone of their words. He rather thought they had abandoned their clan, striking out after Jarli on impulse rather than with any settled plan for finding him. They did not seem to be very skilled travellers, to Helm's mind. He did not know a great deal about the outclans, as by their very nature they had little to do with the tribes. He knew what he had learned from his mother: that outclans were groups of tribesfolk who had, for one reason or another, decided they no longer wished to follow tribal ways. Some resented the structure of the tribe that gave ultimate authority for decision-making to the huntmaster; some found tribal life not structured enough and preferred set roles for all their members; some wished to leave the annual tribal circuit and settle in one area, hunting less and growing more of their own food. No tribe ever prevented any of its members from choosing another path, though they mourned their going. What worried Helm now was that the young wanderers of the Owl appeared to have lost their way completely. They seemed to him as uncivilised as wild men, and even less able to fend for themselves Outside.

He stumbled at last onto ground that was mostly level to find Rasti in a lopsided sit, waiting for him with a grin on her face. A tired and thirsty grin, truth to tell, Helm thought, looking at how her pink tongue lolled so far out of her mouth and the hurried snatches of air she was taking.

'There you are,' he said. 'You set us quite a pace.'

The rat terrier seemed to be growing stronger, or perhaps they were getting closer to Feather. Whatever the reason, Helm found that Rasti was now setting a speed he found quite taxing.

He went down on one knee and pulled out the waterskin that hung from one of the straps of his gear. He cupped a little water in his hand for the terrier and then took a small swig himself. Water was heavy to carry, so there was not much in the skin, and there was also precious little good water to be had on Broad Plain as a rule, as far as he knew. On the other hand, those autumn rains, so unusually heavy, would have filled some of the sinks and hollow places. Helm had no fear of going short. He gave Rasti another handful of water and another; she lapped at his hand neatly and then sat back, still panting, but less distressed.

Helm stood and looked about, wondering where they should aim for next. The weather was crisp and dry, with a sharp taint of frost in the shadowed places. As far as he could see, the red dirt of Broad Plain billowed and tapered—very much in the manner of the unevenly shaken rug he had imagined when he looked down on it from the Broken Ranges—as far as the horizon in almost every direction. He noted a handful of starved saplings and the tottering skeletons of what must once have been colossal trees, their blasted trunks leaning a little, blackened branches like the broken limbs of giant men beaten, routed, vanquished. He could see irregular heaps of something smaller, too. Bodies? Bones? Well, he would find out soon enough.

He wondered which way Rasti would lead them now. Behind them was the thorn-strangled tongue of rock they had just overcome. Ahead he could see nothing so solid. Unless … He shaded his eyes with one hand. At the very edge of his sight, an uneven silhouette broke the straight line where the ruined land met the stark light of the sky. That could be a mountain, or perhaps the remnant of an old caldera. Helm looked down. Rasti was on her feet again, her whip-thin tail high over her back, her black nose pointing directly at that shape on the horizon.

'So that's where we're going.'

As usual, Rasti sent him nothing in return beyond her habitual chant of 'Feather, find Feather'.

Helm nodded. 'All right, I'm coming. A couple more hours, mind, and then we need to start looking for tonight's shelter.'

Rasti trotted east without looking back.

* * *

'I am sorry, my lady. We have done what is possible. The weather, you see.'

Brettin Danesdottir, Lady of the Temple and chief of the Settlement, paced in front of her desk, the embodiment of her station.

'I believe you need to explain.' She peered up into the stolid face of Olinna, who claimed she had been asked to inform her about the latest disaster. As if some sorts of news required a special reporter. The notion was ludicrous, thought Brettin. Disaster! She could not believe that the situation was as dire as Olinna reported, so dire that Brettin needed to be informed gently. 'I find it difficult to believe what you are saying. There have never been flood waters inside the walls of the Settlement, I am sure. There is nothing indicating even the remotest possibility of such an inundation in the archives of the singing screens. I have just looked. You may see if you wish.'

Brettin gestured the screen on her desk, inviting Olinna to read the section she had highlighted. Prolonged rain had on occasions made the going quite heavy underfoot, but that could not be the case now.

'It is no longer raining,' she went on. 'Olinna, I do not see why such a simple thing as ploughing is not possible. Surely the ground cannot be too wet for an equo or two to walk over? For a couple of strong helots to turn with a spade? I do not understand what you mean by "the weather". There is nothing amiss with the weather. It is in fact quite crisp and dry. I noted that this very morning.'

Olinna, who had not moved to look at what the singing screen reported, lowered her eyes and indicated the chair behind her. 'May I? Thank you.' She said no more until Brettin had resumed her seat behind the heavy wooden desk that had once been Valkirra's. Then, her hands neatly folded in her lap, she went on. 'It is a matter of the river rising, you see. The rain has ceased but the water continues to rise. Brettin, it is even now flowing over the river gate. The lower town is more than ankle-deep in water.'

'How? I do not believe—' Brettin paused. She had no real reason to doubt what Olinna told her, Olinna who was one of her closest allies, except that she had never heard of such a thing. A flood inside the walls of the Settlement? Why would Olinna make such a claim if it were not true? She took a breath and strove to compose herself. 'This doesn't seem to make sense,' she went on more mildly. 'If it no longer rains, why does the river still rise?'

Olinna shrugged, pursing her small mouth elaborately. 'We cannot know what goes on upstream in the Outside,' she said. 'Though the sky looks clear enough to the south, and to the west, rain may still be falling at the headwaters.'

Brettin frowned at her. Headwaters indeed. Olinna sounded rather too much like Talis, with his habitual assumption that he knew more about everything than anyone in the room. She wondered who Olinna had spoken with to make mention of headwaters and rain upstream. One of the herdsmen, perhaps, who cared about such details as weather and water, clear skies or cloud. Another thought struck her. Talis had spent altogether too much time in the archives before the Settlement had split, and had indeed taken away with him—along with a dozen or so deluded acolytes—most of the older records. Perhaps somewhere in those documents there was mention of the Founders River flooding. Talis had found old archival materials that had never been sung onto the screens, records so out of date as to be meaningless, worthless. Well, she decided, old records were of no value now. The situation would be faced with settler courage and settler determination.

'Perhaps it would be wise,' she told Olinna, 'for me to come down to the Lower Town and see for myself. Indeed, the Temple should assess the condition of the Lower Town, and inquire whether any of the lesser folk need our help. And if the ploughing can soon begin, that will be well. That land cannot be left fallow any longer.'

'No, my lady, but indeed today is not the day for working the soil. The mud, one would say.' Olinna rose to her feet again, her bulk making her appear clumsy beside Brettin's ascetic form.

Brettin walked ahead, not at all disconcerted by the contrast. As they went down the stairs, the Lady motioned for her assistant Blazej and a couple of the lesser notaries to follow. She also beckoned the young acolyte Jenna to her side. Jenna was a most useful creature. Brettin was glad of her decision to send Esteri, the fussy old son of the previous Lady, back to the main Temple halfway down the rise. There was no need for him to remain at the chief's house. His business was Temple business. Hers was now the running of the entire Settlement.

They made a stately progress through the gardens of the chief's residence and down the steep, close-set steps to where the major marketplaces were situated. Brettin looked about. The weather had not changed since she had made her round of the garden that morning, though perhaps the air was a little more chill now that the morning clouds had dispersed. There would conceivably be a frost tonight. Fine weather indeed for the start of winter, she thought, and fine weather for trading, but she could see that the market activities were sluggish, the squares unusually quiet. Brettin was surprised. Now that Temple duties took up most of every morning, she had expected trade to be quite brisk during the afternoon. Certainly the merchants paid a great deal of money to the Temple for their stalls, so there was little sense in not using these expensive spaces to the full. She frowned, noting that not only were customers scarce, but there was little in the way of goods for them to buy. She drew Jenna closer with a short gesture.

'Find out why the market is so slack today,' she ordered. 'Then meet me down at the river gate.'

'My lady.'

She and Olinna continued their descent, going by ever-sloping ways through the quarters of the merchants down to the furthest reaches of the Lower Town, where the elders, labourers, beadsmen, villeins, and helots all resided. Of course, this district was somewhat under-populated now, because many of the non-standard workers had left the Settlement to join Valkirra's exodus to the inappropriately named Newkeep Port. Brettin suppressed a smile, as she often did at the thought of the runaways in their makeshift home. She wished that she might live long enough to see them erect a keep! Or even to make a decent working port. But there, they had made their choice and she would not have such people living within Settlement walls again. Folk who walked away from their responsibilities whenever circumstances did not suit had no business expecting to be coddled whenever the Outside grew too large for them.

As surely it would.

They reached the last yard of stone-flagged way and Brettin saw that ahead, the unpaved paths of the Lower Town were slick with mud. Lifting her skirts above the mire, she somewhat regretted not having changed into her outdoor clogs. Although it was no longer raining, Olinna had warned her to expect inundation. She had not believed it.

Brettin stepped delicately down the shallow incline toward the next corner, expecting to see ahead of her the last of the workers' cottages and the empty ground she wanted ploughed, with the path winding through various market gardens and sheds toward the river gate. But all she could see was water, swirling nearer to her in a murky, rippling tide.

Even Olinna gasped. 'This is worse than I thought!' she exclaimed.

Brettin had no words. Water was flowing over the steps of the river gate in a steady surge, bringing with it all manner of torn-out tussocks and broken branches. There were bodies, too—a handful of voles, a patchwork hare, a sand rat floating on its back. There was a water snake, too, swimming with the flow, its head reappearing every so often as it fought to surf the current. As they watched in horror, the snake slipped under the water and they did not see it again. Brettin's skin crawled as she looked about, wondering where next the snake would surface, and hoping that it would not be too close to where they stood.

With a great crash, a huge branch thudded against the river stairs and for a moment its bulk acted to raise the level of the steps above the flood. Perhaps, thought Brettin, this floating tree will act as a dam against the influx. The next instant, another great branch thumped against the first, shoving it back into the larger current. The rushing side stream that had entered the Settlement faltered and then regathered its momentum.

The water kept coming.

For another long minute, Brettin stood silent, watching, while Olinna muttered to the notaries and Jenna ran up behind them, hopping about, waiting to speak.

'What is it, girl? What do they say?' Brettin could not tear her eyes away from the rising level of the floodwater.

'Told me they sell everything they can, my lady,' Jenna reported. 'Said if they had more they would sell more.'

'What nonsense.' Brettin's mind, though, was distracted by the scene of devastation around her. Jenna fidgeted, waiting for another order. Waiting to be told what to do. In her heart, Brettin knew that this was the moment for Valkirra, who had never faltered in a crisis, never stood back while others ran to face any danger. Valkirra was always at the forefront, first into whatever trouble threatened. Brettin well remembered a certain incident with a crazed mob of ovines, and of course the terrible fires that burst through the Settlement at the time of the last aftershock. She knew herself, at that moment, small and timid in the face of this incursion by the untamed forces of the Outside.

So. Small and timid she might be, physically no match for Valkirra and her ilk. Brettin reminded herself that there was more to leadership than raw, unthinking courage. Somebody had to shoulder the burden of decision-making. Someone had to choose the best way to combat any threat. A true leader made the difficult choices quickly and well. A true leader acted for the best, no matter the cost. Lifting her chin, Brettin raised her voice.

'We will go back,' she said, 'back to the paved ways. There we make our stand. Jenna, Blazej: go ahead and tell the market stallholders. They are to bring their wagons, their packs, and their tables—whatever they have. They are to make a barrier here, at the top of this flagged path. We will not allow the water to enter any higher into the Settlement.'

Jenna set off at a run.

Olinna plucked at Brettin's sleeve.

'What is it?'

'My lady, what of the folk down here in the Lower Town? There are, ahem, some who cannot easily walk up this hill. The aged, the ill, the very young—'

'A good thought,' Brettin said. 'Perhaps the Temple notaries may knock on some of these doors and then join us as we retrace our steps. Let the people here know what is happening. Tell them to make what shift they can to get away from the floodwaters.' Brettin paused as another thought struck her, a most fortuitous one. 'Indeed, District

Representative Olinna, as we make our way back up the town, we will direct any of the villeins and helots from the Lower Town to go back and help.'

'Of course,' said Olinna, signalling with a flip of her hand to the lesser Temple notaries, who began to pick their way along the mud-slick paths of the Lower Town.

The two women began to walk back up the muddy way to the paved way. There they met Jenna again, shrilly commanding various traders, none of whom looked too happy to be deploying their wares as a flood barrier. Blazej was being a bit more explicit about his orders, taking one merchant by the shoulders and turning him, with his armful of boxes, back toward the river gate, where every mite that could add to a makeshift barrier would be needed.

Brettin paused, raising her voice, speaking loudly but with an intense calm.

'My good people, I thank you for your service. Together we will ensure that no lasting harm comes to our community. Traders, we implore you to do your utmost to halt the flood at the bottom of the flagged way. You others of our community—those of you who live in the Lower Town—now is the time for you to show your gratitude to the Settlement, to offer thanks for the homes you have made here. I implore you, every one, to go into the Lower Town. Go among the cottages and shelters, find everyone you can. Do your best to bring the elders, the ill, the helot children—do your utmost to save them from the waters.'

With that, and with Olinna nodding this way and that as they passed others on their way down to help fortify the defences, Brettin picked her way up the path. They were the only ones going up the town, proceeding at a painstakingly slow pace as around them set-tlers, villeins, helots, and non-standard workers pushed down to see what could be done to save the Lower Town. Brettin walked past them, raising one slim white hand now and then in blessing, and continued toward the Temple. That would be a good place, she thought, to await news, in proper reverence to the powers that ruled the land.

Powers that even now could be sluicing the vagabonds Outside completely off the face of the earth, and would just as surely wash away some of the dangerous people of the Lower Town. Brettin smiled, only a little, as she swept into the courtyard of the Temple.

CHAPTER 9

'What is happening? Have they reached the target yet?' asked Adaeze.

Jaxon was sitting with the rest of the senior council in the throne room, bearing as patiently as he could with his queen's repeated questions. Adaeze liked to have daily—hourly—updates on the progress of the troops, although he had explained to her more than once that they would hear little of value until the raid had taken place. It made no difference. Adaeze had, perhaps, a short attention span.

'There has been no further rain, but the going is still rather heavy,' Hokulani told her, as he had the previous three days. 'This is all the feed I can show you.'

They all looked at the mottled picture on the screen at the far end of the room. To Jaxon's mind, it resembled an art installation rather than a live feed. So many bleeding colours, so many unpredictable surges of light and fizzing shapes. Interestingly, they had discovered that Hekili's link with the raiding party became inactive within one day's march. Hokulani, as head of the service, retained his connection for longer, but even he reported that communication was weak. Despite the fact that the eight Wereguard on the Outside had fully functioning wrist screens, no sense could be made of the visuals that Hokulani attempted to relay onto the screens in the regent's throne room.

'Perhaps the signal has been interrupted by storm activity,' Hekili said. 'An enormous storm can break up the transmission.'

'You are right, of course,' Jaxon agreed. 'But no such storm exists between our travelling citizens and the bulwarks of the Pale: the weather is clear and cold. We have sunny days and windless, frosty nights. Perfect transmitting conditions, one would say.'

Strange that communication had become so difficult. There was silence in the room as everyone present stared at the flickering screen · and tried to garner sense from the shimmering shapes, the wavering colours. They had not imagined they would be unable to communicate with the troops across the flattened terrain of Broad Plain, despite the distance.

And yet, as Jaxon had reminded them only yesterday, it was many, many decades since any troops of the policosmos had travelled so far away. Once the Pale had been made complete and secure, there had not been the need. The walls had kept out all threats, and the omnipresent ferals had literally driven fresh live matter right to their gates. For quite a few generations, the Pale had been able to thrive by harvesting the remains of feral kills and undertaking the occasional sally against some of the more troublesome of their neighbours on Broad Plain. Jaxon could remember a particularly successful offensive against the pantheras that had once prowled the Outside in bothersome numbers, and there was the spectacular summer when they had culled the mastodons and brought down several mammonites. Many decades ago now, of course. Since then, there had been no compulsion to do anything quite so energetic. What need, when they had a stable population and a steady biofuel supply?

This futile meeting every day with the senior officers no doubt added spice to Adaeze's rather boring and circumscribed existence, he thought. Jaxon would much prefer to have the time to concentrate on their current difficulties. They would know the result of their raiding soon enough. At least Adaeze had none of the ugly, dangerous tastes of some of her predecessors, who had entertained themselves with some rather revolting, and very wasteful, pastimes. Just as well, thought Jaxon. Now that they had sent off all their excess citizens, and eight of the Wereguard in addition, their restricted food reserves were almost enough to keep their rations at the accustomed level. Almost. Yet, for as long as the biofuel supply was compromised, every activity of the policosmos was limited to a matching degree. Service staff on half rations could not deploy their usual amount of strength and endurance, so less work could be carried out, despite the dire need for repairs and backfilling. The fault line through the heart of the Pale continued to grow, and it was evident that sooner or later most of the buildings on the far side of the city would fall. Already many were leaning dangerously away from the rest of the policosmos, as if priming themselves to crash their length down onto the crusted red sand of Broad Plain. The fabric of the Pale was being ripped apart from beneath.

Jaxon had an uncomfortable thought. Perhaps there was no interruption to the signal being sent by the raiding party. Perhaps their wrist screens were functioning perfectly. Perhaps the fault was inside the Pale—the screen itself, the receivers, the signal between them, the power source? Unnerving as the thought might be, he had a duty to follow it up. He gave a little cough, indicating he had something to say. Adaeze turned quickly from the screen, her shining eyes fixed on him in hope. Gratifying as it was that she depended upon him to find a solution, the situation was more difficult than he could readily convey to her. He kept his expression neutral, nodding to Adaeze, but turning to face Quauhtli, who sat in his usual cramped posture as though trying to sink through the seat of his chair.

'Chief of the Teshniks,' said Jaxon, 'I wonder if your staff would mind running some tests? We would be glad to know that all our receivers and screens are functioning perfectly here inside the policosmos.'

Quauhtli lowered his head, a sulky expression on his angular features. 'Above our usual testing, you mean, Senior. We will do so. As you all know, our comms systems have never fully recovered from the PPA.' He stopped, having uttered more words than Jaxon recalled hearing from him in many decades. However, the result was gratifying, as Adaeze clapped her hands.

'Ah, that is a good thought. Do you know, I have never experienced our communications at their best? So many of you tell me how effective, how clear and crisp our signals were before that aftershock. How I wish I had been progressed before the PPA! What different lives you must have led.'

'Yes, my lady,' Jaxon said, a little reluctantly. 'We have known our policosmos to function better. We are going through some rather difficult times.'

'But you have set my mind at rest, Senior. I have been worrying about the welfare of the troops, you see. Those images! So muddled, so inconstant. But perhaps it is nothing more than our faulty comms.'

'Indeed it may be nothing more than that, my lady.' He wanted to say that just a little more patience, a little more time, and their questions would be answered, but he said nothing more. With no other topic to be discussed, the senior officers soon dispersed about their duties, while the regent went to inspect some changes to her rooftop garden. Of course it was foolish to deploy service personnel on such inane work when there were other more pressing needs, but the planning and decoration of her new home was keeping the regent reasonably occupied while she awaited the outcome of the raid. That was to be counted as a good. Jaxon had enough to worry about without spending every hour soothing his queen's anxieties.

The weakness of the Service in general would need to be addressed very soon, if they were to have any certainty about their safety over the winter. Jaxon had also noted that many recyclers, also now on minimum rations, appeared to have neither the wits nor the skill to effect any worthwhile healings, let alone to progress eggs at the rate the policosmos required. He found himself considering some very radical possibilities, such as recycling all but a handful of citizens and beginning the entire post-Conflagration cycle afresh. He had even gone to the length of calling up dozens of old maps, maps that pre-dated the building of the Pale. There were extensive notes on why certain sites were unsuitable, but little detail about why the present site had been chosen, apart from its perfect siting in terms of solar energy harvesting. There was a note about access to a stream of bio-energetic flow somewhere deep beneath the surface, but it was not clear how this had been opened, or whether it was still active. The first citizens, content that they had discovered the best setting for their new abode, had omitted to record the full text of their decisions. Although the exact reasons for choosing this place were unclear, Jaxon had to admit that it had served them well for over two hundred years. To be fair, the first citizens no doubt had their hands full carving out safety from the ruins of the Conflagration. Until they had created the Wereguard and had their walls in place, there would have been little leisure for record keeping. He should be impressed that there was so much material for him to study. He should, but Jaxon was beginning to know fear. As the buildings beyond the fault line began to tip toward the Outside, he was worried the remaining sectors of the policosmos would also fall.

The Pale was collapsing under his feet and he had very little notion of what to do about it.

* * *

There had never been quite so many creatures gathered about the den of Hippolyta, leader of the ravine canini, Feather imagined. Hector had carried Mashtuk to the meeting place, and lowered him down gently beside Thestia. Jarli had brought his twin sons, followed by the gambolling cubs, and together with Hector they sat around Mashtuk, looking up at the crowd. Most of the canini were present, and all of the Storm. At the back of the assembled tribesfolk, Feather was surprised to see that Pinto and Violeta were standing with a half-dozen fellow members of the equii herd. He frowned. Something about the closeness of the equii to the humans of the tribe made him uncomfortable. Not that the tribesfolk would ever treat them as the settlers had—as dumb beasts of burden to be controlled, beaten, and confined—but still he knew that he preferred to see the equii running free at the other end of the ravine, far away from human interference.

Feather stepped into the clearing, aware that many waited to hear what he had to say. Whether he liked it or not, the Storm looked to him for direction and advice. He had never quite got out from under the influential shadow of his grandmother Kilimanjara, so that the hint of her wisdom clung around his heels. Feather did not feel that his words warranted so much attention. No matter; he had felt the weight of the tribe's expectations lie more and more heavily across his shoulders in the seasons since her death, and he knew that it was one reason he had been avoiding life with the Storm. Well, today he had news for them that may just alter their views of him. He had carried with him the secret of his father's return, had kept it to himself. He knew that now was the time he had to face the wonder, the blame, the marvelling, and the guilt.

'Good morrow, fellow tribesfolk of the Storm,' he said formally, inclining his head. It was the kind of greeting he would offer on completion of an errand, the traditional reverence that tribal heralds made to the elders when they returned with reports from beyond the tribal circuit.

Nobody replied, and Feather looked about, frowning, wondering what could be amiss, that no one gave him back the customary invitation to tell his news.

He saw that Callan was sitting with Hippolyta, and that both they and Thestia held themselves at attention, their ears pricked forward, waiting for the tribesfolk to speak. Marin and Willow stood to one side of the senior canini, but merely looked about them, as though they had no role to play in this meeting. Feather felt a tiny prick of annoyance. Why could Marin not accept his position as huntmaster with a good grace? Why did he always look so diffident and uncertain? It was rare, even when disagreements flared among the tribesfolk, that Marin spoke up in command. Ah well, perhaps when he realised that the position belonged to him for good, he would carry the burden more willingly. He had all the capability he needed, Feather was sure. He had to stop waiting for someone—Feather—to come and lift the cloak of responsibility from his shoulders.

'Leaders all,' Feather said into the continuing silence. 'I come to wish the tribe safety and good companionship on their journey back to the paths of the annual circuit. Once more, I beg the boon of travel. I must return to Newkeep Port to confer with my partner Jana. I hope, in a few weeks at most, that Jana and I will join the circuit.'

'Probably not until spring, would you propose?' asked Willow, her brows raised in inquiry, or maybe disapproval.

'As you say,' agreed Feather. He kept his tone quiet, his manner mild. There was no need for heat over this small matter. Of course the elders were by now accustomed to his habit of spending large portions of the year with his partner. He was sure they would agree that the makers of Newkeep needed his help more than the experienced tribesfolk of the Storm did.

'So you will not travel with us now?' confirmed Marin. He looked haggard and old. Feather was sorry to see that the matter of Jarli's twins weighed so heavily upon the foremost couple of the tribe.

'I cannot,' Feather replied. 'I wish you all speed and safety.'

Marin shook his head slightly and turned to Jarli, sitting at the feet of the assembled canini leaders. 'And you, fellow Outsider, scion of the Owl, what do you say? Do you bring your family with us, or no?'

Jarli cleared his throat, but Feather was pleased to hear that when he spoke, his words had the clarity and weight of decision. Jarli had done some growing in the weeks he had spent with the canini.

'We do not travel with you,' Jarli confirmed. 'I thank you from the depths of my heart for the offer, and for your care and concern. I am forever grateful for the help you have given me as I take up the role of fatherhood. However, for the moment we stay in the ravine. My children need safety and stability. They have bonds with the canini. I have grown some bonds with the canini too. For now, we stay.'

'You do not go to rejoin your clan?' asked Willow.

'No. Hippolyta and Thestia have agreed that we may share this sanctuary, at least for the short term. As Romulo and Remo grow, things may change. The future will unfold in its time.'

Feather nodded his approval at Jarli, who lowered his head, his tale told and the difficult decision made. Marin and Willow conferred privately, he saw, but they appeared to accept this state of affairs. Now was the time for Feather to give them the rest of his own news.

Yet before he could continue, his daughter Freya spoke.

'Huntmaster Marin, I too would ask leave to stay,' she said. 'I have formed something of a bond with these infants. If it is acceptable to you, and if my father agrees, I would welcome the chance to remain at least another season or two here in the ravine. Hippolyta has granted me leave to stay, if I have the approval of my pack.' Freya smiled at this description of her family, and Hippolyta grinned at her. They evidently had a good understanding, better than Feather had realised.

He recovered first from the surprise of this request. 'Are you sure, daughter? It is quite a restricted life, here in the ravine. It is not in the least like travelling the circuit.'

'It is a little more like the Settlement, only much better,' Freya agreed. 'I am sure I could be of help to the canini, and to the twins' father. I would like to help, if you give me leave.'

Feather inclined his head. At fifteen summers old, he had known his own mind very well. He had no doubt that his daughter was just as certain, and that it was his duty as a father to allow her to make her own choices. Kilimanjara—his grandmother who had been the only parent who mattered to him—had always taken his notions seriously.

'My leave you may gladly have, daughter,' he said. 'If the huntmaster agrees?'

Marin looked doubtful, but in the tribes' unspoken rules of politeness, the authority of parents over their children was taken seriously. That was indeed why they gave so much weight to Jarli's choice.

After a moment, Marin nodded. 'As you wish, Feather, but I begin to fear that your family is forming its own outclan.'

That waiting silence fell again as all the tribesfolk looked to Feather. He saw that Freya had put her hand over her mouth, surprised at the serious turn the conversation had taken. Hippolyta, pack leader of the ravine canini, climbed to her feet as if she feared a disagreement was about to erupt.

Feather raised both hands. 'Peace, fellow members of the Storm,' he said softly. 'I am sorry if that is how it seems. I know I have not been the most reliable of tribesfolk since the passing of Kilimanjara.' Even now, months later, he had to stop and take a breath at the mention of her name. Callan, too, whined in sorrow, and Feather sent him an understanding look. 'Yet I would say to you,' Feather continued, taking a deep breath and speaking a little more loudly, 'that the matter of the mastership is settled. Marin is by every measure a fine huntmaster. I tell you this now, as I have told you before, it is a mantle I shall never wear. I also say that for as long as I live I will help you all I can. I will always help the Storm, but I will never be huntmaster.'

'Feather, son of Helm, please, won't you reconsider?' Marin asked as many of the elders began to speak at once.

Feather shook his head. 'The matter is settled.' He held up a hand as more protests rose. 'Peace, there is more I must say. Tribesmen of the Storm, there is news. One who was lost has been found again.' He turned to face Marin and stepped closer to put a hand on the older man's shoulder. 'Huntmaster, I must tell you that my father Helm, son of Kestrel of the Storm, has returned to us. He has made the journey back from madness and exile, and even now awaits my return to Newkeep. Marin, your old friend returns. I will bring him to the Storm, I swear, in the spring of this turning.'

* * *

Talis believed that the worst had passed, and Valkirra was inclined to agree. For many hours, there had been no further advance of the Founders River into Newkeep. The makers had watched through a fearful night, but they were encouraged by the sights that met their eyes as the rays of the rising sun flooded across Broad Plain toward them. Nothing had grown worse overnight. Nothing had been irreparably damaged, and they had managed to save all their stored foodstuffs and all their livestock, thanks to the quick thinking of Iver and the industry of all the makers. Talis hoped that this would be the worst they had to withstand, for this season at least. They had faced and passed their first serious test of life on the Outside without the centuries-old protections of the Settlement.

Jasper, Valkirra's son, was filled with an energy that only twelve-year-olds could possess after such an eventful couple of days. While the adults gathered in the main hall, doing their best to sweep the thick, muddy water out into the courtyard, each with their trousers rolled up to their knees, Jasper volunteered to do a run around the inside of the walls, checking to see if perhaps a high tide mark might be visible. Who knew? By now, perhaps it would be possible to see that the height of the flood had passed and the water levels were on their way down. Talis hoped it was so. At the moment, they were trapped inside by their own moats on three sides and on the fourth by the lake-like expanse of water where the river should be.

'Go on, then, and be as quick as you can. Don't go through anything higher than your knees, though,' he added.

Jasper hardly waited to hear this, but ran splashing through the broom-wielders to the door. Cushla squealed, splattered a little by the mud of his steps, and Talis reached out to lift her into his arms.

'There now, darling, you're all right. It's only water.'

'I want to go with Jasper! I want to go outside!'

'Of course you do,' said Valkirra with a hint of exasperation. 'You can go later, sweetheart.' Cushla had kept them awake all night, screaming whenever the water touched her, and also whenever she imagined the water might touch her. They had all done their best to keep the children completely out of its reach, but every table and bench and shelf was already overloaded with food that had to be kept dry. Humans, rat terriers, and ovines could withstand a little wet; stored grain could not. It had been an uncomfortable night for them all.

'I want to go now!' Cushla was sobbing. 'I want to go home.'

Talis met Valkirra's eyes as he shushed his daughter, turning her face into his shoulder. Her tears could hardly make him wetter than he was already. 'Perhaps something to eat,' he suggested.

'A very good notion,' said old Ahrenkild. 'Such a pity we can't have a fire. Hot food would be even better.'

'All in good time,' said Iver. 'We have here a whole tub of sour pears, dried and ready to dip into the honey in this jar. What do you say, children?'

As the other youngsters gathered around him, Cushla turned her head to watch. In only a minute, Talis was able to set her down to join the others at Iver's side, her fears forgotten in her enjoyment of the rare sweet treat. Of course, that one big jar of honey had been meant to last all winter, but this was as good a time to use it as any. Jana joined Iver, promising the children that they could help her make a song about the Founders River Flood as soon as they had finished their treat. Talis pulled Valkirra close and planted a kiss on her forehead.

'Don't worry about Cushla. She'll get used to living here. It was a pretty horrible night for us all.'

'It was.' Valkirra put an arm around her partner's waist. 'I didn't realise she missed our old home so much.'

'Cushla is frightened. I'm frightened!' Talis declared. 'I don't blame her for thinking of her old bed, up in the High City. Don't tell me you wouldn't prefer to be watching all this from up in your office?'

'My old office,' Valkirra corrected him. 'Maybe. No, not really. Remember everything else that comes with that safety. Ugh! The Temple with its sticky hands on everything of value, assessing us settlers out of existence with their foolish notions of untainted humanity.'

'You're right, of course.' Talis shook his head. 'There is no such thing. Untainted humanity! No amount of careful breeding can strip us of our inbuilt Conflagrationist genes. All that bio-engineering has coloured our blood.'

'Even if most of it ended up inside the Pale,' agreed Valkirra. 'We can't undo so many generations of tweaking and bending, no matter how many years we've spent refusing every technical accessory. Every one of us has pre-Conflagration legacy.'

'We do. We have done away with nano-engines and implants. We might even have bred out the fliers and the mind-readers, but I wouldn't be surprised if there is still some of that animal-language ability among us.'

'Do you think so? I thought only tribesfolk could mindspeak the canini.'

Talis walked a few steps with her to the entrance of the hall. The day was fine and clear, though still cold. The sweeping had made little dif-ference to the ankle-deep level of the water inside the hall, but at least the broom-pushers were a bit warmer. They looked around their new home, now one or two hands under water. The level indeed seemed to have stopped rising, and the indignant fowl hanging in cages from the walls could soon be pecking about in the mud. How soon—and when the water would actually start to recede—were the questions that rose into Talis's mind. It was difficult to say. Jasper would be able to tell them more, once he had checked all the muddy marks on the walls. Talis put the thought aside and returned to his conversation with Valkirra.

'My heart,' he said. 'I don't think we can say that those bio-alter-ations exist only in the Outside—only in the tribes or the outclans, or the wild men, of course. Some of us are quite good with animals. Look at Tammas and the ovines, for example. Even better, Tammas with the equii.'

Valkirra scoffed. 'He doesn't mindspeak them, surely. He just cares for them with respect. No settler has mindspeech!'

Talis lifted one eyebrow. 'No settler would say so, in any case.'

'No, Talis, really, that's nonsense. If you're trying to distract me from all this mud with your foolish talk, you are succeeding.'

Talis grinned. 'Good. All right, say I agree with you. Yes, I believe that the tribesfolk have the best mindspeech, and that they value it.

I suspect they use far-sight too, and are glad of anyone who has it, despite the fact that the Temple would call it an 'un-human' skill. None of us knows what the humachines of the Pale are like, except that they have the advantage of every pre-Conflagration modification of weaponry and strength.'

Valkirra grew grave. They both remembered the unsuccessful attempt the settlers had made on the Pale in the months following the last aftershock, the terrible PPA.

'Yes, well. Let us hope that we never find out any more about them. Let the humachines keep to their end of Broad Plain and we will keep to ours.'

'A good notion indeed.' Talis frowned. 'Where can Jasper have got to? It doesn't take this long to run around the inside of the walls. Newkeep is not so big.'

They stepped further out into the shallow, muddy water of the yard, looking about for any sign of Jasper. Talis walked in one direction and Valkirra in the other, until they could both see around the hall to the full extent of their grounds on either side. They turned as one back toward the expanse of the river.

Jasper was nowhere to be seen.

CHAPTER 10

Everyone began to speak at once—everyone human, that is. Feather saw the canini withdraw a little as he fended off the questions and exclamations of the tribesfolk. One good result of his news was that Freya pushed her way through the crowd to throw her arms around him, evidently moved and thrilled to hear of Helm's unexpected return. As Feather answered questions and made promises, Freya hung about him. For this if for nothing else in his life, Feather was glad of Helm's influence.

Yet his announcement made a very long event of the tribe's leaving. All the elders had questions, some of which Feather found annoying, some of which cut him to the heart.

'Helm is alive,' cried Willow, a spark in her eye. 'That is wonderful news! Oh, Feather, why did you not say so?'

'I am only slowly becoming accustomed to the news myself,' he answered. If truth be told, he thought, he would say that for most of his life, his father's name had been dust in his mouth. 'I am sorry for the delay,' he went on. 'It has cost me some pain and many days, nay, weeks, of striving to accept his return myself.'

'I think I understand,' said Marin. 'Helm's reappearance must be even more of a shock to you than to us. Is he well? Is he in his right mind? Poor fellow! How he must have suffered.'

'I believe him to be well, now,' said Feather, blinking. The notion of his father's suffering was one that made his heart sting. 'We spent time together at Newkeep, with Jarli, helping the makers to prepare for the coming winter. He is quite strong and his mind appears sound.'

Willow looked across at Jarli, who returned her look with a mild but self-assured stare and a lopsided grin at Feather. If she had expected him to tell her anything that Feather chose to keep buried, Jarli's look said, she underestimated him. Outclan-bred he may be, but he knew loyalty and love as well as any of the tribe. Feather was sorry that Willow was hurt by this, but a little warmed by Jarli's unspoken pledge of trust. He nodded to the outclansman.

'Helm must be much changed, though,' Marin continued, frowning. 'Ai! How well I remember the day he left. What sorrow! What anger! That measure of grief must put its mark on a man.'

Feather kissed the top of Freya's head, feeling her arms tighten a little around him. He released a long breath and glanced away, but no amount of calming himself could change the truth. 'I cannot say as to changes. I have never met the man before.'

Willow gasped, a little outraged by the bald severity of his statement, and opened her eyes wide at him.

Marin only nodded and spoke mildly. 'It is so,' he agreed. 'You never knew him. Well, that may be mended. He is a good man, you will find. The best friend I ever had. Feather, you have provided us with good news, and much to talk about on the journey. I thank you for that. I am sure we will have much to say of this, another time.' He reached forward to pat Feather kindly on the shoulder and then clapped his hands for attention. 'Come, tribesfolk of the Storm, we really must leave now if we are to reach a good camping place before nightfall. Join me in thanking our gracious hosts for this time of plenty, of sharing, and of companionship here in the ravine.'

Feather thought that this was something Marin did extremely well—he was very adept in all the politenesses that endured in the Outside. Despite the fact that his own mindspeech was weak, Marin respected and valued the canini. Feather was glad of it. With Freya by his side, he stepped out of their way, only then noting that Hector had climbed to his feet. Towering over everyone there—his head even higher than that of Pinto, the tallest of the equii—it was no surprise that all speech came to a halt at his action.

'Marin, Willow,' said Hector. 'I too am remaining with my pack here in the ravine. Here I believe I am of most use. Here I have the strongest bonds. I thank you for your friendship and for all you have taught me about being human.'

Willow gave a little cry of dismay and quickly covered her mouth with her hand. Feather thought that she must have been counting on Hector to stay with the tribe. It was a shame, really; there were few couples better suited to parenting than Marin and Willow, but it seemed they were never to enact that role.

Marin put his arm across Willow's shoulders as he replied. 'Hector, son, you are quite human enough without any learning from us. We wish you well, and we will always be happy to see you, any time you care to visit.'

Willow went forward then to embrace him, and Feather shook his head sadly. He knew that she had come to have love for this strange creature, who listened to her and valued her. What a shame that Hector's parent—whoever that person may have been—had not left him at the camp of the Storm all those years ago, instead of at the gates of the Pale. At the same moment, he realised he was pleased that Hector was staying. The big human-humachine would use all his power to keep every living creature in the ravine safe. Freya could not be better cared for anywhere in the Outside. He looked down at his daughter.

'So you will have Hector as well as Jarli to give you some human conversation.'

'Oh, yes,' Freya answered, waving a slim hand toward Hector, who was now talking quietly with Paolo the scout and some of the elders. 'I don't mind him. I'm glad he is staying. Father, we can talk later. I'm going to help Jarli with Mashtuk and the babies.'

Feather raised his brows at this but said nothing. He believed it was better for young folk to manage their relationships without the interference of parents. He had thought that Freya was particularly friendly with Paolo over the last summer, but he saw now that she regarded his going with seeming indifference. And if, he thought, she is she was now becoming attached to Jarli, then that too may well end in disappointment. Like Helm and his beloved Alia, Jarli had buried his heart with his dead partner Magda. Freya is young yet, Feather reminded himself. It may be years before she knows her own heart. Not everyone makes a heart choice at fifteen.

He went to join the group gathering by the senior canini, offering thanks and farewells. Feather spoke up too, stating his gratitude for their hospitality and care of his kinsmen the Storm.

Callan grinned at him. 'They did not do it for you, my friend. The canini of the ravine are very attached to me,' he said dryly. 'Of course they welcome my two-legged friends.'

Thestia turned to stare, as if about to chastise him for his impoliteness, but then realised that he was sharing a joke with Feather. She wrinkled her nose. 'Callan, you have a strange way of showing your love for this fellow.'

Callan flicked an ear at her. 'Feather and I are old friends. He likes my twisty speech. He understands me.'

'I do,' Feather said. 'And I love him like a brother. Besides, our minds are open to each other, for the most part. I see the love that his words hide.'

'Enough, my friend,' said Callan. 'You will make my pack fellow here squirm. Thestia is not one for soft language.'

Thestia showed her teeth in a mock growl. 'You are so mawkish that I have to leave now or lose my last meal.'

Callan laughed as she turned tail and headed, like many of the pack, to follow the tribe through the thorn forest and to watch them make their way down the steep path onto the sands of Broad Plain.

* * *

Gavino looked over the edge of the parapet atop the walls of the Pale, making sure to take his time scanning everything within reach of his wristscreen. Since the day they had exiled his year-mate Hector—no, since before that, since Hector and his experienced partner Tad had met that cursed live canine and let it go—let it run across Broad Plain and home into the damned ravine—well, ever since that happened, nothing much had gone right for the overworked service staff of the Pale.

Gavino brought his wristscreen close to his visor and sifted through the images he had captured, zooming in and out repeatedly to try to make sense of what he could see. The pictures were grainy, as though they had been recorded in the worst kind of fog such as they got sometimes in the middle of winter, but there was no fog today. After those big autumn rains stopped, they'd had nothing but fine clear days and freezing nights. Not even a wind to dry off the sodden plain and raise the usual dust. No reason for his wristscreen to record everything so hazily, unless there was some problem with the recorder, or maybe with the power source. At the thought, he let out a frightened yelp, quickly suppressed.

Not quickly enough. A moment later, Supervisor Laylene had stepped smartly up the ladder to his perch on the wall. She tugged impatiently at the back of his tabard, the thick metallic fabric scraping against the unprotected skin of his neck as she pulled it too hard.

Making sure that nothing of his dismay showed on his face, Gavino turned to look down at her. 'Ma'am?'

'What did you see? Is there anything out there?' Unusually for Laylene, she did not sound angry. She sounded rattled, as if she expected him to report that a thousand ferals were massed under their walls.

Gavino shook his head. 'No, ma'am. Nothing to be seen. Well, nothing alive.'

'Nothing? Don't talk rubbish.' That sounded more like her. 'There must be something,' she continued. 'The Outside is teeming with life, we all know that. We've lived off it long enough, with everything the ferals drive in our direction.'

'Yes, ma'am. I know, ma'am. The Outside and the ferals provide us with our harvest from the base of the walls. The flesh for the biofuel pits, and the metal for the stacks. I do know that, ma'am.'

Supervisor Laylene scowled at him, her arms folded across her thin body, one long finger tapping rhythmically against her armour. 'Don't try to tell me what I already know, Serviceman. I am not a fool.'

Gavino knew what she was thinking—what she was always thinking and sometimes said aloud—that he had trained with the human Hector, that he had been progressed in the same pod. She sometimes reminded him that he had partnered with Hector after Tad had been ostracised, and that he had too much softness, like Tad did and like Hector did.

Laylene asked him about both Hector and Tad many times, but he had nothing to say that she did not already know. Was he soft, like those two lost ones? He didn't think so. Why, his liveware was based on Tangshi genes, like the senior forecaster Jaxon Tangshi! He could not possibly be harbouring any over-human quirks like empathy or compassion. He couldn't, Gavino told himself. It was not feasible. These moments that came over him, these twinges of fear and grief, were mere blips in his wiring. Maybe they would disappear, once the policosmos resumed its regular schedule of enhancements, which was suspended just now while they dealt with the loss of the Acrocomplexa and the whole western half of the city.

He just wished that he could control his words, and his face, a bit better. Then no one other than himself could possibly realise the depth of his knowledge and dread: the Pale was fading in power, with no reliable comms anymore and no working viewfinders in any sector. On top of that, Gavino also suspected that his own internal power sources were failing. He was terrified that Laylene would notice his weaknesses and assign him to be recycled. It had happened to others. He took pains to stand straight and to look the supervisor in the eye.

'Ma'am, I'm sorry to say that I can find nothing alive, and no wrecks nor bodies either within easy range.' He did not say that the wrist-screen images he had gathered were so crude that he couldn't tell the sky from the sand. 'It may be as you supposed, ma'am, that the ferals are dying off.'

Supervisor Laylene's impressive scowl grew more pronounced. 'I don't remember saying that.'

Too late, Gavino realised that he was quoting a rumour back to her, one that was doing the rounds of the service oikos. Someone, it was said, had overheard Hokulani Head of the Service tell Laylene that the ferals were coming to the end of their half-machine life. That the ferals had been made before the Great Conflagration, that they were old, very old technology, and that was why they couldn't last much longer.

'Ma'am, your pardon, please. I'm just saying what I've heard in the piazzas. That the ferals are old and worn out.'

'Hmm.' Supervisor Laylene turned her back on him and began to make her way down the ladder. 'The ferals provide much of our raw food source, Serviceman. You would be wise not to underestimate their resilience. They have been around much longer than we have. They will continue to provide. The Pale will survive.'

'Yes, ma'am. Save the Pale, ma'am.' Just as well to give her the formal words. Gavino saluted, remaining in the respectful position until Laylene had reached the inner go-way and resumed her round of the perimeter, even though she never once glanced back at him.

He turned again to look out over the parapet. It was true, what she said, that the ferals had been working the land since before Broad Plain existed. The ferals had been made as fighters before the Great Conflagration brought an end to all the battles, before it took down all the cities and all the mighty go-ways and all the forests and all the mountains and … and everything. Ferals had been made before the Conflagration and all its aftershocks had reshaped the land into the starved, dead-dry, lifeless desert it was today. The ferals were way older than Broad Plain, way older than the whole of the Outside, so of course they were older than the Pale. Ancient technology for sure.

Not like us, as one of the youngest of the service personnel had said, not built with proper technology to last the ages. Not like the service staff, she had said, as if that could convince her of their own continuing existence.

Only a youngster could say that, was what Gavino thought. Only a youngster would not know that all the service staff were beginning to fail, because she'd never known anything else. It was no fault of the Service; it was not that they worked less or didn't try as hard as ever. But on half rations and suspended upgrades they could not keep up to their usual standard. There was, after all, a reason why they had routine intake levels in the first place: they had always been supplied with the minimum they needed to undertake their duties.

Same as every citizen in the whole policosmos. As an egg you were given what you needed, in liveware and hardware and software assignment. Then when you got progressed and trained, you got fed what you needed to play your role in the Pale, and you got the regular upgrades and refits that you needed. For the first time, Gavino realised that every single citizen still alive in the Pale was on reduced provisions. That meant that every single humachine was only able to do part of their usual assignment of duties. It stood to reason.

Gavino bit his lip, frowning out onto the darkening shapes of the Outside. He could reason things out, he knew, a little bit too well, because of his Tangshi genes. He had more reasoning than he needed. He had been told so many times, and it had rarely brought him anything but surprised praise. The fearfulness he showed, though, and the way he couldn't help the odd nervous shiver, was something he had often been scolded for. He didn't think it could be explained by any of his other splices, or at least, there was nothing amiss that any of the recyclers had found. He wondered, though, whether it was a matter of his reason beginning to fail, just the same as the power of his equipment was also diminishing. He couldn't capture clear images on his wristscreen, and neither could he stop fearful thoughts running through his mind.

Gavino was very afraid.

* * *

Daku, Jarli's brother of the Owl outclan, was now wishing he had never set out after his brother. He remembered being very angry with his father, and with the rest of the clan. They had no feeling for Jarli at all. Not only had they condemned him for taking up with a Settlement girl, they had closed their hearts to him. Their own father had told Jarli never to return, to make his home with the filthy settlers if he wished, folk who sat astride their own sewers and pretended that their Temple could save them from death. Idiotic nonsense, of course. Everybody died.

Daku put his head in his hands, doing his best to stem the tears that leaked from his eyes. He had never been so alone or so scared. Everybody died, it was true. Not that any of his kin at the Owl would care. They had let Daku and his friends leave—had told them to go, in fact—said that if they wanted to mix with settler types, they were welcome to do so. Full of indignant anger on his brother's behalf, Daku had done just that, and three of the other young men of the clan had gone with him. What they had been thinking, Daku no longer knew. What they had hoped, he was no longer sure. What they had expected—ah, that he knew. They would follow Jarli across Broad Plain to the Settlement, and speak with him. Jarli said his partner Magda was the sweetest woman ever born since the time of the Great Conflagration. A foolish notion, of course, though their father had not needed to dismiss it in quite so definite a way. Spitting in Jarli's face, telling him to check where he had left his brains: that was no way to talk to Jarli.

Talk to Jarli. Daku wished that he could. 'Jarli, my brother,' he whispered. 'Jarli.'

There was no answer. There could not be. At Daku's feet, one of his companions groaned softly. Daku patted his shoulder. 'Hush now. Not long now,' he said. 'Not long.'

Around them, around the two dead youths and the two yet living, a dozen over-confident pantheras made a lazy circuit, waiting. Waiting for them to stop moving. Why fight further, Daku supposed, when they could feast in a few minutes?

'Not long,' he said to the pantheras.

Chapter 11

The search for Jasper drew everyone forth from the hall, first out into the enclosure and then, desperately, into the Outside proper. Every one of the makeshift buildings was searched from its mud-slick floor to the height of its thatch—or bare beams, in some cases—but no trace of the boy could be found. Iver directed the older folk to walk slowly through the grounds, pushing a broom or a rake, checking that there was no clue hidden by the sludgy floodwaters, now less than ankle-deep. Not deep enough, in truth, to drown in. That's what Talis kept telling himself. There was not enough water in the compound for Jasper to have come to grief.

The moats around their walls and the purling, opaque water of the swollen Founders River were another matter. They could see clearly now that the flood level was falling, but that was scant comfort. Talis came to stand beside Valkirra, waiting forlornly at the edge of the swirling water. He put his arm across her shoulders.

'He is gone.' Her voice was harsh.

'My heart,' replied Talis, 'we do not know that for sure.'

'Talis, please. Don't pretend. Look at the river! For certain it has swept him away. Either that, or he went Outside when he knew better, and stepped into one of the moats by mistake. Stupid, stupid boy!'

Talis bit his lip. This anger of Valkirra's was one face of her grief. He knew it well. She had been so angry, many years before, when their foolish raid against the Pale had ended in disaster, when a score of their best and most promising settlers had been razed to dust in an instant. And then again, when their eldest child Charm had fallen to his death on the steep stairway that led to the Lower Town. That time she had raged for days. Charm's fatal tumble was the event that had begun Valkirra's abiding antagonism against the Temple, who had suggested there had perhaps been something wrong with Charm, some unnamed genetic flaw that had turned his simple fall into a deadly event. Talis knew his own brand of anger at the Temple, but he wished that, just once, Valkirra would show her grief in a way that would allow him to comfort her. Her anger only drove him to contradict her.

'We don't know that,' he said. 'Don't give him up so easily. Jasper will be safe somewhere. We will find him.'

Valkirra rounded on her partner, her eyes red and her face blotched with tears of fury. 'Don't make promises you can't keep! He is gone, I tell you, gone!'

She pushed roughly past him, striding back inside the compound without looking at or speaking to the dozens of folk doing their best to find some clue to where Jasper might be. Talis watched her retreat until he saw Ahrenkild, the oldest of their community, gather Valkirra into an embrace and take her back inside the hall. He let out a long breath, closing his eyes against the flat, bright light of the sunny day, light that reflected gaily off the turgid surface of the damn water.

'The dam water? We have no dam, Talis.'

Talis opened his eyes to find Jana standing in front of him. Of all the makers of Newkeep, it was Jana who had the clearest vision of what their home might become. She had the gentlest of ways with words, too, befitting her station as singer, the poet of the community.

Talis shook his head. 'Apologies. I was thinking aloud, I suppose. Damn this water, was what I was thinking.' He gasped, choking down a sob. 'It has stolen my son! My only—'

'Hush,' said Jana, tucking her arm through his elbow and turning him about, away from the river, away from the built-up mud and the wreckage of plants that now lined the banks, away from the bloated, twirling bodies of hares and hop rabbits and sand rats. At least they could see the banks again; that was something.

He put one hand over Jana's. 'I'm sorry. I've been trying so hard to be positive, to believe that we will see our son again. But it's hard.'

Jana began to walk with him toward the hall.

Talis looked up and pulled away. 'No. I don't want to go inside. Let Valkirra have some space.'

'As you will. Talis, we are making a bridge of sorts, across the moat.'

'A bridge?'

'Yes. So that we can get across and onto Broad Plain. Tammas thinks that Jasper may have found a way out there. He thinks the lad may have gone after a hen or an ovine, or even one of the rat terrier pack. They are not all accounted for. All our animals, I mean, except for the equii.'

Talis frowned. There were only five equii at Newkeep, and they were plainly visible, standing up to their hocks in their enclosure. Someone—Tammas, he supposed—had filled their manger with an extra ration of hay. Probably the equii needed reassurance, too, that the danger was past and everything was back to normal.

Everything was not back to normal. Jasper was gone.

'What is it?' Jana interrupted him.

'Nothing. Just thinking,' Talis answered. 'Jana, you say all the animals are not accounted for?'

She nodded, her slightly curly hair now a frizzy mass, like tangled sheaves of ripe wheat about her head, over her shoulders. Jana's eyes, a gold-tinted hazel, perfectly matched her skin, which had the colour of darkest honey. Talis looked at her and shook his head. How could such a perfect creature have a child who had been designated as non-standard? The Temple's measures made no sense. They were right, he and the other makers of Newkeep, to drag themselves out from under Temple rule.

But the cost! Talis closed his eyes, closed his mind to the thoughts that battered him. Animals, yes. Think of that, he told himself.

'I thought the ovines had been penned.'

'Tammas says one of the young rams is missing. It's a flighty, nervous creature. Tammas said it possibly leaped over the fence of the pen and swam across the moat to where it could see pasture.'

Talis looked to where Jana was pointing. A distance away on Broad Plain, several humps of raised ground showed above the shrinking floodwaters like soggy dumplings in a murky soup. Although the Outside looked flat and almost featureless, there were of course areas of higher ground, and places where the sands were hollowed out right down to the clay bedpan or the bedrock. Nothing was ever completely flat in nature. Of course, Talis told himself. He knew that. Now that Jana had put the idea in his mind, he could not shake it out.

'And Jasper may have gone after it?'

'Tammas says he is the most diligent of the children, where our animals are concerned. That Jasper seems to know and to care about every one of the ovines, and he has names for each of the fowl.'

'That I did not know,' Talis replied. He stood for a moment, wondering what to do next.

Jana touched his arm. 'Talis, I know what it is like, waiting for Feather to come back from the Outside. It is terrifying, but at least I know that he always has good reason to be out there, and I trust that reason to keep him safe. We hope—Tammas and I—that Jasper is the same. If he is trying to save one of our stock, he will do everything he can to return to us.'

'You are right.' Talis looked toward the north edge of the compound, where Tammas with Branimir and a few of the herders were wrestling with lengths of wood, doing their best to span the murky brown waters that swirled within the confines of the moat. 'Ah, we can do better than that,' he muttered. 'We don't need a bridge to keep our feet dry! Jana, tell them I've gone to fetch the barge poles. They are strong and will cover the distance across the moat. Even if I have to go across hand by hand through the water, I am for searching in the Outside.'

'I will tell them,' Jana answered.

Without a further word, Talis slogged through the mud back into the compound, racing to find the poles that had been stored in safety on the roof of the hall, the longest building they had constructed. In only a minute, Branimir was by his side, helping him to pull down a couple of the sturdy shafts. Together they hefted the long poles over to the moat, where Tammas and the herdsmen waited, all of them soaked to the skin and covered in mud.

Talis did not stop to think how, when the water had been even higher, Jasper could possibly have crossed the moat to chase a hen or an ovine or a rat terrier onto Broad Plain. He only knew that he had hope once more in his heart.

Hope could keep him going.

* * *

Callan saw that Pinto was going to delay the departure of the Storm even further. Difficult as it was for the equii to traverse the twisted, narrow paths of the thorn forest, they had managed it once when they first came to the ravine, so really it should be no surprise that they could do it again. With Violeta and the handful of youngsters behind him, Pinto appeared at the top of the entry path. Here a shallow depression made a clearing of sorts, and here the senior canini were gathered to watch the tribe on their way.

'Wait,' called Pinto. 'Wait, tribesfolk. We wish to ask you a boon.'

Callan, who was the most adept at speaking with the equii, nudged Thestia to pass on the message. 'Pack mate, the equii want to say something to the Storm.'

'Those leggy things, you mean? The ones who do nothing except eat every green leaf in the ravine? The ones with the big eyes and the silly blunt teeth? Those equii? Your equii?'

Callan nosed her in exasperated affection. Thestia pretended that she could not hear the equii, and often made mock of Callan's decision to save them from being hunted to exhaustion and death on Broad Plain. He had to admit that there was little the equii added to the life of the ravine, and they also caused quite a devastation on the shrubs and grasses that, in truth, every other creature depended upon. Still, they were harmless in themselves, and their lives were precious. He was sure Mashtuk would agree.

'My equii!' he scoffed, and then turned his attention to the tribesfolk. 'Paolo!' he mindsent strongly. 'A word before you go.'

The scout made his way back through the people and packs that crowded the area. Marin had already begun the steep descent down the path with the rest of the elders—Callan now knew that the tribe travelled like the canini did, with the aged and slow setting the pace in the lead while the others managed the bulk of the baggage and guarded the whole column. Paolo and the rest of the scouts would range both ahead and behind, maintaining the safety of the route and also choosing the most likely campsite for the tribe to spend the night. At this rate, thought Callan, they would be camping in the first stand of trees they encountered. He had never seen such a palaver about a journey. The Storm repeatedly said that they were going, but they did not seem to be very urgent about getting on their way. He wondered about that, because he and his pack had spent many years travelling with this very tribe. He had never known them to be so dithering, so indecisive. But then, he reminded himself, in his day Kilimanjara was the huntmistress. Kilimanjara always knew what she was about. Perhaps it would be best if Feather did take over leadership of the Storm. But that would never happen; Feather had just as much decision about him as his grandmother. Ah, maybe Helm, the lost-and-found father, could relieve Marin of the burden. But that was a matter for another day. By the stars, he was becoming as philosophic and absent-minded as Mashtuk. That was what came of spending time in the ravine!

'Callan?' Paolo spoke as if he had already said the big white canine's name more than once. 'Callan? There is something you wish to say?'

'Yes, Paolo, thank you. It is to do with the equii. They wish to ask something.' The scout, after initially being a trifle wary of the canini, had quickly developed his latent mindspeech, possibly from his close connection with Freya. However it had happened, it was extremely handy for the canini to have a strong mindspeaker present. There could never be too many of them when it came to negotiating with humans.

'The equii? You can talk with them too?'

'Somewhat,' Callan explained. 'They have only recently begun speaking to us again. They stopped, you see, after the Great Conflagration.'

'They did? That is something I didn't know.'

'They preferred not to put things into words,' Callan went on. 'Fears, hopes—you understand.'

Paolo had the tolerant look of an adolescent cub being politely patient with an elder. 'Of course. What is it they want now?'

Callan lifted his nose toward Pinto. 'The tribe waits on your request, Pinto my friend.'

The big parti-coloured equo looked down, his huge sooty eyes almost hidden by the long black lashes that were just one of his many points of beauty. Such a pity, Callan thought as he had often in the past few months, that some idiot settler had decided to geld such a magnificent creature. Ah well. There was nothing to be said of that now, and here in the Outside, no equo would ever suffer the same.

'These younglings,' Pinto told Callan, 'are wondering if they may accompany the tribe on their circuit.'

Callan could not suppress a tiny yelp of surprise. There were equii who wanted to leave the ravine, who wanted to travel on Broad Plain?

'Are they sure?' he asked. 'Are you sure? It is not very safe for your kind in the Outside, brother of the land.'

Pinto shook his long mane. 'This we know. Still they wish it. If the tribe will allow. These juveniles feel the constraint of grazing one paddock only, no matter how safe, no matter how large.'

'I suppose they are quite young.' Callan could not think that experienced creatures would be so sanguine about danger.

'What is it they want?' Paolo interrupted. He was shifting his weight from one foot to the other, keen to be on his way. Behind him, all the tribesfolk had left the clearing and were going down the long, slippery path that led through the sentry point and further downhill onto the sands of Broad Plain.

Callan, still doubting that this was a wise request, nevertheless passed it on. 'Paolo, these young equii would like to travel with you. They want to live near the tribe and walk your annual circuit.'

Paolo stood up straight, taken by surprise. He looked behind Pinto and Violeta at the five young equii, who stood with their heads up, their large dark eyes fixed on him with hope. Two bay colts with identical white blazes that Callan found impossible to tell apart, a neat grey mare with black shins, a brown filly, and another young mare who was piebald like Pinto himself.

Paolo lifted both arms wide. 'We would welcome them,' he said simply. 'I remember the two equii who lived with us many years ago, when I was young. They were lovely, gentle creatures.'

Pinto blinked his long lashes at the scout. 'I thank you,' he said.

The velvety brown mare Violeta nudged her rump against the big piebald. 'Speak clearer,' she advised. 'The tribe can't hear us.'

'I heard that,' said Paolo with a grin. 'Almost as clearly as I can hear Callan.'

'Then hear this,' said Callan. 'These youngsters are not hardened like the old cart horses who lived with us. They may be a liability. They are not safe on Broad Plain, and the Storm may not be able to make them so.'

'We would still welcome them,' said Paolo. 'If they wish to travel with us, to live with us, I do not see that we can have any objections.'

'Tell him they will attract all sorts of predators,' prompted Thestia. Callan had almost forgotten that she sat beside him, bemused by the complex interchange.

'They are prey, Paolo. Fiercer creatures will hunt them, and that could be dangerous for you.'

Paolo lifted a hand in acknowledgement. 'Then we will do all we can to make them safe and to keep them so,' he said. 'Life is perilous for us all on the Outside. Even so, we welcome new members to our tribe. We would not turn them away. I am sure, very sure, that the elders will say exactly the same.'

'So be it,' said Callan, lowering his snout to cede the point. 'Pinto, the Storm welcome your brethren.'

Pinto, too, lowered his head, his nostrils almost touching the ground, in a kind of salute to Paolo. 'So be it,' he echoed. 'Come, little children of the land, greet your new brother. Then you had better all make speed to catch the end of the convoy.'

'We are fast enough,' said the brown filly. 'Just watch us!'

With only a bare touch of their noses as farewell, the five young equii pushed past their elders and tackled the treacherous slope out of the ravine. Callan had no doubt that they would keep up with the tribesfolk, and perhaps make themselves useful as well. The last tribesman left in the clearing, Paolo dropped to one knee and opened his arms. Touched, Callan walked forward into the embrace.

'Farewell, brother of the land,' said Paolo.

'Until we meet again, farewell.'

They watched as he too started down the incline. Pinto and Violeta turned without a word to make their way back through the paths of the thorn. Callan was glad that, for once, Thestia curbed her sharp tongue. In silence, they watched the empty space until all sound of the tribe's departure had vanished.

Chapter 12

Helm was perched most uncomfortably in the topmost branches of a bloodwood tree, with Rasti tucked against him in the carrying sling that Jana had made for Feather back in Newkeep. Back in those weeks when they had all been busy and content, working alongside the makers of the new settlement. The better settlement. The one with a true community. The one without the Temple.

The one where he wished he could be, just at this moment.

Rasti whined and he ran one hand over her skull, feeling her skin furrowed in worry. 'Quiet now,' he mindsent. 'Quiet and still.'

Below them, a pair of half-starved ursini quartered the ground, picking up and putting down their huge shaggy paws with a single-minded deliberation that was setting his teeth on edge. The ursini looked confused, as well they might be. They had sighted Helm and his companion clear on the path before them, and given chase. Luckily for Helm and Rasti, these ursini were not at their hunting best. Their coats were so thick with dirt they looked more red than white, more like overgrown drop bears than the fierce hunters of the snowy south. They must have slogged their way through those long days of rain, trudging through the sodden sands of Broad Plain, unable to find food or shelter. In the south, as Helm knew from his years of self-driven exile, these creatures would look fat and sleek, and they would move with the slow majesty of surfeit at this time of the year, seeking a den where they could hibernate over the worst of the winter, and only waking when the days began to lengthen again. Ursini never seemed to mind the cold, which varied little across the year in the southernmost reaches of the land, but as the days grew shorter they disappeared into their lairs. What they might be doing, traipsing around Broad Plain several days' north of their usual range, Helm was not sure.

He had noted some of the creatures moving north on his return from exile, on his own journey to find Feather last season, but he had not seen any this side of the Settlement. Not previously, that is. By the look of them, these ursini were not managing very well in this territory. Although they were too big to be prey for anything other than a whole pack of canini, or an entire nest of pantheras, or several collected gangs of strikebeasts, they were also too slow to catch most of the animals of the plain. To be small and quick, and expert at hiding; that was the way to survive on the Outside. Helm was tall and slow, by the measure of most of the creatures of Broad Plain, but he was quick-thinking and good at hiding. The ursini, poor creatures, were not very clever. They were much more suited to sit beside a stream or a hole in the ice and dangle their huge paws for passing fish. They would never think to look high for prey they had seen on the ground.

Unfortunately, they were also stupid enough to keep searching the same place over and over as if they had not nosed it only a minute before, and a minute before that, and a minute—

Well. Safe though they were, Helm felt that he and Rasti could not stay in this treetop refuge for many hours, not with two hungry ursini plodding around and around below, going over and over the same ground. Stupid they might be, but no matter how large and fluffy their paws looked from up here, they had long, dagger-thin claws that could pierce a man's ribcage and make short work of tearing his heart out. He looked about their perilous sanctuary, hoping that perhaps a cluster of old, hardened bloodwood nuts would be within reach. He had some idea of throwing the heavy seedpods into the distance, distracting the furry menaces so that he and Rasti could make good their escape. There was nothing within reach. He was thinking over the contents of his gear, and had almost decided that the half-empty water pouch would be best for the task, when the rasping noise of an engine feral sounded, very close.

Helm froze, and a part of his mind noted that Rasti in her panic had urinated all over the front of his tunic. At least she made no sound, and the engine noise would distract the ursini from the sharp scent he was sure was now perfectly obvious to any predator of worth. While he held his breath, he saw that the ursini, too, had heard the approaching feral.

'That's it,' he whispered, looking down past his boots to where he could see the ursini lifting their heads to look in the direction of the noise. 'That's it! Away with you, now.'

As if they had heard him over the grinding and crashing of the approaching live machine, the ursini turned and began to lumber back the way they had come, back to the west of where Helm had met them. It was clear to him, now that he had a better sight of their gait, that they were footsore as well as starving, and would not long walk the plain unless they found something of value to eat soon. Well, the something would not be him and Rasti—that was one comfort.

Now he had all his hopes pinned on the feral deciding to chase the ursini rather than to sniff him and the rat terrier out of their bolthole. Judging by the sound, this was a large feral with a substantial engine, large enough to strip the limbs from the bloodwood and bring them to ground. Large enough to rip the tree off its roots. Large enough to—

Rasti yelped, and Helm stifled his own cry of surprise. Coming into clear view was not one but two engine ferals, locked together in a futile battle from which neither could escape. That explained the magnitude of the grinding and mechanical screeching. Multiple articulated limbs tangled inextricably, the raging creatures approached, lurching first this way and then that, each rolling the other onto its back and then being furiously dumped in its turn. They tumbled and growled and struck sparks off each other. They had no eyes—no whatever senses such half-alive machines depended upon—for anything but their own fight.

Helm watched and waited. He was good at hiding, and good at waiting. As soon as the rampaging ferals reeled far enough past the base of the tree, he began his slow descent, Rasti in her sling held firmly in the crook of his arm while he climbed down with an agility he had never lost. Once on the ground, the sounds of the staggering feral combatants first grew and then faded. As if they came close, and then suddenly pitched off into the distance. The clanking simply ceased. It seemed like the two engines were running down. Stopping, dying. They had seen many a dead feral on their journey. Were ferals killing each other now, instead of everything else that walked Outside?

'THIS WAY!'

Rasti had no patience with his musings. Her little claws scratched wildly as she did her best to escape the wet sling and jump to the ground.

Helm grinned, pulling the material away from her limbs. 'You are right, my small friend,' he said. 'There is no point staying here. We should go.'

She did not wait to hear what he had to say or to see if he was following. With her skinny tail curled high over her back, Rasti was cantering confidently across the ragged country, always heading east. Always heading toward Feather.

Helm shook his gear into place and followed.

* * *

Mashtuk lay at his ease, just within the shelter of the den. At his back, Jarli rested against the rock wall, quite content to have the big canine leaning on him. Although Jarli had declared more than once that he was a mere outclansman with no mindspeech, Mashtuk found that they understood each other well enough. They had scant need of words. Just as well, thought Mashtuk, because his own words had dried up as if he had never had language at all.

He could use words for thinking, that was still true. He could imagine and worry and plan. He could remember Zélie and, as far as he knew, every word she had ever spoken to him. His lip lifted a little, recalling the dry affection of her conversation. Gone. But he remembered those words.

He had enough language to fear for his cubs and wonder about the choices that Hippolyta, their pack leader, was making. Hippolyta and Thestia, pack leaders, he reminded himself. The two packs of the ravine were now one. He had to stop living in the past. Zélie was gone. The world was not the same, and there were many ways in which he wished he had not survived into this new life. Another thought, one that came often to Mashtuk's mind as he considered all that had happened since last he spoke with his beloved.

He could recall with great clarity every story, every song, every verse, every saying of wisdom. Every word that he had ever learned from the canini elders, from listening to the humachines inside the Pale, and most recently from overhearing the conversation of the tribesfolk, was clear in his mind.

He had words. He had thoughts. He had knowledge.

What Mashtuk no longer had was the way to share these.

He could make some limited sense of what the other canini said to him, at times when they spoke slowly and in simple terms. Otherwise he found that, after just a few phrases had jangled into his skull, a whole cascade of memories and worries crashed onto them, drowning the words in so much noise that he could not tell one from the other. Sense was lost. No, he corrected himself, sense was not lost. Sense overwhelmed him.

He shifted in discomfort and immediately Jarli lifted an eyebrow toward him as if to ask if anything was needed. Mashtuk blinked at him slowly. Rest easy. Nothing is needed. I am thinking.

That is what he would have told his companion, if he still had the words.

Then Jarli sat forward, and Mashtuk realised that the tribesman Feather had entered the clearing, carrying both of Jarli's children. With him was the girl Freya and Hector. Hector the great shining human-humachine whom Mashtuk loved like a son. Ai, Mashtuk, who with his partner Zélie had longed for many years to raise young, was now in the joyful and terrifying position of having more than one cub to care about. There was Enis, now partnered with Tsendi and soon to be a parent himself, and there were Rhosyn and Niccolò of Zélie's last litter. Mashtuk knew himself to be the sire of Hippolyta's cubs too—Mared and Aled. Not that he would ever tell anyone about that. It was Hippolyta's business after all. Ai, not that he could ever tell anyone, he remembered. His words were gone.

Hector crouched beside him, rubbing his large hands over Mashtuk's back. Mashtuk groaned in pleasure. Nobody else could quite match the strength and certainty of Hector's touch on his aching muscles. There were words of greeting between the humans. Mashtuk did not pay these words much attention. His whole focus was on Romulo and Remo. Of all the creatures who lived in the ravine, it was Jarli's twins who had the best mind communication with him. Released to the ground from Feather's arms, they tottered and crawled, staggered and fell, and picked themselves up again, making their way into the den. As usual, they made no difference between Mashtuk and Jarli, clambering over them both with a great familiarity. We are indeed pack, thought Mashtuk.

Romulo, as was his way, spoke first into Mashtuk's waiting mind, though he sat tucked onto Jarli's lap. 'Papa, they have gone.'

'All gone.' Remo had a tendency to repeat everything Romulo said. Perhaps that was a help, thought Mashtuk. Clear, sharp little voices and everything said twice. 'Gone,' Remo then said aloud.

Jarli nodded. His dark curls had grown enough now to fall into his eyes, and he had started wearing a headband to contain them. Mashtuk recognised the work of Freya in the weaving of the long dried grass strands. She had woven the band in the same pattern that she braided Feather's hair, and her own. Was she claiming Jarli as pack too? Mashtuk narrowed his eyes. Huh, an enquiry he could never make, not unless his speech returned. Still, answers were often given even when questions went unasked. It was always possible to learn by watching and listening. Mashtuk looked in turn at each of the creatures gathered by his den. Feather, son of Helm of the Storm, a tribesman. Freya, his daughter, a child of the Settlement. Jarli of the outclan Owl. Romulo and Remo, rescue cubs of Zélie. Hector of the Pale, a puzzle that had never been solved. And himself, half-ruined scout of the ravine.

Mashtuk shook his head, relaxing somewhat as conversation flowed above his thoughts. Romulo and Remo stayed close to him, at least one small hand always clenched in his thick coat. Most of what the adults spoke about was mere noise to him, but every now and then he caught an echo from the infants. The tribe returned to their circuit. Equii on the trot. Winter shrinking the hunt. Feather going. Freya not going.

Too much to listen to, he decided, and he needed more rest. The life of the pack went on, and he was not quite part of it. Mashtuk closed his eyes, thinking hard. Life, alive. Pack.

As soon as he could, he must find a way to live again as one of the pack. Life meant work and help, care and toil. He would get better, he would. If he could never again speak mind to mind, still he had a big body and a loud bark. He would maybe never have the strength to hunt again, but he could watch.

He resolved to walk again, walk well enough to make the journey across the clearings, through the twisted thornbush path, down the scree slope to the sentry place. He could never scout again but he could act as lookout. That would be his place from now on. At the cursed and sacred pinch point where Zélie had met her death, Mashtuk would guard the ravine.

CHAPTER 13

Teiuc, Foremost Ingeneer, was impatient for news. Jaxon watched with interest as Teiuc and Quauhtli, chief of the teshniks, each tried to blame the other for the failure of communication with the raiding party. Seated beside the regent, Jaxon had an excellent view of the petulant argument playing out before them. What interested him most was that Teiuc's silvery face was becoming quite red, almost as if lit from within. Fascinating. Jaxon had not realised that the ingeneer had as much liveware as all that. He made a mental note—which is to say, he dictated a direction to himself: Check liveware allocation of Foremost Ingeneer. Oversupply?

The debate continued, as such debates would unless Jaxon interfered. The regent was still too diffident to control these meetings, even when she had suggested the agenda items herself. Really, he must never, never again saddle himself with such a juvenile. More than once in the past few days had Jaxon wished for the return of the decisive and terrifying Élin Patraena. Too late for such thoughts now, he told himself, after he had spent so much time plotting with Adaeze to effect Élin's downfall. Ha. A neat turn of phrase, considering that Adaeze had pushed Élin over the edge of the regent's terrace to her death in the crevasse below. That could indeed be described as a downfall.

But Jaxon's mild amusement was short-lived. Most unfortunately, he had not foreseen the unprecedented dangers that the Pale was now facing. Indeed, there must be some fault either in the forecasting data or in the procedures that failed to consider the possibility of treachery from the land beneath them. How safe was this particular slice of Broad Plain? What anomalies lay under its seemingly benign surface?

Jaxon allocated himself another task for after the meeting: Review data regarding the selection of the site chosen for the policosmos. Compromises?

There was no end to the small chores that filled the day of a ruler, especially one who did not rule in name.

Jaxon cleared his throat, a delicate enough sound but one that immediately brought the attention of all the senior officers of the policosmos, as well as the regent and the handful of servants, back to him.

'Chief of Teshniks, Foremost Ingeneer,' he said mildly. 'You speak of problems that we cannot easily investigate until our raiding party returns. I suggest to both of you—to all of us—that we would do well to wait upon events. By all means, continue to run your tests and check your readings, as often as you care to. It makes no odds to the rest of us. Debate it between yourselves in your own time, if you happen to have such time. However, I would ask you not to bring these profitless reiterations into our regent's meeting. Our queen has no need to listen to your half-formed arguments, and could much better spend her time otherwise engaged.' He indicated Adaeze with one hand, and—like a good student, he thought as he hid a smile—she inclined her head in obvious agreement with her senior adviser. As she should. Excellent. Together they were a force to face down any or all of the staff gathered around the meeting table.

He waited a few moments while the other officers wriggled in their chairs and looked away, at the flickering screens, at the nervous servants, down at the table. No one spoke.

Into the pause, Jaxon clapped his hands together. 'An opportune time, perhaps, for some refreshment. My lady?'

'Thank you, yes, Senior. A good notion.'

Adaeze could always be relied upon to welcome the provision of goblets of the finest biowine and plates of her favourite sweetmeats. She rose from her carved chair with the dignity of an empress, and then strode with all the power and grace of a panthera over to the table of refreshments. Ah, though Jaxon. Such a perfect combination of strength and beauty. A pity she was not more learned, or even more intelligent. Time enough, he reminded himself, to address that matter once the current crisis had been put behind them. An inept regent was an annoyance he could solve quite simply, either by enhancing Adaeze, or by promptly progressing a more suitable candidate. Another thought struck him and, first collecting a goblet for himself, he made his way to where Ailani, head of recycling, stood a little apart. She was staring at the fizzing display screen as she sipped her biowine.

'A shame we cannot have more news,' Jaxon commented quietly.

'Pah! Useless, these screens. What's the point of even calling them up?'

'Quite.' Jaxon touched her elbow, gently steering her to where a large arched plate of plexiglass had been inserted into the stonemetal fabric of the regent's stronghold. The former home of the recyclers had been modified and adapted to serve its new purpose. Numerous windows of plexiglass, an extensive rooftop garden, and various embellishments of gems and rare metals—rescued from the imperilled walls of the regent's tower in the now abandoned Acrocomplexa—had been added. The stronghold was now a perfectly acceptable residence for the Pale's regents. At least, Jaxon amended, until more prosperous, more stable times returned.

The view from the arched window was extensive. At least two levels had been unmade from every nearby building in order to provide the regent with an uninterrupted prospect east over Broad Plain. It was wise to keep the Outside in clear sight, considering that their view-finders no longer functioned at all. True, service personnel had been detailed to keep watch around the perimeter, but they were no match for the equipment they replaced. Jaxon shook his head. This spreading failure of all their technology! Not one of the citizens responsible was able to locate the problem, let alone address it. He started as Ailani sipped her wine a little more noisily than was polite.

'You had something to say, Senior? Something to ask me, perhaps?'

'Indeed.' Jaxon took a draught from his own goblet, feigning ease. Keeping his true feelings from every other citizen was second nature to him, and not at all difficult. They believed him, after all, to be wholly machine with the merest semblance of liveware—a little more life-like than the Wereguard, but actually no more alive. So with his misgivings well concealed, he smiled at Ailani. 'I wondered, Head of Recycling, whether conditions have improved to your satisfaction. I believe you have recently enhanced several of your staff.'

Ailani frowned. 'We did so, but our results have been mixed. I must admit, though, that a handful of my staff have been brought to more useful status.'

Jaxon nodded. 'I am pleased to hear it.'

'Others did not survive.'

Jaxon choked and coughed. Blinking his watering eyes, he pretended he had not heard. 'I beg your pardon, Ailani, what was that? This biowine is not as smooth as it might be.'

'I said that of those staff we attempted to enhance, not all survived.'

'But how is that? Enhancement, as I understand it, is no more difficult or dangerous a process than gene stripping.'

Ailani nodded, a wry twist to her mouth. 'Such as when I, a former paramount, was rid of my Patraena genes. My understanding matches yours. That was an uncomfortable process, but scarcely life-threatening.' She turned back into the room, facing away from the view, but made no move toward the rest of the group. 'I have wondered, though, Senior—'

Jaxon moved so that he too could keep an eye on the other senior officers gathered around the spread of refreshments. 'You have wondered?'

Ailani was given to questioning her role, her staff, the effectiveness of the entire recycling process. Her dissatisfaction with arrangements had often irritated him, because no previous recycler had ever found anything to criticise in the Pale's carefully planned procedures. Now, however, he was interested to hear what she might say.

'You have wondered?' he repeated as she remained silent.

'Myself, for example. Were all my Patraena genes eliminated? I am surprised that I remember so much. And Milo—you remember Milo, who unwisely tried to insert himself into the hierarchy and had to be recycled? The former paramount who malfunctioned to the extent that he thought himself fit to be head of the service?' Ailani looked up at him, her eyes wide.

Jaxon nodded slowly. 'I remember everything, of course. I have access to every data set in the policosmos, as you know.' As well to remind her just how much of a machine he was. There was no way, in any case, that he would ever forget Milo, the ex-paramount who had tried to usurp Hokulani as Head of Service, an attempt that Jaxon had suppressed by the simple mechanism of recycling the stupid, over-ambitious fellow immediately. Milo's superior genes were more valuable in the recycling pool than in a pushy young citizen with no proper sense of his new station. But the head of recycling was looking at him with something of a glint in her eye, as if she suspected that Jaxon's hand had lain quite heavy on Milo's career aspirations.

'Of course you do!' Ailani agreed with some enthusiasm. 'Well, what I wondered was whether he came to have such grandiose ideas because he retained too much of his Patraena legacy? Whether the gene stripping failed, you see.'

'Ah!' said Jaxon, who had thought the same, but many months earlier than the idea appeared to have occurred to the Head of Recycling. 'That is a very interesting notion. But, my dear Ailani, you were about to tell me something of the failed enhancements.'

'I was. It seems to me, my dear Senior, that many of our recycling practices are now ineffective. I am told that they have operated faultlessly for over two hundred years. Now it seems they are less reliable in their outcome and more dangerous in their application. Of seven citizens put through enhancement, two were so damaged that they had to be recycled, and two more show no change at all. So we have only three staff who are somewhat improved.'

Jaxon had worked hard to restrain another choking fit at being addressed as 'my dear Senior', and now took a moment to consider. To seem to consider what Ailani had suggested.

'I see. Fewer than half. That is worrying. I will reflect upon it, and study all the relevant data.'

'Thank you. Was there, by any chance, anything else you wished to ask me?'

Jaxon assured her there was nothing, and together they made their way back to where the members of the meeting were once more taking their places at the table. As he resumed his seat beside the regent, though, Jaxon was preoccupied with a torrent of problems, plans, and possibilities.

Had recycling somehow been degraded? Was there a fault with the gene material that had been stored in the Navel since the Great

Conflagration? Well, since the Navel was built, very soon after that dire event. How much success could Jaxon expect when he asked, as soon he must, for the progression of some paramount eggs?

Most of all, though, his mind turned over another possibility. Could Ailani be renovated to become the next regent?

* * *

The hunt for Jasper had taken a new direction. Talis and several of the other weapon-trained makers of Newkeep had crossed the moat by means of the long barge poles and had made their way warily into the Outside. They had several reasons to be cautious. Not only was the earth of Broad Plain saturated and shifting, there were large depressions in which the water from the flooding Founders River looked set to linger for many days or even weeks. With the onset of bare winter, Talis imagined that these unusual lakes might freeze, with the water unable to penetrate the hydrophobic clay pan under the red soil, and unlikely to evaporate until the sun resumed its summer-time climb into the sky.

The deepest of these bow lakes, or billabongs as Tammas named them, might remain on Broad Plain as an almost permanent feature.

The deepest of them would freeze the hardest.

The deepest of them could well conceal the slender body of one lost boy.

Talis shook his head. They were searching in pairs, doing their best to find any clue about Jasper's disappearance, while at the same time keeping an eye out for any of the manifold dangers of Broad Plain. Strange, Talis reflected, that his fear of Broad Plain today seemed so baseless. What could possibly happen on Broad Plain that could be prevented by hiding inside the makeshift barriers of Newkeep, or the sturdy palisade of the Settlement, for that matter? Death visited all mortal creatures eventually.

'Talis! Here!'

A shout from Branimir brought his head up, and his heart rate too. After almost two hours of slogging through the silt and mud around their walls, at last there was news. Talis made his way as quickly as he could to where Branimir was crouching to look at something on the ground, with his search partner matching her steps to his.

'What? What is it?'

Branimir looked up, both hands plunged into the red mud at his feet. 'I think, just let me—' He tugged hard at some object trapped in the sodden soil, and then suddenly fell onto his backside as it came free.

Talis helped him struggle to his feet. Cupped in both hands, Branimir held a boot. A distorted and muddy boot, clogged with red earth and bent out of shape by the movement of water and soil over it. A narrow boot, with an overly long sole and some rather untidy laces, knotted unevenly by an impatient and inattentive wearer.

Talis fell to his knees beside Branimir, while their search partners whistled and called to the other pairs.

'Jasper's boot! We've found Jasper's boot!'

'The river didn't take him. He's somewhere here on Broad Plain.'

Talis, on his knees beside Branimir, put his face in his hands. There was a chance, then, a chance that Jasper was still alive. That he hadn't been carried downstream by the flooding river. That he had gone the other way—why, nobody could say. Nobody could yet say.

Branimir shook him by the shoulder. Talis expected some words of comfort or encouragement, but Branimir just held his shoulder in a tighter grip. Around them, the score of searchers had grown eerily silent.

Talis rose to his feet, the tallest among the group. Over their heads he could see what Branimir was trying to show him, out on Broad Plain.

A shining column of soldiers was marching steadily across the ground, headed in the direction of the Settlement. Talis knew immediately who—what—those soldiers were, though he had never sighted one before. The Pale had sent out an army of its half-alive, half-machine citizens. At the moment, the column was moving at an even pace and straight across the corrugated plain as if they were on a smooth road, the humachines not at all inconvenienced by the rough terrain, the sodden earth, the numerous water-filled depressions. Well, they wouldn't be. They were machines.

They were deadly.

Any moment now they might look to the west and notice the small band of searchers on the bare red sands. Talis made a hand signal, motioning the search party to crouch as low as they might. To lie on the ground out of sight. To move slowly and silently as they did so. They were all plastered liberally with red mud, so they could just pretend to be red mud.

The search party waited immobile for long minutes, hardly daring to breathe. Talis cautiously lifted his head now and then, but he could see nothing. When he felt that enough time had passed, he rose slowly to his feet.

There was no sign of the army. The humachines had passed by, intent on whatever their mission might be.

'They're gone,' Talis said.

As they all got to their feet, Branimir with the muddy boot still in his hand, one of the searchers let out a soft wail. 'The Settlement!' she said. 'They are going to attack the Settlement. We must warn them.'

Talis drew a deep breath. 'You're right. But how to manage it in time, that's the question.'

'Can't pole up the river, it's too high,' said Branimir. 'Can't run there in less than a day. One of the equii, maybe?'

'Perhaps. We must try. All of us have someone there, someone we know and love. Come, let's take this news to the others.'

As they turned to make their way back inside Newkeep, Talis felt his heart contract painfully. Jasper was still out there somewhere on Broad Plain.

Chapter 14

Brettin had been in her old quarters in the Temple for two nights and a day, receiving reports about the flooding of the Lower Town and leading all the Temple acolytes and scores of worshippers in long hours of prayer and numerous litanies. They prayed for succour for those settlers and inhabitants of the Lower Town who had not managed to escape up the paved stairs before the water reached the barrier erected in such haste by the merchants and their servants.

In due course, they would learn how those villeins and helots and elders below the barrier had fared. Brettin reassured many a petitioner that the people down there were most likely safe but hungry, probably sitting comfortably in their upper rooms or at the worst, clinging to their roofs. Quite safe in this fine weather. There was not even a wind to dislodge them. Some, perhaps more than they cared to think, may have fallen victim to the power of the flood. Brettin warned the settlers that there may be deaths to mourn when news at last arrived from the Lower Town. There was no profit to be had in endangering anyone further, so she had also decreed that no one else was to enter the Lower Town until the water had completely ebbed. The hungry ones down there could wait a day or two; there was no help they could render to the dead. The majority of the settlers were safe, and for that they must be grateful.

The water had risen higher and almost overtopped the barrier at the nethermost end of the paved way, but now that it could be seen to be receding, more and more people had come to the Temple, gathering to share their news and their fears. They wanted to join Brettin's supplication to the powers that ruled all of life, and they wanted permission to enter the Lower Town. The weather remained unusually fine and bright, so despite the flood situation, they had no need to ask for the rain to stop.

'We should have been asking the powers for a halt to the rain some days ago,' Brettin said tartly, sick of hearing Esteri bless the fine weather as though it was some sort of special boon. 'We should have been praying for fine days before whatever deluge that fell upstream gathered itself into such a flood.'

'My lady, we would, we should,' Esteri agreed earnestly. 'But how were we to know? We cannot find a single mention of any such event in all the two hundred years since the first settlers built our home here.' He lowered his head again to the screen he was notating, singing a record of the damage reported by one of Anielka's merchants.

A shame, really, that the merchants had used so many of their wagons and stall tables and barrels and boxes to form the flood barrier at the base of the paved way, thought Brettin, though she was surprised at the amount of material being reported destroyed. She had not thought the barrier so extensive, but she had yet to see it in its entirety. So much damage, so much to be restored. The Temple would have to find the means to assist the affected settlers, if anything like normal trading were to be resumed. The problem of where to source the necessary materials, and the skilled craftsmen to make the repairs and fashion new items, was one she was leaving for a later day.

'What you say is true.' Brettin looked over Esteri's head. Beyond the double doors to her reception room, a distressingly long queue of anxious settlers waited to speak with her on this second morning. 'But what you should say is that is there is no mention of the Settlement ever seeing such a flood on any of the singing screens.'

'Yes, my lady, and nothing in our archives either.' Esteri nodded his head as if that settled the matter. In his mind, they could not have known that such a raging of the Founders River was at all possible.

Blazej, who stood as ever beside Brettin's chair and had begun to call forward the next supplicant, suddenly held up his hand to stay proceedings. Brettin looked at him in surprise.

'My lady,' he said with some diffidence. 'I have a thought. Talis may know more.'

Brettin pursed her lips. She considered Talis Jarisson, who had

scored so highly on his Assessment at puberty that it was small wonder that Valkirra the chief had taken him to partner. Taken him very
gladly, it might be said. Talis was as beautiful as the carved statue of
Light that graced the inner sanctum of the Temple. Yet Talis, handsome and well-made as he was, sadly cared more for reading than for
anything else. Talis found much more in the archives than anyone
cared to, or needed to, discover.

Unbearable, irritating man.

Brettin now knew, as did all the settlers, that more events, more
stories and guidelines, more songs and verses, more of every sort of
possible knowledge, existed in the oldest of the written records. Many
of those records had never been sung onto the screens. No one would
have known anything about that hidden history if it had not been for
the meddlesome ways of the chief's research-obsessed partner. The
former chief, of course, she reminded herself.

'I do not think,' Brettin said coldly, 'that we could ever be expected
to consult with any of the runaways—ah, what is it they call themselves
these days? The makers, that is it. I do not believe that we can be expected
to ask the makers of Newkeep Port to advise us on any matter here in
the Temple Settlement. They may have taken the oldest of the archives
with them, and a gaggle of our most deluded historians, but the Temple
hierarchy made the decision long ago that the information in those old
records had absolutely no value. If the knowledge they contained had
been useful, it would have been sung onto the screens. Blazej, I thank
you for your thought, but I believe we can dismiss the notion.'

With a decisive nod, she indicated that she was ready to continue
her audience with those settlers seeking help and advice. Counselling
others was a role Brettin rather enjoyed. Strange, she thought, how
few people are able to see their way clearly through a problem. Always
being distracted by messy emotions, when all they needed to do was to
follow the rule of the Temple.

As Blazej raised his hand to resume his summoning of the next
petitioner, a ruckus arose in the doorway. There were shouts and
someone screamed. Esteri got to his feet, but he could no more make
out what had caused the commotion than the other two up on the dais.
All that Brettin could see was that the crowd was pushing through the

doorway, carrying the Temple guards with it, and that all these noisy people milled around a still point somewhere in their midst. A small but determined voice was raised above the exclamations of the crowd.

'Brettin! Lady Brettin! I must see you. I must speak with you.'

Long moments of confusion and disorder eventually ended when a filthy, barefoot, mud-caked lad, his long hair loosed from its braids and hanging in rattails over his tear-streaked face, pushed his way to the front of the settlers. As he staggered up the stairs to the dais, everyone could see that he was—that he had been until lately—one of their own. Tall for his age, skinny with too-quick growth, covered in mire and close to collapse with fatigue, this sorry boy was without doubt the son of Valkirra and Talis.

'Jasper!' said Brettin, astonished by both his abrupt arrival and his state. 'What is it? What has happened?' She felt her heart give a great, thumping leap in her chest. 'Nothing wrong, is there? Are all your people safe?' For a moment, she imagined her prayers answered, and all the irreverent runaways swept off the plain by the force of the Founders River in flood.

'We are safe,' gasped Jasper, 'safe at Newkeep, but you are in peril here. All of you. Brettin, there is an army of humachines marching this way!'

Screams and cries of horror resounded through the Temple. Someone began to wail as if they would never stop. Brettin closed her mouth, which had dropped open, and looked about. Then she shook her head, mortified to realise that she had been instinctively looking for Valkirra. She rose to her feet, calling above the turmoil.

'Guards! Fetch me Anielka and Olinna. Then get to the walkways and see what is to be seen. Quick as you can, then report back here. Everyone else, to your homes. Fetch your families, grab your belongings. We cannot resist an attack by the Pale. The humachines are deadly. We must save ourselves, save what we can. Go! All of you! Run!'

'But—where can we run, Lady? Where can we go?'

Brettin looked at the crowd, the multitude of hopeful faces in front of her. She could think of no other word but 'away'. Before she could gather her panicked thoughts into more sense, Jasper turned about and raised one arm.

'Go to the river path,' he shouted. 'Go toward Newkeep! The Pale doesn't know we exist, they won't even look for us there. Go to Newkeep. I can show you the way. Gather your people and follow me.'

The son of Valkirra and Talis in truth, thought Brettin.

* * *

Feather was finding his farewells rather trying. While he had often left his daughter behind, all the years of her life, he had never left her so alone. Ai, she was not alone, he reminded himself. She was safe in the ravine, safe with the pack. Callan was there too, and Feather trusted Callan to the last drop of his blood. He trusted all the canini of the ravine. But for human company there was only Jarli of the outclan Owl, who hardly spoke, and his infant sons. And Hector, of course, who had once been a humachine of the Pale.

Hector was a puzzle indeed. He seemed entirely human, except for his great size and the silver under-tint of his skin. And the inbuilt weaponry of his forearms, and the hinges that protruded from his ankles—something to do with attaching wheels to his feet, Hector said. Feather liked him well, but every now and then, one of those reminders of the Pale made him shiver. Hector, whatever his origins, could never be solely human. The Pale had left its marks on him.

'When will you return?'

Feather blinked and looked down to find Callan sitting before him, head tilted quizzically.

'What makes you think I am returning to the ravine?'

Callan grinned. 'Freya.'

Feather crouched down to lay one arm around Callan's neck. 'I see my heart is never hidden from you.'

Callan was startled. 'Did you ever think it could be? We are pack.'

'You are right. When you canini left off running with the tribe, I lost the habit of revealing my heart. I'd forgotten how easy it is to share my feelings with you.'

Callan nosed him. 'Kilimanjara died about the same time. She broke both our hearts beyond sharing.'

'True.'

When Feather said nothing more, Callan pushed his nose more strongly against the tribesman's shoulder, unbalancing him. 'You did not answer my question, pack brother. When will you return to the ravine?'

Feather rose to his feet, smiling. 'I do not yet know, my friend. Some weeks it may be. Winter comes on. First I must go across Broad Plain to Newkeep, to see Jana, and to check on Helm. It may be that we travel first to meet up with the Storm, I cannot say. I will also collect my new companion Rasti, who will now share my travels.'

'A rat terrier, you said?'

Feather heard the amused tolerance behind Callan's words. 'I did.'

Callan snorted. 'You will have to carry her, you know. These town-bred creatures are hardly canine at all. I hope she will be worth your trouble.'

Feather laughed aloud. 'You don't fool me,' he told the big white canine. 'You would never forgive me if I abandoned her. She does not need to be "worth" anything. She is my friend, and precious.'

'I am sure it is as you say.' Callan made a pretence of disbelief, but Feather could read the warmth in his heart.

Feather kneeled down to hug his friend one final time. 'She is precious as all life is precious, as precious as the pack. As precious as your equii.'

'My equii!' scoffed Callan. 'I only brought them here because it's what Mashtuk would have done.'

'I did not know Mashtuk before his change,' said Feather. 'Yet even though he now has no mindspeech, I feel how big his heart is. Yours is the same, however you try to deny it.'

Callan shook his head. 'Enough soft words. It's time for you to go.'

Feather grinned. 'Time and more than time. Will you come to the sentry point?'

'Of course. We will all watch you safely onto the plain. Freya will be waiting.'

They matched their steps through the thorn forest path, Callan in the lead while Feather checked over every strap and buckle of his gear, in the time-honoured way of tribal scouts. Just before they reached the head of the path where quite a few were gathered to wish him well on his journey, Feather resumed their discussion.

'If you have had enough of soft words, my brother, you can always spend more time with Thestia.'

Callan looked over his shoulder. 'She has much bite in her speech, that is true.'

'Merely a way to cover her love,' remarked Feather, watching his friend closely.

The thick fur across Callan's shoulders rippled as he gave a surprised skip, almost spraining his left forefoot on the uneven ground. 'She does not speak to me of love!' he protested.

'Does she not?' asked Feather. 'Well, perhaps I will ask again when next I visit the ravine.'

Callan snorted in disbelief, but again Feather read the warmth in his heart, and smiled.

* * *

The rest of the Newkeep makers lingered in the hall. Nobody, it seemed, had the heart to do anything but wait on news of the search for Jasper. When the searchers returned, covered in mud and breathless from haste, everyone in the hall gasped. Valkirra was first to her feet.

'What is it? Have you found him?'

Talis strode forward, putting out both hands to take her by the shoulders. 'My heart, we found something. We found Jasper's boot. We believe that he wandered out onto Broad Plain.'

Valkirra looked about wildly. It was clear that all the searchers had returned, and that she was angry about it. 'Why aren't you still out there? Why don't you go and find him?'

Talis held her a little more firmly as she made to push past him, as if she wanted to rush out onto Broad Plain herself, with Cushla clinging to her leg and no thought for anything else. 'Valkirra, wait. There is more news.'

'What news? Let me go!'

Branimir, always a voice of calm, stepped close to them, barring the way to the door. 'Valkirra, listen. Please listen.' He raised his voice so all in the hall could hear. 'We have news. We have found a clue to Jasper's whereabouts, but we have also seen great danger out on the plain.'

Talis felt Valkirra's shoulders rise under his hands as she took a deep breath.

She stepped back from him, pulling Cushla up into her arms. 'Tell me,' she said. 'Tell us all. What is it?'

Talis lifted his chin, looking about the hall to address them. Every single person who had made the journey with them from the Settlement was gathered within the space, from the former high-placed settlers such as Iver and Branimir and Ahrenkild, to the lowest of the non-standards and non-settlers such as Tammas the herder and Rick the helot woodworker who fashioned their barges. There was no high or low here in Newkeep. There was simply a community, a community that Talis felt the need to protect.

'We saw trouble Outside,' he said. 'We saw an army of humachines marching directly for the Settlement.'

Many voices were raised in alarm, in questions, in fear. 'Are they coming for us?' asked one, silencing the general hubbub.

Talis answered the only way he could. 'I don't know. I suspect they know nothing about us.'

'Well we don't want them to find out,' said another.

Valkirra raised her voice. 'Wait! What of the Settlement? Is there aid we could offer?'

A deep silence fell as the makers looked at each other, some shame-faced, others a little defiant. After all, each of them had a reason to leave the Settlement. It could not be expected that every one of them wanted to help the people who may have made their lives miserable before the split. Talis understood the range of feelings, from those openly weeping for relatives and friends still within the Settlement's palisades, to others whose faces were set against their former home.

'Most of us have kin or at least connections there,' he said. 'Some of us have no reason to love the Temple Settlement—our hurts run too deep. I know not all of us will feel the same.'

'It doesn't matter,' cried Valkirra, always quick to feel and to act. 'Whether we have loved ones there or not, we must try to help. We are the makers of Newkeep, and we must do everything we can to protect our neighbours from danger!'

Talis thought the same, but did his best to bring a note of caution to his partner's enthusiasm. Valkirra had a light in her eye that he did not entirely like to see.

'Valkirra is right,' he said. 'We cannot stand by and do nothing, though we don't wish to bring trouble on ourselves either. I suggest that we try our best to warn them.'

Branimir spoke over the murmurs of the gathering. 'I think we will be too late, Talis. We cannot reach the Settlement before that inhuman army. They move too quickly. We can't get ahead of them.'

'We must try,' Valkirra said. 'The settlers need to know. If they can't get their defences in order, they must run. Their lives are more important.'

'I agree,' said Talis. 'But we must move immediately. Even if we're not in time to warn them of the attack, we may be able to help them fight.'

Iver sounded a note of caution. 'There is no withstanding an attack by a humachine. My dear friends, remember what happened at the walls of the Pale.'

Valkirra closed her eyes for an instant. 'I will never forget that day. Our whole raiding party, razed to dust in an instant. You are right, Iver. We settlers and makers are of human stock and cannot withstand a humachine attack. The settlers must flee. They must be warned!'

Talis spoke decisively. 'The Founders River runs too high; we could not pole against it in time, if at all. The riverside track is sure to be under water in places, and nothing but deep mud in others. Not the best of us could run the distance in time.' He looked at some of the youngsters as he spoke, all of whom seemed to be jostling for his notice, as if eager to be chosen for the mission.

'What can we do, then?' asked Tammas. 'It seems hopeless.'

'Actually, Tammas, it is something I want to ask you. Do you think an equo could manage it? The riverside path, I mean, all the way up to the Settlement?'

Tammas raised his eyebrows. 'Maybe. That's a good thought. I will ask them!'

'What does he mean, he'll ask them?' Valkirra muttered as the herder pushed his way through to the door.

'Tammas has a way with the equii, as we know,' Talis replied in a murmur.

'None of 'em is a riding equo, mind you,' Tammas explained as they followed him to the enclosure where their five equii had their heads lowered to the hay that had been saved from the flood. 'But they'll be quicker than we on that path.'

'They have need to be,' said Talis. 'Even so, we may be too late.'

'We have to try,' said Valkirra. 'Late or not, we must do what we can.'

Chapter 15

Helm decided that his time of comparative rest at Newkeep Port had made him soft. Either that, or his age was truly beginning to catch up with him. No, it couldn't be age, surely; he was only in his middle years and had half a lifetime ahead of him. Half a lifetime in which to get to know his son and his granddaughter. It would be time enough, he promised himself. Still, the going was so heavy across Broad Plain that he found himself calling for rest more often than he liked. Rasti was always pleased to stop, for she found the walk quite difficult, but Helm discovered that her tolerance for rest was short. He had barely found a likely place to sit down, when she would be up and nosing at him to get on the way again.

Or at least, that was how it seemed to him, sitting with his head bent, one hand rubbing at the hollow spot near his breastbone. Not really hollow, no. Helm tried to find a word to describe the sensation. It felt like there was a deep echo inside his chest, with something walled in there and pounding to be let out. Yes, that was it: it felt like he had swallowed a huge passerine that was trying to open its wings and lift into flight within the confines of his ribcage.

There! Again! He had only just sat down, and here was that pathetic little dog trying to shift him on, licking at his face. That miserable whine, as if she had lost all hope and merely waited to die alone on the red sand. As if she would never see Feather again. Really, she had a boundless capacity for despair and sorrow. He had never known such a creature. She was more foolish than he had bargained for. He should have left her with Jana. He should. He should never. Jana. Feather.

Again! This time she was barking. Helm grunted, pushing the rat terrier off his chest. When had she climbed on there? He sat up, shaking his head. He didn't remember lying down. He didn't remember that. He was sure he hadn't done so. He had rested his back against … Helm looked around, moving to his hands and knees. In a minute, he would stand. He would do that. He just wasn't sure where he was, just for the moment. There was no sign of the fractured copse of long-dead bloodwood trees he had chosen for their rest site, unless … unless … over there … that little stand of bleached trunks, a hundred paces to the west. He shook his head. How could—?

'Easy, traveller on the land,' said a deep voice beside him. 'Move slowly. Take my hand.'

Rasti whined, clawing at his shoulder. 'Friend,' he understood her to say. 'Get up. Friend.'

Helm steadied himself and reached out to grab hold of the sturdy arm that was placed there for him to lean on. It cost an unlikely effort to get to his feet. The cold air pierced his bones and the brightness of the light speared him. He took a moment to find his balance, Rasti whining all the while. Then he lifted his eyes to the new friend supporting him.

'Kéhua!' exclaimed the man, an enormous fellow with dense black hair and shoulders as wide as the horizon, or so it seemed to Helm. 'Kéhua! I have found you!'

* * *

Tammas the herder led Talis and the others to the equii enclosure and then stepped in among the creatures. The gate was always left open, because while the equii of Newkeep liked their own space, they did not like to be shut in, and would often wander about the site looking for someone to give them a treat of fruit or fresh greens from the kitchen garden. In a short minute, Tammas returned to the fence with one of the equii, a short, stout animal with a raggedy brown hide. Looking at it more closely, Talis could see that it was a gelding, and that it had stripes of bare, scarred skin across its shoulders and its rump, with a thick winter coat growing patchily over the blemishes. Whip scars, perhaps. He bit his lip. This equo did not look to have had a happy life inside the Settlement. Why would it want to help the settlers?

'Brownie here,' Tammas stated, 'says he will go. He used to pull the barges up to the Wrack Pools, you know. He knows the way.'

Talis looked doubtful still. 'Can he carry me, do you think?'

Tammas laughed aloud, a strange sound in the middle of their anxiety. 'May the Light bless you, Talis! You can't ride him, look at the size of you! One of the youngsters, it will have to be. If it's to be quick.'

That brought a fresh round of exclamations and protests. Keen as the young makers were to go, none of the adults would allow it. They could not bear to send one of the children. Talis closed his eyes. It was exactly the sort of errand that Jasper would have jumped at. But Jasper was not here.

'I am not very heavy,' suggested Valkirra, but Tammas shook his head.

'Still too heavy, my lady, I mean Valkirra, and besides your legs is too long.'

Talis looked around. The makers of Newkeep were right to be afraid. Parents held their children close, unwilling to let any one of them out of sight. Although a handful of younger adults looked willing to take up the challenge, he could see that too much time would be wasted in deciding who, in granting permission, in tearful farewells.

'We won't be sending out any of you youngsters,' Talis said with resolve. 'Branimir, run and fetch me a bow and quiver, and a cloak. Valkirra, quickly, go and write a warning. I will try to reach them myself.'

Without question, they ran to do as he asked. Tammas brought the equo close as most of the makers headed back to the hall.

'Think you can do it?' he asked.

'With Brownie to help pull me through the worst, maybe. I will make what speed I can, and then do my best to hail them from a distance, if I have to. I'm wondering, too, if Brownie might hurry ahead of me with Valkirra's message?'

Tammas scratched his head, looking doubtful. 'He might, if you say so, my lord, Talis, I mean. He knows the way, for definite. And he's very sure-footed, this little fellow. Take hold of this girth strap if you need help through any deep places. Mind you don't get carried away by the water.'

'I won't do that. I'll be careful.'

Valkirra, running up at that moment, thrust a piece of parchment at him and grabbed a fistful of his hair, making him yelp.

'Hey!'

'Just you listen to Tammas! The river is in flood, remember. Talis, if you don't come back safe, I'll …'

'Me too,' Talis whispered, pulling her close for an instant.

To Branimir, who had now come up behind them and was helping him with a sword belt and a cross-wise strap so he could carry the quiver on his back, Talis said, 'If you can, resume the search for Jasper. The water level is falling, even in the moats. I have great hopes of finding him.'

'As do I,' Branimir answered with great firmness, but Valkirra looked away, her eyes full of tears.

* * *

'What is it, Hokulani?'

Jaxon was standing with Adaeze as she greeted their visitor, looking up with some wonder through the plexiglass dome that enclosed the regent's terrace garden here at the stronghold. Jaxon was wearing his silk robes of state, the most formal set with the trim of leonine fur along the seams, the one that made him look as if he might suddenly transform himself into a leon, that most magnificent and fabulous beast of long-ago myth. Jaxon knew, naturally, that leoni were no myth, and that they had been hunted to extinction many long years before the Great Conflagration. Others might think his robe trimmed with panthera fur dyed to leonine colours, and he did not care if that was what they thought. Most citizens knew nothing of the long-ago before-time. His cache of exotic luxuries was his own happy secret.

The regent, too, was dressed this evening in some style, in a tawny, gem-spattered robe that hugged her generous curves and trailed behind her in a glittering swathe speaking entirely of opulence. Those pink diamonds, and those lustrous yellow pearls—Jaxon had been more than happy to provide them for her delight, telling her that they had been stored for many years, awaiting the perfect setting. In general, Adaeze preferred her own fashion of highly decorated but androgynous, practical clothing. To Jaxon's mind, such garb was more suited to the wardrobe of a high-class stage warrior than to a ruler of the house of Patraena, although he had to admit that Adaeze of all the regents he had served had the bulk, the muscles, and the grace to carry it off. Every now and then, though, she revelled in the slippery glory of silk and an extravagance of impractical jewellery.

Neither of them was dressed for the weather, which was so clear and cold that ice was beginning to sparkle on the stonemetal walls of the Pale and to coat the go-ways with a smooth, invisible rime. But then, neither the regent nor her senior adviser had to think much about the weather. Even here on the rooftop, a perfect temperature was always maintained. Under the dome, they were as comfortable as in the throne room, and the view was better.

Hokulani, on the other hand, never looked any different, never dressed differently. Like all the Wereguard, his aspect was that of a man made entirely of metal, as if a gleaming bronze and silver statue had come to life. Weather made no odds to him, either, as he was impervious to it. Jaxon could see no sign of concern or worry on the Wereguard's perfect face. However, if he had thought it necessary to interrupt the star-watching of the regent and her foremost adviser, then he would have good reason to do so.

'My lady,' said Hokulani. 'I must report some further impediment with the Service. To my regret.'

Adaeze glanced at Jaxon, but he only raised his brows. The regent indicated a set of chairs under one of the four bowers of interlaced metal trees that had recently been installed. Hokulani bowed, waiting for both her and Jaxon to be seated before he joined them.

Adaeze was looking at the Head of Service in some consternation, as if not knowing where to start, so Jaxon picked up the discussion. 'There is something amiss, Head of Service?'

Hokulani gave one decisive nod. 'Rations, Senior. I must ask for a greater allotment for the service personnel.'

'How can that be?' asked Adaeze. 'I thought that all the citizens had been allocated what they needed, according to their workload. I wonder why the Service asks for more?'

'Indeed. I too, my lady.' Jaxon opened his hand, inviting more explanation.

Hokulani seemed in no way embarrassed or disconcerted by their incredulous attention. 'Half rations are insufficient for the level of performance that the Service must provide.'

Jaxon and Adaeze waited for more, but Hokulani faced them as if what he had said was sufficient. Jaxon gave a little cough.

'Forgive me, Hokulani, I do not completely understand. When the rations were allocated, you agreed that the Service could operate on half its usual allotment.'

Hokulani gave his single nod. 'I did.'

'But now you say …?'

'That performance is dropping. It is evident in every aspect of our work. Vigilance, strength, communication, defences. All are failing. All service staff are compromised in their utility.'

Adaeze shook her head. 'How can that be?'

Hokulani turned his head ponderously from side to side. 'We have considered this, in the service oikos. We can think of only two possible reasons.'

Jaxon and Adaeze looked at him expectantly, before Jaxon, realising that Hokulani's own performance was at a lower standard than usual, leaned forward and tapped the Wereguard on his heavily armoured knee.

'Two possible reasons, Hokulani?'

Hokulani blinked slowly. 'Two, yes. Amount of biofuel. Quality of biofuel.'

'Extraordinary!' Adaeze said. 'It cannot be the quality, Hokulani. I would have noticed any difference in my own biofuel. I have not had a reduction in my allocation, it is true, but that is for a very good reason.'

'Indeed, my lady,' agreed Jaxon. 'It is our highest duty to maintain the regent, for that is how we maintain the Pale.'

'You are the regent.' Hokulani spoke with decision.

Jaxon looked at him closely. Hokulani's words seemed laboured, apart from being self-evident. Hokulani shared the allocation that was provided to the Service, rather than that provided to the other immortal officers. Although Hokulani was served at full quantity, because he was after all, a Wereguard and a senior staffer, Jaxon could see that his usual stolidity and dependability had begun to slide into a lesser state. Perhaps there was truly something amiss with the quality of that tank. This could well bear investigation, he thought.

'Head of Service, I thank you for bringing this to the regent's attention. She will wish me to look into the matter closely.'

'Indeed I do.' Adaeze favoured Hokulani with a kindly smile, and the big Wereguard rose slowly to his feet, gave a reverential bow, and backed away from them, his errand complete.

Jaxon did not tell Adaeze that her allocation, like his own, came from Jaxon's private store, recovered from the tank at Alpha Gate. The biofuel they were consuming was of the highest class available. It was just possible that the composition of the biofuel supplied to other citizens, such as the service personnel, was inferior. There was a reduction in the supply of raw materials, too, as he understood it; the ferals appeared to be coming to the end of their lifespan, so there were fewer kills to collect. Interesting.

He was glad that Hokulani had mentioned the problem. To Jaxon's mind, the survival of the Wereguard was second only to his own. Adaeze, on the other hand, was expendable. No matter how much reverence he expressed to their faces, he well knew that regents were designed to live and to die, to come and to go, to ascend the throne and then to relinquish it. They were figureheads, after all, and could readily be regenerated from the genetic cache of the Navel. Himself and the Wereguard, on the other hand, were essential to the survival of the Pale. There could be no future for any citizen without the strength of the Immortal Guard and the wisdom of the senior forecaster. There would be no future citizens, in truth. The Service was important too, as they enacted all the necessary tasks determined by the senior staff. Something must be done for them; at least for as many of them as were needed to ensure the essential functions of the policosmos. He would attend to it.

Jaxon cleared his throat delicately. 'My lady, shall we resume our study? The stars are astonishingly clear tonight.'

Chapter 16

Feather had never felt so lonely on the track. He could not count the number of times that he had crossed Broad Plain, quartering it from every angle on his many trips between the Storm on their annual circuit and the fixed point of the Settlement, where for many years, a great portion of his heart had pulled him toward his beloved Jana and their precious daughter Freya. Now Jana, miraculously, was out of the Settlement and living among the makers of Newkeep Port, and Freya was forging her own path, sometimes with the Storm and now at the ravine. These days, he found himself following even more varied lines across the territory he had known well for many seasons. Breaking fresh ground was nothing new. Yet in all those journeys, he had never felt so alone as now.

If only he had Rasti with him, he would not feel so isolated. Yes, he reminded himself, trying to feel more certain about it, this would be the last of the lonely journeys.

'Rasti, I am coming!' he called aloud, and then grinned. Foolish, perhaps, to call attention to himself, but the words made him feel more confident that his isolation would soon come to an end.

He had taken a direct path from the base of the ravine escarpment to the first of the enormous corrugations that wrinkled Broad Plain, and then followed it south. The recent rain, which had soaked him and Jarli on their quest to find the twins, had left its mark on the land. Feather was noticing plants that he had rarely encountered in all his travels. Here he saw silvery broad beans and bushy parrot-cherries, there the soft leaves of rock-lettuce, and now a scattering of pin flowers. There was enough of everything for him to harvest some as he made his way toward Newkeep.

He felt an eagerness to meet again with his father Helm. There was so much, now, that he wished to say to him, so much he wished to discuss. Though his heart still ached with the memory of those years alone, those years when Helm had let his grief conquer his love for his son, Feather could no longer hold as tightly to the sum of his hurt. The childish years, the deserted years, the sullen years. The bitter taste of them was fading from his mouth. He had nothing to complain of, in truth. Kilimanjara and Kestrel had provided all the family he needed. Also, now that he had met Helm and taken stock of the manner of man that his father was, Feather found his resentment fading a little. Perhaps more than a little. Feather could see much now. Expecting a younger Helm to overcome his grief for Alia and take up the mantle of single fatherhood was like expecting the Founders River to turn about and begin flowing upstream. Helm was all quick, deep feeling, and can only have been more mercurial as a young man. Those he loved, Helm loved to the base of his soul. Feather found that he wanted very much to have Helm love him like that.

'Father, I am coming. Father, I love you.' These words Feather whispered, a little more conscious of his surroundings. Broad Plain was not the place to cry his presence aloud.

How would Helm be faring among those settlers, those makers of Newkeep, he wondered. Feather had been away for weeks, and both Jana and Helm, and probably little Rasti, would be worrying what had become of him. He did not imagine that they would be unhappy at Newkeep, which after all was the home of those ex-Settlement folk who were most in tune with what he thought of as true values. Valkirra and Talis, Branimir and Iver—these were folk whose hearts were almost as wholesome as those of the best of the tribesfolk. More than the settlers, the makers cared about each other and the creatures they depended upon for existence, even if they did insist on remaining in the one place for the whole of their lives. To the mind of any tribesman, staying on the one campsite year after year was not to be thought of. To do so would, sooner or later, degrade the area until it became unliveable for human and animal alike. Tribal lore taught that it was important to move on, to spread the load, to step only lightly on the land.

Although perhaps that was not always true, he thought, bent almost double as he moved up the steepest section of the ridge. Feather had now met the canini of the ravine. Unlike Callan's pack, which had run with the Storm across the whole circuit for many years, Hippolyta and Thestia allowed their packs to range within the one territory. The ravine canini seemed always mindful of the effect of their hunting on the land. He admired their restraint and their care for one another. He admired their generosity and their love. Taking in Romulo and Remo, adopting Hector, inviting the equii into the ravine, allowing Freya to stay. Feather was not quite sure what Freya wanted, except that she seemed very attached to the infants. Ah well, time would tell. He was quite pleased that she was casting about for her own path.

Feather looked up, about to crest the height of the corrugation before making his way sideways down the unsteady sands of its western face. On the top of the ridge ahead stood a tall, broad-shouldered man, his arms folded, looking down on him.

Feather stayed still, amazed that there was anyone else on the plain, astonished that he had been caught unawares. That was what came of too much thinking, of not paying attention. He took a deep breath, rapidly considering how he could defend himself. He had never encountered such a big man, and could only think that the stranger must be a wildling. Nobody in the tribes or the outclans had such a girth or breadth, even the tallest of them. This man was more the size of a feral. Or a humachine. He was enormous. He was quite as big as Hector.

'Greetings, fellow traveller on the land,' Feather called in as steady a voice as he could manage. 'You startled me.' He watched closely to see what reaction there might be. He could think of no defence that would count against such a foe, and there was no hiding on Broad Plain.

The big man raised one hand, palm out. 'Peace, brother,' he called. 'I am Kohu of the Shaking Lands. I mean you no harm.'

'I am Feather, son of Helm of the Storm. Peace likewise.' It was well to maintain the forms of politeness. He looked the big man in the eye. 'The Shaking Lands?' he asked, his heart beginning to slow down. 'I do not know such a place.'

The big man inclined his head, smiling. He had thick dark hair that grew in loose curls, falling over his broad forehead and down his thick neck. His skin was a deep and rich brown, rippled with muscles and marked all over in a complex design of deep blue tattoos.

'Unless you can swim very well, you would not find it,' Kohu said. 'We of the Shaking Lands live across the sea to the south.'

Feather raised his brows. 'Then how come you here?'

Kohu laughed, a full and resonant laugh that startled a pair of nearby red-beaked avians into flight. 'We know how to make boats and how to sail them.'

'Boats!' Feather felt a quiver of excitement, a childish delight that responded to Kohu's words. The only time he had ever been on water of any kind was when he had helped the makers of Newkeep to pole one of their barges up to the Settlement. The experience had not satisfied his fascination. 'I have never been on a boat!' He took a few steps to come up to the narrow, level crest where Kohu stood. Where Kohu stood, head and shoulders taller than he was. He smiled. 'A river barge, I have been on once, but to think of a boat that can travel across the sea. That would be something indeed.'

Kohu laughed again. Up close, although he loomed even larger, there was a gentleness about him that put Feather at his ease. 'It is indeed something,' he said. 'And perhaps one day you will see such a boat.' He peered down into Feather's eyes. 'I am glad to meet you, Feather, son of Helm of the Storm,' he said. 'I believe that I could use your help.'

* * *

Jasper was growing very tired, although he was trying not to show it. Foolish boy, thought Brettin, imagining that he could take charge of a settlement full of people, and all the while just about reeling with fatigue. Pursing her lips, she took a couple of longer steps to catch up with him. The deep mud of the river path clung about the hem of her robe, soaking up as far as her thighs. This journey was the most uncomfortable she had ever undertaken. As it was the very first time she had ever been Outside, this was no surprise.

'Jasper, not so fast,' she advised, taking his arm. 'No need to drive yourself into the ground.'

'You didn't see them,' Jasper returned. Brettin could feel him shaking.

'So many! All shining, and every one of them bigger than my dad.'

'So I have been told.' Using a longview lens, the Temple guards had been able to pick out the metallic gleam of the Pale's advancing army as it moved steadily toward them over Broad Plain. There could be no doubt that they were on a direct route to the Settlement. Why they should wish to attack the settlers, Brettin was not sure. It was more than twenty years since that ill-planned raid, when Valkirra had sent the flower of their young people in a futile attempt to steal away some of the Pale's many riches. Just after the PPA, that most significant of aftershocks. Jasper of course was too young to remember any of that. This could not be a raid of retaliation, not after all this time. Though what the Pale could possibly want with the settlers—Brettin shivered. Nothing was too vile to imagine. The Pale was a law unto itself, well known to be no respecter of human life. Usually its citizens stayed safe behind their formidable walls, impervious to any threat from any of the other survivors of the Great Conflagration, yet here they were, in the Outside …

And here she was, in the Outside, a place she had never thought to be. For a lady or lord of the Temple to venture beyond the gates of the Settlement was unknown. Brettin pulled her thick over-robe tighter around her shoulders. Here in the deep shade of the bloodwood trees that lined the river, the cold was vicious, no matter how fast her heart was beating.

'Jasper! Is it much further?'

'A long way to go yet,' the boy answered. 'We're not even halfway.' His words were muffled, and Brettin suspected that he was crying. She could easily cry herself, if she thought too much about their situation. 'Keep walking, Lady.'

Brettin started. True, she had come to a halt. There was so much to think about, and she did not like being rushed. She had not enjoyed the hurried packing, the clamour of escape as the settlers took what they could and made their way as quickly as possible to the river gate. They all had to go down the full length of the paved way, so there was a great deal of jostling and pushing, something she had never before experienced inside the Settlement. At the base of the path they nego-tiated the flood barrier erected only days before, a tangle of carts and trestles and barrels and boxes, lying anyhow all over the area. The barrier had been roughly dismantled by the merchants who had been first to begin the retreat from their home of many generations, and in their rush to follow, no settler had stopped to make the way easier. The Lady had snagged herself twice on the remnants of the barrier as the Temple acolytes and staff followed as quickly as they could, with Brettin in their midst and the most precious of their holy artefacts wrapped into unwieldy bundles. There had been no time to go back up to the chief's palace where her own personal belongings were now kept. Nobody thought to open any of the ovine pens, or release the remaining equii from their stalls. Two of their small pack of rat terriers made a nuisance of themselves underfoot, but most of them must still be shut in, back in their kennels. Just as well. This pair had already almost tripped her, and besides, their yapping was unbearable as they ranged up and down the column of settlers.

As she and the rest of the Temple staff hurried down through the plazas and onto the paved way, Brettin had seen panic on the faces of the settlers. She did her best to reassure them with her calm, wishing to be a focus of confidence in this alarm, but with Blazej on one side and Esteri panting in haste on the other, she had no opportunity to speak as she wished.

Then the Lower Town! Brettin had never imagined that water could do so much damage. She did not care to dwell on the sights she had seen there—the carcasses of animals, the bloated body of an unlucky elder. What was to be found inside the flood-drowned dwellings, she did not dare think about. There was an emergency of greater proportions to be faced. The army of the Pale threatened the Settlement itself, high-assessed and workers, villeins, helots, elders—every living thing. First to save the community, and then to worry about the damage that the flood had done.

Before that, though, they had to outrun the Pale's humachines with their diabolical weaponry. Fortunately, as Jasper had pointed out, the river gate was completely invisible from the plain. The Pale's soldiers could have no idea that their prey had escaped. If they found the tracks—impossible not to leave tracks in the soft ground—then perhaps they might follow. Who knew? Did the humachines want the settlers, or did they want the Settlement? No one could say. The settlers' only chance of survival was to flee, to escape down to Newkeep and ask for sanctuary.

Much as she disliked the thought of asking for help, Brettin was sure that Valkirra Adelriksdottir with her sympathetic heart would welcome them into safety and do all she could to help. She would not close her gates against her former community. Valkirra could be relied on to make the soft choice. A thought struck Brettin.

'I suppose your mother sent you?'

No answer. The boy was stumbling along in the wake of a handful of merchants, who needed no guide to show them how to follow a riverside path, wet and heavy as it might be.

'Jasper?'

'No,' he answered, quickening his pace until he was a length ahead of her. 'She didn't send me. She doesn't know where I am!'

'What is there to cry about in that?' Brettin called after him. 'Think how pleased she will be to see you.'

Again no answer.

Brettin frowned. 'What is the matter, boy? Do you think Valkirra will be angry?'

'No! Don't be stupid. You don't understand anything!'

That was certainly a comprehensive dismissal. Brettin let him hurry ahead. She had endured quite enough of the boy's rude ways. Slowing her steps, she allowed Blazej to come up beside her.

'Are there many behind us, Blazej?'

'A great many. We are not far from the front of the column, I think, my lady.'

'Truly?' Brettin shook her head. 'We have been walking for hours, but I cannot see the head of the line.'

'No, my lady.' Esteri hurried to put in his share of the discussion. 'The river turns somewhat between the Settlement and Newkeep.'

'I see.'

'And we will not be able to travel the usual route, my lady,' Blazej informed her. 'With such a burden of water in the river, no doubt there are places where the path is flooded. We may have to walk around quite a way.'

They trudged on for a while in silence, looking only at the sodden ground in front of them and the mud-caked feet slogging the path ahead of them. Brettin had to hold her soaked robes up with both hands or risk tripping and falling into the knee-deep sludge. She was not burdened with bundles as all the other settlers were, but even so she found it almost impossible to keep lifting one foot after the other, pulling herself through the mire like a laden equo ploughing heavy ground. One hour, and then a second, went by, Esteri behind her intoning the seven hundred couplets of the formal incantation to the Power of Light. He then muttered and gasped his way through an entire recitation of the verse annals of the history of the Settlement since the time of the Great Conflagration, no doubt to raise their spirits as they all struggled to keep pace through the heavy ground. The chill wind had strengthened and was blowing directly into their faces, moaning through the twisted branches of the bloodwood trees interlaced above them. Brettin had never been so cold, so dirty, or so frightened.

She had not imagined, either, that her situation could grow any worse. When Blazej beside her stopped walking, she lifted her head to see what he was doing. Only then did she realise that the whole procession in front of them had halted. There was clear sky ahead of them, which could only mean, surely, that they had come to the end of the path.

Those two bothersome rat terriers darted right past her, once again almost knocking her off her feet, their barking even more high-pitched than previously. For once, they may have a reason for their maddening noise. No doubt they too could see the end of this repulsive journey.

Brettin let herself enjoy a surge of relief. 'What is it, settlers? What is happening? Have we arrived at last?'

Certain that she should be the one to lead the settlers into Newkeep, Brettin squirmed her way through the people in front of her. For once she wished that she had the bulk of Olinna, who would have been able to make a much better path through the press of people—tiresome people who seemed to be edging back, shoving against her, babbling nonsense, almost forcing her off the muddy path and into the deeper puddles beside it. Why didn't they just stand back, if they didn't want to be first to hail the runaways in their flimsy enclosure?

'Let me through, let me see.' Brettin found Jasper ahead of her. No mere boy should be at the forefront in a matter of this importance, she thought, grabbing him roughly by the shoulders. She forced him to the back of the adults as she demanded right of way. Exasperating child, thinking that he was the most important member of this convoy, or perhaps in a hurry to see his mother. Very affecting. Very aggravating.

'Let me through!' Brettin hissed as now one of the merchants tried to stop her, grabbing ineffectually at her saturated robes as she thrust her way to the front.

'My lady, wait!'

It was too late.

Too late for Brettin, and too late for most of the settlers at the front of the column. There was no place to run as a huge section of the riverbank began to collapse from under them, plunging them into the tumbling waters. In the blink of an eye, several dozen settlers, the Lady of the Temple, and most of her acolytes and Temple guards among them were swallowed whole by the power of the Founders River.

Chapter 17

Only two days' trek from the ravine, the Storm had found a camping site that would suit them for the winter. Although they were accustomed to making a similar circuit around Broad Plain each year, they regularly chose new places for their seasonal camps. Part of the tribes' lore was the necessity to walk lightly on the land, so they took care not to tread too often over the same ground.

Kilimanjara, in her last weeks with them, had urged them to return to simpler ways. The truth was that since the enormous upheaval of the PPA—the post-post aftershock that had ravaged the land and destroyed decades of work, apart from causing many deaths among the tribesfolk—nearly every one of the tribes had become more cautious and less certain about the wisdom of their chosen path. For over two hundred years they had followed what they believed to be the best way to survive in the post-Conflagration world. The careless shaking of the land under their feet had reminded them of something they had lost sight of: nothing was certain, nothing was safe. A lifetime spent caring for the land and its creatures, making sure they did nothing to disturb the fragile balance between life and death, no more ensured a safe life than the reckless, exploitative ways of the humachines of the Pale.

Marin was responsible for choosing the site. The place he had chosen was further north and further east than their usual wintering grounds, but he was satisfied that there was enough game, enough water, and enough shelter to keep them healthy over the cold season. Some of the elders remembered this place, or something like it, from before the last aftershock.

'You will find salt water just over that little ridge,' they told the hunters.

'You can bring us fresh fish. Salt fish are delicious,' said another.

Paolo, the young scout who led the hunters whenever Feather was absent—which as everyone knew was all too often—listened with his head cocked to one side. He had been brought up too well to argue with the elders, but Marin noticed that he rarely led the hunters east. Paolo's focus was mostly on the prey that lived around the edges of Broad Plain. After a summer spent in the ravine, the tribe's hunters had acquired some of the canini ways and relearned some of the canini wisdom. Marin remembered when Callan and his pack had first run with them in the lean years following the aftershock. In those hungry days, fibrous tubers and skinny lizards had been welcome. The stay in the ravine had reminded them that they did not need to bring down big prey to feast. If they didn't bag a longneck deer, a sack full of juicy arthropods would feed the tribesfolk just as well.

Willow elbowed him. 'What are you thinking, husband?'

Marin shrugged. They were sitting side by side at the central meeting place, peeling boiled land yabbies. A large clay bowl sat on the ground between them, gradually filling with the chewy, tasty white meat. At some distance, a couple of the wisewomen and an older man were baking flat-cakes over a small brazier. Although the day was cold, they would not light the big fires until after the sun had set. Until then, every able member of the tribe could keep warm by staying busy.

'I was remembering to be grateful for our stay with the canini. They reminded us to make the most of small things, not to rely on our favourites. They reminded us that it is good to be alive.'

'All life is precious, we know that.'

Marin nodded. He peeled the last yabby in his basket and dropped its shell back in with the other empty ones. The shells would be used to flavour broth. He was not very fond of thin yabby soup, but he had to agree that it was better than hot water.

'You are still thinking, and not about how good it is to be alive.' Willow did not look up as she spoke. Marin put one hand over hers. She let it lie for a moment and then pulled her fingers away from the contact. Marin raised his brows at her.

'I yearn for Romulo and Remo,' she whispered. 'Why can't I have them? I do not understand how there can be two orphaned children, two, waiting for care, and the pair of us so ready to look after them, only to have them snatched away. It is not fair!'

Marin bit his lip. This was not the first time they had covered this ground. Willow knew as well as he did that the twins had not been snatched or stolen, and that they were not orphaned. Nobody denied that Willow and Marin would make good parents to the boys. Everyone agreed. Everyone felt their longing and their pain and was sorry for it.

None of that would bring them children of their own.

Much as he hated going over and over the same words, Marin could not help himself from saying, 'Their father came for them. They are not orphans.'

Willow made the same answer as she did whenever the topic was raised, and it was something she said all too often for Marin's peace of mind. 'It is not fair!'

He had given up arguing with her. 'It is not fair,' he repeated.

Willow glared at him. 'The next thing we will hear is that they have gone to live with that dreadful outclan. They will not even be safe. That Jarli fellow will not know how to care for them.'

Marin looked down. 'You like Jarli. You said he is a good father.'

'You don't even care!' cried Willow, beginning to cry.

He reached to pat her shoulder, but then put his hand down without touching her. 'I am sorry, my love,' he said quietly. 'What you fear may come about. It may be that Jarli takes them to the Owl. It is nothing to do with us. Romulo and Remo are with their own family. They are not ours.'

Willow stood, her own basket of cooked yabbies spilling to the ground, and walked away from him. With a little sound of pity, Marin collected them again and continued where she had left off.

For himself, he liked to think of the twins growing up with their father. True, when he thought of them, he imagined them in the ravine, surrounded by the care and love of the canini packs, kept safe by them and by the impressive and capable human-humachine, Hector. Ai, that was the name that made his own heart clench in pain. If he had ever had the chance to have or to adopt a child, he would very much like to have called Hector his son. But Hector, like Jarli, had felt more kinship with the canini than with the Storm. It was a sorrow to Marin, but he thought he understood it a little better than Willow did. Like all the Storm, Marin had lived for many years cheek-by-jowl with the canini, with Callan's pack, and Waleen's. The canini made good hearth-companions. He wondered briefly—no, Callan looked to be settled in the ravine now. Marin would have liked to have the big white canine travel with him. All of the tribesfolk had improved their mindspeech during their season in the ravine, and Marin had begun to enjoy his discussions with Callan, Hippolyta, and Thestia much as his predecessor Kilimanjara had.

Kilimanjara. He missed her. They all missed her. Such a huntmistress came along all too rarely.

Marin finished pulling the flesh out of the last yabby and took the clay pot over to where the elders were preparing the bread. There would be good eating this evening. He only wished that Willow might enjoy it.

Not for the first time, the old people were speaking of salt fish. Marin did not ever recall having tasted it. For as far back as he could recall, the tribes had stayed inside the shallow rim of Broad Plain, a rim that sometimes reared into a mountain-like outcrop—such as the ravine of the canini, for example—but mostly formed a kind of thin, ragged crust that divided Broad Plain from the bounding sea. He would not mind looking at the bounding sea, and he told the elders so.

'You would be frightened, if you could see it,' said one of the wise-women. 'There are rolling hills of water on it, laced with white spray. It is never still. You would drown if you tried to walk through those water hills.'

'I know of those who can cross it, though,' added another. 'I am sure that we once had visitors from the bounding sea. It was when you would have been very young, Marin.'

'Oh, the Shaking Landers! I remember,' said the first, clapping her hands. 'So handsome—Beris, do you recall?'

Old Finn, a shrunken little fellow who had recently become a great-great-great-grandfather, and liked to boast about it, laughed at her.

'Don't talk nonsense, Nita. They were good, big fellows at least, very good hunters. But that was before Marin was born, surely?'

'Perhaps,' said Beris. Marin looked up at the odd tone of her voice. Beris slowly raised herself to her feet and lifted one hand to point across the meeting place. Nita and Marin turned to see what she had seen.

Their scout Paolo had arrived at the other edge of the clearing. With him were all the young hunters, and behind them came a crowd of tall, broad-shouldered people. It looked like a whole tribe had arrived on their doorstep.

'Shaking Landers,' whispered Nita.

Paolo raised a hand. 'Here is my huntmaster Marin,' he announced formally. 'Marin, these folk have sailed across the bounding sea to find us.'

'We have!' said a large woman with a wide band across her brow, a ribbon woven with an intricate pattern of black and white. 'Marin of the Storm, I am pleased to meet you. I am Kiri Ana Rea of the Shaking Lands. We seek our old friend Helm of the Storm, but Paolo here tells me he is not with you. Huntmaster, we come to warn you. The Shaking Mountains have erupted and the ice wastes are melting. People of the Storm, you must leave for higher ground.'

* * *

'What are those creatures, do you know?'

Callan, standing at the pinch point of the ravine path, looked back over his shoulder. Enis and Tsendi had come to relieve his watch. He had been so intrigued by the scene below him on Broad Plain that he had not heard them arrive. Foolish. Well, it would have been madness at any other sentry post. Here in the ravine, he had grown accustomed to the idea of safety. Nothing could come at him from behind. That was a dangerous notion he had adopted all too readily. Mentally berating himself, Callan lifted his snout in acknowledgement.

'I do know,' he answered. 'I think they are ursini. I have heard tell of them, though I have never seen them before. Your father would know of them, Enis.'

Enis, watching with narrowed eyes as Tsendi made her careful way to the guard post, grunted. 'I wish he could talk.'

'Perhaps he will,' said Callan, saddened to hear the grief in the young canine's mindspeech. 'In time.' However, he felt in his heart that Mashtuk's command of language was a closed matter, and that nothing would bring him to speech again.

For long minutes, the three canini watched as two filthy, ragged creatures prowled listlessly among the broken ground at the base of the trail. They did not appear to have the energy to look up, let alone to think of trying the path into the ravine. They did not seem to be aware that they were being watched. For all their great size and the impressive length of the dagger-sharp teeth protruding from their mouths, to the canini they looked like prey. Enis tilted his head to one side, his over-size ears flicking with the movement. Evidently he could not comprehend why the ursini continued to rummage around the scattered rocks, when they must know that they had already searched in all the places they kept going back to. Callan saw him relax, satisfied that the wretched creatures were no threat, before seating himself neatly beside his partner.

'What do you know of them, pack leader?' asked Tsendi. Enis's mate was coming close to her birthing time and carried herself with the caution of impending parenthood. This would be her first litter; it was no wonder she was a little anxious and awkward in her movements. Callan gave her an encouraging nod. She had a brave heart, he well knew, having heard of her adventures with the humachines. He was glad about the young couple's expectations, though he worried a little about raising newborn cubs through the depths of winter. No matter. Canini had done so before and would do so again. If there was any safe place left to raise young, it was here in the ravine, which seemed to him full of hope. Hope and love, sharing and care.

'Callan?'

The big white canine shook himself alert again. 'Ah, I was thinking. Ursini, yes. They mostly live in the south, beyond the Broken Ranges. At the time of the PPA—you won't remember that, neither of you being born then—at that time, when the canini were left homeless on this barren land, we all made choices. Hippolyta and Thestia led their packs here; Waleen and I found a home for our kin, running with the Storm. Another of the packs, led by Brynt, decided to seek a new territory in the south. I remember old Tinashe—that's your father's grand-dam, Enis—Tinashe warned Brynt that the ursini had moved south. She said they were big and dangerous, and would fight canini for the same prey. That's all I know.'

Enis tilted his head again. 'What are they doing here?'

Callan yawned, rejecting the notion that he had much knowledge of this. 'They look to be starving, that's what.'

Enis grinned. 'That much I can see. Why are they here?'

Callan sat and scratched behind one ear. 'Who can say? Others of their kind chased them from the hunting grounds? The autumn rain washed away their prey? The Broken Ranges fell down? They do not look to be a threat to us, in any case.'

'I should think ferals will pick off those two soon enough.' Tsendi did not sound disturbed by the thought.

'And do you not want to offer them sanctuary, Callan?' Enis asked with a gleam in his eye. 'Shall we invite them to run with your equii?'

'My equii!' scoffed Callan, shaking his head at the jest that never seemed to lose its currency among the canini of the ravine. 'To answer your question, no, I do not want them to join us in the ravine.'

'Could we perhaps eat them?' asked Tsendi.

The other two stared at her, and she blinked and looked away. 'Hungry,' she muttered.

Enis nosed her. 'You are always hungry, dear heart. We ate, just before we came down to guard.'

'Blame your cubs.'

Callan rubbed one paw over his snout, hiding a grin. In a serious tone, he added, 'They are very big, and their claws and teeth look sharp. We do not need them for meat, so we should let them go their way. We have good enough hunting as it is.'

'Hector could fight them,' Enis said thoughtfully.

'No need to put him in danger,' Callan replied quickly, the thought of Hector going down to challenge the shambling ursini making his ruff prickle with discomfort. He set his teeth, recognising that Hector was pack. Of course the thought of him at risk would hurt. 'I say we let them take their chances down there with the ferals, or with the cursed vulpini.'

Both Enis and Tsendi shivered at the word 'vulpini'. Callan didn't blame them. Though it was many months since the death of Zélie and Memandi in the vulpini attack on the ravine, the grief of the pack ran deep.

'I will tell the leaders what we have seen.' Callan turned to make his way back up the scree-slick slope. 'Should those pitiful creatures think to look up, or offer any threat, give voice and we will come.'

* * *

Talis struggled along the half-drowned path, more than once reaching for the wide, flat strap that was fastened around the equo's barrel-like girth, where a plough harness or a saddle tack would usually go, and kept in place by a strap of narrower width across his chest, a bit like a riding breastplate. Brownie was a stocky, short animal, but as Tammas had promised, he was very sure-footed. He put his head down and heaved his way upriver, regardless of how deep the mud was or how many times he had to crash through tussocks and bushes, carving a way forward past the places where the flood had washed out the regular trail.

Brownie's pace was steady, and a little quicker than Talis could well manage in the conditions. That was good. Though he was heaving for breath and his legs felt like they could melt from the sensation of fire in every muscle, Talis knew that he was making good speed. Their errand was urgent and the equo seemed to know it.

He remembered, years ago, Feather telling him that the equii had language, like the canini. A little bit like the canini, he had said. Not as complex, because they had never been modified to speak with humans, but they had still communicated readily until the time of the Great Conflagration. After that, according to tribal lore, the equii had preferred to keep their thoughts to themselves. Too many fearsome memories, too much pain, too much grief. Not putting those feelings into words, Talis supposed, was one way of keeping them in check.

Lifting the pace of his slogging steps a little, he came up beside the rough-coated equo and tucked one hand under the width of the chest-band. Maybe there was still comfort to be had in words. Whether or not the equo understood what he was saying, Talis felt the need to express his indebtedness.

'Brownie, I'm so grateful that you came with me.'

The equo snorted, lowering his head and raising it again. To Talis, the sound was almost as if the animal was laughing.

'You don't seem frightened or overwhelmed by this flood,' Talis went on, his words coming in snatches as he matched his stride to the steady jog-trot of his companion. It was quite a pace, and the going was heavy, but with one hand on Brownie's gear, he was able to keep himself mostly on top of the worst of the path.

Brownie. Talis shook his head. It seemed a poor name for such a strong, generous beast. Brownie had no reason to help him, and no reason to love the settlers, judging by the look of his thickly scarred hide. Yet here he was, putting himself in peril, uncomplaining and, it seemed, untiring.

'You shouldn't be called Brownie,' Talis told him, panting, his breath harsh. He had settled into a league-eating half-run, though he wasn't sure how long he could keep it up. Just keep going, he told himself. Keep going. The equo flicked his long mane out of his eyes, the mud-splattered strands swiping against Talis's shoulder. Talis kept going.

'I think your name is not Brownie,' said Talis after another couple of hundred labouring steps. He was sure he was talking to himself, but somehow the sound of his voice, and the heavy, steady rhythm of the equo beside him, helped maintain the pace. 'You should have a new name, my friend,' he gasped. 'A new name for a new home. Would you like that?'

Talis told himself that he was nearing the edge of fatigue. He was beginning to imagine things. At his last words, he was sure the equo had flicked a glance at him, one large dark eye gleaming for an instant.

Tired, yes. Dreaming they were having a conversation. A good conversation. Carlo was a good companion. Carlo would never let him down. Carlo—

Talis pulled on the girth strap, asking the barge-pony to slow down for a bit. He moved forward, now walking alongside the equo's head.

'Your name,' he said, 'is Carlo. That's your Newkeep name. What do you think?'

Carlo came to a complete halt, turning his head so that he could look Talis squarely in the face. Something happened, though Talis could not be certain what. Was it a particular depth in Carlo's eye? The flickering of those long lashes? The smile-like lifting of that soft lip?

He couldn't say. The thought that came to him, though, was that Carlo had always been the name of this equo. The settlers just hadn't known it.

'Well, Carlo, shall we press on? We've a way to go yet.'

Carlo shook his mane, and then bobbed his head up and down as if in agreement with this statement. Talis smiled, and with a word of caution or thanks every now and then, resumed his taxing half-run, half-stumble along the route Carlo chose. Keep going, keep going. That was the trick. He was amazed to feel that he and Carlo had formed a sort of partnership, that they were in complete lockstep in their hearts as well as in their stride.

The day was duller than any they had recently enjoyed, or, Talis realised, maybe it just seemed so under the shade of the crisscrossed branches of bloodwood that lined the usual course of the river. It was difficult to see very far ahead, but Carlo appeared to have no doubts about where it was possible to hug the bank and where they needed to detour several yards inland. Talis could not always understand whatever it was that compelled Carlo to change direction. Sometimes the path was completely under water, so taking an alternative way was sensible. But at other times the way ahead looked entirely clear, and yet Carlo pulled him doggedly away from the edge. Talis wondered if Carlo could tell that the riverbank was undermined in those places, or if there was something else that made him turn aside. Another ghastly floating body, perhaps. They had seen quite a few drowned, bloated ovines and one longneck deer, its body deformed and torn by the steady power of the current. He left the choice to Carlo and just kept going, head down.

They had been pushing on for so long now that Talis was beginning to doubt they would ever reach the Settlement end of the river way. His breath was rasping in his throat, but he had no choice but to continue dragging himself along, trying not to lean too heavily on Carlo's girth strap. The equo had not changed pace, but kept jog-trotting toward the Settlement as briskly as the flood-scrubbed terrain would allow, until suddenly he didn't, coming to a full halt and breathing out a kind of snorting confusion.

Talis raised his head, lurching to a stand as his feet caught up with the idea that they had to stop. Around them, the trees had opened their canopies to the afternoon sky. No, that wasn't right. He could see the afternoon sky, a broad sweep of blue deckled with flimsy white clouds, because they had come to the end of the trees. The trees that lined the Founders River all the way between the Settlement and Newkeep Port.

Except they didn't anymore. An enormous chunk of the riverbank had simply disappeared, creating a filthy, muddy bay several dozen feet across. The wide breach in the bank was swirling with angry floodwater, floodwater that was thick with all kinds of broken branches, half-submerged bodies, bobbing packs and floating bundles. Everything was unravelling in the eddying tides of the new bay, heaving and gulping where it met the flood-force of the river, debris being swept into the main flow, replaced immediately by incoming surges of filthy floodwater.

His mouth hanging open, Talis looked across the impassable gulf of filthy, corpse-filled water. On the far side, he could see a crowd gathered. He could hear screams and shouting, but he could not make out any words.

And between the milling crowd and the water, his son Jasper was waving his arms above his head, trying to get the unruly mob to attend to him.

Chapter 18

Feather, astonished, looked up at Kohu. 'You need my help?' The big man seemed to recognise his name. Feather could not imagine how this could be so.

'If you will. Over here.' Without further explanation, Kohu started to make his way down the western slope of the sandy upthrust. His huge feet splayed out, he managed the uneven going just as well as Feather with his small, staggered steps. Arrived at the base, Kohu immediately began to jog toward the next uplifted corrugation of rock and sand, this one striped with layers of all colours from deep orange and dark red to the palest pearly ochre. Feather admired the play of colours as he followed the Shaking Lander, seeing how each band of pigment exactly echoed the meandering shape of the ones either side of it. The drift of colour was as like to water as stone could be. Feather thought it looked as if one of the salt-painted lakes had been suddenly made solid, its many shades set into this flowing rock shape.

Kohu made no attempt to climb over the upthrust, but led his companion to a fold in the rock, where a leaning stand of thornbush created a cove of shade. Here Feather could see that there was another man, just as tall as Kohu but rather more slender, and that he was bending over something, someone, on the ground. What could be wrong? Had one of their group been bitten by a rock-adder, or stepped on a scorpion, or fallen afoul of a strikebeast? There would be nothing Feather could do to help them if anything like that had happened. He opened his mouth to ask what was the matter, when an unearthly, high-pitched scream erupted from the little gathering under the thorns.

Feather stopped in his tracks, but Kohu only laughed. 'It seems you are known, brother of the land.'

About to turn and ask for an explanation, Feather gasped as the squealing ceased and a minor explosion of sand burst from the place. A small, pointy-nosed, black and white, furry explosion on four legs.

Feather dropped to his knees, arms opened wide, as Rasti flung herself toward him, her yaps of welcome somewhat fractured by the heaving breaths she needed to cover the little rolling sand hills that separated her from Feather. She took the last yard in a single jump, landing awkwardly on his shoulder, her claws scratching his face as she scrabbled to get as close as she could, panting and licking, setting up a choked kind of whimper that was half delirious joy and half despair of separation. Feather could not suppress a laugh, even as he reassured the rat terrier and did his best to calm the wild ecstasy of her greeting.

Over her head he looked at Kohu, watching with a half-smile on his face.

Kohu nodded. 'Yes,' he said. 'The traveller who needs our help is your father Helm.'

* * *

'We have found it! My lady! Senior! We know where the problem is.'

Jaxon covered his astonishment with a show of politeness, bowing as low as was proper between senior officers of the policosmos, rear-ranging the planes of his face as he did so.

'That is very good news indeed. Please, tell us more. Ah, Hekili and Hokulani too! Quite a gathering. Please, come and tell us what you have found. I am sure the regent is eager to hear your news.'

He and Adaeze had been busy planning a further raid into the Outside. Which is to say, he was telling Adaeze about his new plan, and ensuring that she was able to add something to it by the judicious introduction of rhetorical questions and self-evident comments. This was a particular skill of his, Jaxon knew: the able handling of a ruler while allowing such rulers to maintain belief in the excellence of their own judgement and ideas.

For Quauhtli and Teiuc to interrupt such a discussion was unknown.

Adaeze stayed seated, only now managing to close her mouth, which had fallen open in surprise. She stared at the delegation that had burst through the door of the throne room. Her back was pressed against the highly polished tourmaline insert, and every line of her body said that at the first sign of danger, she would spring into action. Jaxon had risen to his feet, a move that came to him without thought, his deeply ingrained instinct to protect the regent at all costs momentarily overpowering his rational mind. He deliberately relaxed the scarce-used weapons that had sprung out from the backs of his hands, reined in the hyper-alertness of his sensors, and settled himself down to his position by his queen's right hand.

There was a minute of suspense and awkwardness as the others drew out chairs and seated themselves with every sign of excitement. Such an attitude was unprecedented in the throne room. Jaxon waited, bemused and a little shaken. He did not appreciate the inference that others of the Pale's senior officers had been able to discover something that he had not found. After all, his data set was the most complete in the whole policosmos.

The regent, too, had caught the note of enthusiasm. So young, Jaxon thought for perhaps the hundredth time, or was it the thousandth? Never again, he promised himself—also for the hundredth or the thousandth time—would he promote such an unformed ruler. He bit his lip as she stammered into speech.

'What is it? What? Please say, Teiuc. Have you found something good?'

Something good, indeed. Such eloquence. Jaxon hid his smile of derision in the same brief instant that it appeared. Then with all the gravity he could command, which was of course formidable, he added his own invitation.

'Please, do tell us what is this marvellous discovery. We await your words.'

Teiuc, usually so taciturn, was bubbling with enthusiasm. The over-generous portion of liveware in his makeup gave his speech a breathless quality. 'It is one of the parent plaques! The one in the Acro-complexa, the Palatine plaque!'

Jaxon looked to Hekili. 'What is he talking about?'

Hekili shrugged. 'Listen. Learn.'

Just as well, thought Jaxon, that I have an excellent command over my own liveware. Every biowire in his body tingled with outrage at the Wereguard master's tone. Hekili sounded defeated, as though he and Jaxon had failed. None of this made any sense. Jaxon, rejecting Hekili's abrogation of duty and the imputation of failure, attempted to gain control of the discussion.

'I fear you must make yourself more clear, Foremost Ingeneer. Something about the Acrocomplexa parent plaque? The plaque in the Navel, you would say?' As he spoke, Jaxon called up the relevant data set. An old one, this, from the very first days of the Pale. Ah. While he could bring the information points ready to hand, Jaxon realised that the structure to which they referred pre-dated him by some months. The term 'parent plaque' was one he did not recall ever having accessed before.

'You know the parent plaques, yes?'

'I know the term, of course,' replied Jaxon, because now he did. 'However, I doubt that it means much to our current regent, who is very young in her position. Perhaps you could explain?'

Teiuc nodded enthusiastically, the copper-threaded red-blond tufts of his hair flopping quite amusingly around his silver face. Nonetheless, Jaxon listened carefully.

'Last time we spoke, you advised us to run all our usual tests and checks. Both of our arms have done so, the ingeneers and the teshniks. We started at the most obvious fault—the shutdown of the comms systems—and worked our way micron-by-micron back up the line to the energy source of all our technology. Eventually, as you will understand, we arrived at the parent plaques. The plaques! One parent plaque in each sector, you recall. Seven in all. Palatine, Aventine, Capitoline, Esquiline ...'

Quauhtli interrupted, growing impatient with Teiuc's careful recitation. 'Viminal, Quirinal, and Caelian. Yes, that much even a non-teshnik knows. Get on. There is work to do.'

Jaxon and Adaeze exchanged surprised glances. For the chief of teshniks to speak uninvited was an event of some amazement. For him to upbraid a fellow senior was unheard of.

'Indeed there is!' agreed Teiuc with undiminished enthusiasm. 'And now we know the extent of that work. Dangerous, yes, but it can and it will be done.'

Jaxon help up one slender hand. 'So far all you have done is to recite the names of the seven districts and say "parent plaque" over and over. There must be more to your great discovery. It is not as if these plaques are a secret.' As he spoke, Jaxon interrogated the information. He then relayed it to the regent as though he had always had it at the forefront of his mind, instead of calling it up for the first time just now.

'My lady, the seven parent plaques were created at the same time as the Navel was built. They were meticulously installed on the same plane, at the lowest level, to form a circuit that …' Jaxon stared at the senior officers and the Wereguard, an excess of knowledge suddenly flooding his immediate thoughts. 'Ah. The plane!'

Hekili nodded, putting one large hand on Teiuc's shoulder to keep him from bursting into excited speech again. 'You see it too, Senior, do you not?'

Jaxon took a deep breath. 'Yes,' he agreed. 'I'm sure we can all see, now that it has been brought to our attention.'

'I still do not understand, not completely,' Adaeze said. In truth, she looked thoroughly baffled.

'If I may?' Hokulani rose and tapped the screen wall. Nothing happened, but instead of giving the command again, Hokulani faced the rest of them. 'My lady, Senior. This is the situation. At some time in our past, a fault began in the under-levels of the policosmos. When I say our under-levels, I do not mean that this had anything to do with our building techniques or the blasting and shaping that was required to form our site's foundation into the perfect shape we enjoy today. This was not caused by our actions. Much more likely, this is a geological fault of many aeons' existence. It is this fault that has ultimately affected our comms systems.' Hokulani gestured briefly to the weakly flickering screen behind him, which looked like a dying avian still trying to fly, or perhaps a dead avian with wings made to flap by a passing breeze. Then he resumed his seat.

Adaeze turned to Jaxon. He immediately understood that nothing but the most complete, step-by-step explanation would suffice.

'Let me put it this way, my lady.' He was glad to hear that his voice sounded firm and full of authority. The fact that internally he was desperately asking himself how he had missed this fault for years—for centuries!—he kept private. 'The parent plaques underlie all our technical systems: power, light, heat, weaponry, comms, sanitation, biofuel processing, and so on. However, they were designed to work in concert, in perfect harmony. This harmony is achieved by their careful placement on the same plane. In the Navel, this is on the lowest level, where most of the data was stored, just below the bulk gene storage. In other districts, the parent plaque may be situated higher or lower in the relevant edifice, depending on the underlying contour of the site on which each was built. The important factor is that each plaque co-exists with its six partners in a meticulously level plane.'

Adaeze nodded. 'And the plane has been, what would you say? Disrupted? Broken?'

Teiuc was fidgeting, eager to leave this discussion and begin work. Jaxon admired his appetite for danger.

'Yes, my lady, for want of a more teshnik word.' Jaxon permitted himself a tiny smile. He invited Hokulani to add more, but again it was Quauhtli, who rarely opened his mouth, who jumped in to speak.

'The fault, you see. We thought it was the PPA—the most recent aftershock—because that's when the comms began to fail. Now that the entire area is becoming even more disrupted—buildings beginning to fall, you see—we have even worse failures. No viewfinders, no screens, no functioning comms pillars.'

'It is true.' Even Hokulani spoke with some vivacity. 'Some service personnel have noted that their wrist screens and their weapons begin to fade.'

'So it is not the biofuel?' asked Adaeze.'

'No, my lady. The biofuel rations are adequate. The quality is adequate.'

Jaxon spoke into the brief pause. 'So our course now is clear. We must bring the plaque in the Palatine, in the old Navel building, back onto the necessary plane. Dangerous work, but essential.' He nodded at Teiuc. 'The wonder is, truly, that the plaques have functioned so well for so long with this underlying fault.'

'The wonder is,' Teiuc said, 'that nobody thought of this in all the years since the PPA.'

'If you had undertaken a micron-by-micron assurance process—you or your predecessors—perhaps this would have been discovered some years ago,' Jaxon answered with some asperity.

'We are not immortals,' protested Quauhtli. 'We are mere huma-chines. You, Senior, and the Wereguard, must always have known about this, this planar arrangement of the plaques.'

Before Jaxon could answer, Hekili held up one hand. 'Let us get on with the business of reinstating the plane.'

'Indeed,' said Jaxon. 'I am sure that is what our regent wishes. She has no need to hear us debating who knew what, and who is responsible for what. Neither the Wereguard nor myself are accountable for the day-to-day functioning of the Pale's technology, whatever our access to data may be.'

Adaeze sent him a grateful look and smiled with real pleasure. 'Do you know that in my lifetime, I have never known our comms to function properly? Teiuc, Quauhtli, I thank you for your service. Let us not keep you here talking when you could be working. Please keep us updated on the progress of the issue.'

Jaxon joined her in her farewells to the other senior officers, and then took his own leave. He had matters to think over, data to sort. Under it all, his liveware leaped and shimmied in a manner that was testing to conceal. Revive the plane, and the Pale could once more reign over the land as it should.

Jaxon was very happy.

* * *

Hector was first to notice that the equii were missing. Well, not missing. He simply realised that he had not seen either Pinto or Violeta for a while. True, he had taken quite a few stands of sentry duty over that time, but even so. He liked Pinto in particular, a creature whose head stood near as high as his own, with gleaming dark eyes that seemed to have a haven of kindness in their depths. For some reason, Pinto reminded him of Tad, though what connection there could be between a parti-coloured cart equo out of the Settlement, and a metal-moulded humachine entirely of the Pale, he couldn't say. All he knew was that he liked Pinto and missed seeing him about.

He asked Callan, 'You seen Pinto lately?'

Callan wrinkled his nose, as if sniffing the air. 'I do not think he has been to this end of the ravine for a few days. Why do you ask?'

Hector shrugged. 'Just wondering.' He rose to his feet, towering over the canini gathered around the sward of Mashtuk's den, where they were sharing a play hour with some of the pack's cubs, and made his way up to the path to Hippolyta's den. She was out with the hunters, so he spoke to Thestia. Thestia had a sharp way with words that made him smile, but she never used that tone with him. To Thestia and the members of her pack, Hector was the one who saved Tsendi. The story of how he and Tad had released the young canine from beneath the carcass of an engine feral, right under the walls of the dreaded Pale, was one of their favourite tales.

Hector squatted beside her. Thestia was engaged in shredding the rib bones of a brace of patchwork hares, making meal-sized portions for later. Hector took a moment to admire her neatness, the way she used her paws—he very much approved of the thumb modification that all the canini had—to hold the carcass steady while she cut into it with her sharp teeth. She flicked her glance to him, and made a mental prod of enquiry.

'Greetings, pack leader. Could I ask you something?'

Thestia rolled her eyes. If more words could be said than were needed, Hector would find a way to say them. This was something she had told him more than once.

Hector grinned. He liked how the canini used so many ways to communicate—their mindspeech, their voices, their bodies, their faces, their eyes. For someone who loved to exchange ideas, living with the canini was perfect. Sometimes Hector wondered how he had lasted over two decades inside the Pale, where the citizens used the least number of words they could, and even the comms pillars hardly lived up to their name, spitting and squeaking and shrieking with static more than communicating. But the nagging absence at the back of his mind pressed him into more immediate thoughts.

'Pack leader, I have not seen Pinto or Violeta for a while. I was just wondering about them. Maybe I missed their visit?'

Thestia spat out a mouthful of fur and fastidiously licked her lips. 'You'd be able to smell them, if they'd been here. Even with your blunt nose, our Hector.'

He liked that too: 'our Hector'. He also knew that his sensors were as keen as those of the canini, however much they liked to joke about the flatness of his face. As Thestia had said, there was no fresh scent of equo anywhere near.

'You're right, of course—'

'Of course!' Thestia agreed with a twist of amusement in her mind-voice, as though to say that she was always right. She went to work on the second hare. 'Is there a problem? You need their help?' Again, her mindspeech was tinted with wry amusement. Hector was as strong as any of the equii, as all the pack well knew, and the equii counted more as pack members to be given help rather than providing it.

Hector shook his head, but could not shake off the feeling of unease. 'No, I don't. It's just that—it's just, hmm. I don't know what it is.' He rose to his feet, and was surprised when Thestia dropped the carcass she was working on and stood with him.

'Actually, Hector, you have made a good observation,' she told him. 'The equii go their own way so much that I rarely give them a thought. We keep to our own hunting, after all.' She meant that the equii and the canini were never in competition. They lived beside, rather than with or against one another. Hector could see the notion clear in her mind. To Thestia, the equii were of minimal account. They lived in the ravine, and they were not prey or predator or rival. They were, to Thestia's thinking, a quirk of Callan's soft heart.

Hector looked down. 'Think I should go and check on them, pack leader?'

Thestia threw him a glance, her mouth working a little, her thoughts private, with a dark tint that increased Hector's unease. 'Yes,' she said at last. 'Please do, our Hector. And take Callan with you. The equii are his particular project, and a trot into the deep ravine will be good for him.' Although her words lay lightly in his mind, Hector could also sense that he had raised an issue she considered important. Now that he had mentioned it, Thestia too seemed worried about the absence of the equii from the dens of the ravine.

'Thank you, pack leader, I will.' He gave a sketchy salute and jogged back to Mashtuk's den, all the while tuning his sensors into the deep of the ravine. Strangely, he could not detect any hint of the equii.

CHAPTER 19

Talis called with all his might, but it was clear that nobody on the other side of the roiling inlet could hear him, any more than he could make a single word out of their scream and cries. He took a step closer to the edge of the broken bank, but Carlo shouldered him aside, setting himself between Talis and the shattered earth. Talis yelled in frustration, looking about for the best way to reach his son. Jasper, it seemed, was trying to bring the settlers down to Newkeep. Jasper, may all the powers bless him, must have seen the advancing army of the Pale when he went out to check the water levels. The boy had wasted no time, not even the minutes it would have taken to alert them at Newkeep. He must have run his heart out, rushing to the Settlement with the news. Now the Founders River, for so long the basis of the settlers' existence, had turned against them. They had managed to escape the confines of their home before the Pale's attack arrived, but now they were trapped by the ravages of the flooding river.

Talis looked to his left, inland. The only action he could think of was to go around this new inlet on the river. It would take a long time, much too long, but there was no hope of getting across the water. He narrowed his eyes, trying to see a way through the tangle of fallen bloodwood trees, their roots washed from underneath them. Just as he was about to clamber over the first trunk that barred his way, a horrendous roar from the river warned him to step back. Another great chunk of the bank on his side of the rift collapsed with a mighty crash, raising a huge jet of dirty water and completely drowning out the noises from the other side. The bucking of the ground that followed as the earth subsided dropped Talis to his knees.

Carlo reared and trumpeted, a sound Talis had never expected to hear from the little barge-pony. He staggered to his feet and looked across the gulf, the churned up water looking like the famous waves on the bounding ocean he had read about in the archives. On the far side, the settlers were milling about, coming close to the edge and then pulling back. He could just make out a second split in the far bank—the escapees would soon be standing on a tongue of land reaching into the fast-flowing river, surrounded by angry water on three sides. They had no option but to go back, as far as they needed, until they found solid ground again. He watched helplessly as they crowded at the edge, some of them much too close. There was Olinna, he could see, and with her a crowd of people from her manor. All of them looked too terrified, too frightened either to go forward or to retreat.

'Go back,' he yelled. 'Back to firmer ground. Try to make your way around!' And even though he knew that nobody would hear him, he kept yelling, jumping up and down, waving his arms while Carlo reared up beside him.

Nobody paid them the least bit of attention. They were too busy arguing on the far side, that much he could see, though he couldn't hear the words. He saw Anielka, another district representative, push her way through to the front. Jasper was still there, but he had his back to the water and hadn't seen Talis. He had both arms raised, imploring the settlers to move back from the edge, but he was immediately hidden by the surrounding adults, all arguing and pointing. None of them even looked at him.

Talis saw Jasper worm through the crowd again. He grabbed at Anielka as she shouldered past him, wrapping his fingers around her upper arm. No doubt he was trying to make her see sense. Talis waited with his heart in his mouth, a part of him dreading to see what he feared would happen next.

Anielka thrust Jasper away from her, and he tumbled backward into the surging waters of the river gulf.

Talis screamed, but nobody could hear him. On the other side, a woman flung out a hand, trying to catch hold of the boy, but she snatched at thin air. Jasper had already disappeared beneath the surface.

Carlo flung himself off the bank and into the tossing waters, his shaggy hooves throwing huge lumps of dirt into Talis's face.

'Oh no, oh no!' Talis was yelling, nonsense words, stupid words, words he hardly knew. He threw himself onto all fours as close to the crumbling edge as he could, but the sodden soil was disintegrating under him so that he had to crawl backward or fall in himself. He stared desperately at the thick tawny water, trying to see some sign of life among the floating, spinning debris of corpses and clothing, trees and gear. He could see nothing alive, nothing!

No, wait! Carlo's head and shoulders rose above the tossing water. He could almost have been rearing up on his hindquarters, his forelegs high in the air as he battled the water. The equo's nostrils were hugely distended, showing a shocking red against the darkness of his saturated brown coat. He made some sort of squealing sound and went under again. Talis groaned, unable to look away from the disaster unfolding in front of him. There was nothing alive, nothing—by the powers! There was Carlo again, about four lengths away from where he had last appeared. This time he seemed to flatten out along the rocking surface of the flood, only his questing head and thick shaggy neck visible, all his legs out of sight. He had righted himself this time with his nose toward the bank where Talis crouched, and there—there, clinging to the strap around Carlo's girth was Jasper. With his eyes closed and gasping for breath, Jasper was using all his strength to hang on to the struggling equo.

Talis found he had no words to match the crushing pain that sat inside his chest as he watched Carlo fight against the fickle current. Huge washes of water were bashing at the banks, with others carving their way back to the main flow. Heavy water was running both in and out of the gulf while the barge-pony tried to swim across the mouth of it. Any one of those unruly tides, all choked with debris, could have forced him out into the full force of the Founders River or smashed him against the newly formed, unstable walls of the gulf. Or simply twirled him like a leaf into one of the large random eddies that were circling through the flow. Talis could only watch helplessly. Any moment now, both boy and equo would be pulled under. Could be pulled under, he told himself. They might make it. They might. They were getting closer. They—

He cried out in agony, seeing both boy and equo disappear from sight. The bound his heart gave when they came back into view a moment later was almost more than he could bear. Talis staggered up and back, his senses nearly overwhelmed by mingled fear and hope. Then he remembered where he was, what he was doing, what was at stake, and he crawled to the edge. There he slipped and slid too far down the crumbling wall, but was able to plant his feet at last against a ledge of bedrock, thigh-deep in the churning inlet. Carlo was close now, almost close enough to touch. The equo's eyes were wide, showing white all around, and there was blood streaming from both nostrils and from his open mouth, curling thickly through the muddy water.

'Here! Here!' called Talis, even though he knew it was stupid, knew that Carlo was doing all he could to make the bank. Here! If only he was wearing a headstall, Talis would have been able to reach him, to pull him closer. As it was, he dug both hands into the equo's mud-slick mane, and felt Carlo find some sort of unstable footing under the water. The equo stumbled and struggled, went to his knees, and rose again, all the while doing his best to swing his hind quarters around through the confused currents, trying to bring Jasper in far enough for Talis to pull him out onto the bank.

They were all screaming, it seemed to Talis, gasping for breath. Now! He let go of Carlo's mane and reached out both hands to drag Jasper ashore. Talis sank to his knees in the crumbling soil, but Jasper was safe, Jasper was sobbing and filthy, Jasper was clambering up the disintegrating bank on all fours, Jasper was reaching the top. Jasper was lying full length on solid ground.

Talis, breathless and sobbing himself, heaved himself through the mud to turn about. He felt he had used the last of his strength, boosting Jasper up the bank, keeping himself out of the water. Carlo was scrambling for the shore, making no progress as his footing collapsed again and again under the flood-line, and Talis wished once more that the equo had a halter on. He reached out to grasp Carlo's mane just as another great incoming wash of debris-filled water overtopped the little equo.

Behind him, Jasper screamed, higher and more shocking than anything Talis had heard yet. The sound, so shrill and intense above the clamouring of the river, the muffled shouts from the other side, and the steady rumble of the soil disintegrating around him, hit his ears like a blow. Talis fell backward, slamming his head against the rotten clay of the dissolving bank, and struggled up again. Carlo made one more surge toward him, his eyes wild. But the equo's strength was gone and he could not get within arm's reach, despite Talis leaning out into danger again. Carlo went under.

Father and son wailed aloud, scrambling along the bank, watching the river's currents in horror as the shape of the struggling brown equo showed now close, now far, under the muddy, rubbish-filled surface. In moments, even that dark shape was lost among the muddled, careless swell of water.

* * *

Mashtuk was taking his first unaided walk toward the main meeting place, the clearing where the pack leaders Hippolyta and Thestia denned together. That much he had worked out from the discussions around him. Since the day Zélie had been killed by the vulpini, the two packs of the ravine had come together. Strength in numbers. Mashtuk understood that. The deepest part of the ravine, the meadow sward, had been given over to the equii. Callan had invited the equii into the ravine. Callan told Mashtuk he had done so. Mashtuk was glad the creatures were safe, but if he could exchange their safety for Zélie's return ... he did not follow that thought. Zélie would have snapped at him. Zélie would have lifted her lip and growled. Zélie would have—

He remembered in time that it hurt to shake his head. Something to do with the way his torn-and-mended ear hung and pulled at his scalp, the way the blood throbbed through its thickness. He usually remembered not to scratch it either. Not always.

He had woken from one of his frequent sleeps to find his own denning site deserted. Jarli must have taken the twins out, and the cubs usually accompanied the hunters in their morning quest. Time for him to return to independent action, he thought. He was going to walk down to the meeting place and show them—because it seemed he no longer had the language to tell them—that he was well enough to take a turn of sentry duty at the pinch point. He was glad, in a way, that he did not have the words to say 'pinch point'. It was bad enough that it was the best place from which to defend the ravine. If Zélie had been alive, she would tell him not to make a show of his mourning and just do his duty. Stupid thought, that. If Zélie was alive, he would not be in mourning. His brain was truly muddled. Ah—he remembered again not to shake his head.

His duty was to protect their cubs, along with all the rest of the pack. Rhosyn and Niccolò were almost fully grown now, both of them tall and rangy like their brother Enis. They had all their meat teeth, and if they retained the overblown energy of youth, that was fitting for their current place in the pack. Rhosyn had a busy, active personality, and was warm in all her emotions. Quick to laughter, quick to anger, quick to pity. She had a great deal of her mother's clear, incisive judgement. Rhosyn might have the makings of a leader in her, if she managed to survive her zealous enthusiasm in the hunt.

Niccolò was much quieter. Perhaps he would be a thinker, like Mashtuk himself, except he did not seem very interested in talking things through or solving problems. Mashtuk felt that Niccolò missed his mother too much. He had never resumed his puppy playfulness after Zélie's murder. He was an anxious, nervy youngster. Mashtuk was not sure what pack role would suit him best. Niccolò was too edgy to make a good sentry, and too tentative to make a good hunter. A den guard? But that required patience and calm, and Niccolò did not have those strengths either.

Mashtuk slowed his steps, beginning to feel tired. He did not recall that the main den had been so far away from his own, from his and Zélie's place. Huh. Of course it seemed further now. He couldn't walk any better than a half-eaten arthropod, spinning around on its remaining legs, not realising it was dead. His ugly, awkward, pain-filled trot seemed to bring him no closer to the cleared space by the leaders' den. Perhaps if he sat for a while. That was better. He wasn't expected. No one was waiting. He could take his time. He could—

Mashtuk lifted his eyes, searching for something familiar in the scene around him. Surely the path between the dens could not have become so overgrown since last he made this trot? He swivelled his head to look over his shoulders, each one in turn. Where was—He couldn't see the path he had used to get here. There was nothing but stunted sourpear and tangled bindvine, all seeming to enclose him. How had he arrived in this twisted snarl of undergrowth? There was no way in. There was no way out. There was hardly room to stand.

Mashtuk stood, swaying and unsteady on his three good paws and his other worthless one. He had walked the wrong way, somehow. He had been thinking too much, not paying attention. He had got himself confused, turned about, off trail. Huh. His muddled brain. Then perhaps it was true, as Callan had said recently, that it was too early for him to walk on his own. He lifted his nose, sniffing for some clue of the safe den he had left behind. He sought for the scent of Jarli, pungent and human; for the twins, sweet and dung-smelling at the same time; for Hector, who retained a clean tang of metal even as his human-tartness grew the longer he spent out of that benighted Pale. He smelled the air for Callan, his thick coat always a little muddy and his maleness so distinct and defined. Or Freya, Feather's daughter: her scent was precise, a mingling of the herbs and leaves she braided into her hair and the sweat-tainted sweetness of her hunting trots. Perhaps he could find the trodden-earth taste of the air by the den.

None of them. Nothing. Sourpear, bindvine, wet rock, saturated dirt. Water not too far away. And—

And the sudden overpowering blast of strikebeast stench behind him. Strikebeast? Sometimes one or two snuck into the ravine. Zélie hated them, feared they would be after the cubs. Whenever she left him with the cubs, she told him to check for wood-adders and scorpions and strikebeasts. He had never found a strikebeast near their den, but occasionally one had been seen inside the deep. Mashtuk couldn't understand why the smell was so strong around him. Surely there was no strikebeast here? With a grunt of effort, he swung his body about, his damaged paw held awkwardly off the ground.

Noiseless to his swollen ear, inescapable with his crippled leg, a gang of three of the ugly dappled creatures awaited his next move.

Mashtuk prepared to fight for his life. He roared his defiance as they all rushed him at once. They seemed large, as large as the cursed yellow vulpini, those monsters that had killed Zélie. He had not fought like this since that day; he had not fought alongside Zélie then as he did now. He felt her shoulder pressed against his, heard her clear snarl of challenge, knew that she would never leave him. This was right, this; Zélie's mind open to his, the quick to-and-fro of their words, the warmth of her heart, the love never-ending.

* * *

The news from the Palatine was good. Jaxon was amazed at how quickly the service crews, leading and protecting the team of teshniks and ingeneers, had found their way into the damaged district, and inside the leaning tower of the Navel. As Teiuc had explained, it was dangerous work. Jaxon more than any of them knew how perilously close to collapse the buildings in the abandoned districts were. After all, he had the best access to the plans and construction notes. These were not matters he had very often had occasion to study, but of late he had found himself accessing that particular data set obsessively.

The comms systems worked well enough for the council of senior officers to track the progress of the working party. Gathered again in the regent's throne room, they had persisted with their commands until the screen had reluctantly glowed into life. A find-bot had been attached to the gear of each of the working party—old, unreliable technology from the early days of the policosmos. Hekili had unearthed them from a cache of artefacts he kept from those pre-Jaxon days. The senior forecaster had been surprised to learn of this—first, the memory cache itself was such a sentimental idea for a Wereguard who had only the bare minimum of liveware, and second, the operative status of the old technology was astonishing. Jaxon had never suspected that pre-Conflagration gadgets not only existed, but could still function. A testament to the ingenuity of the first citizens, of course. He really should not be startled by that.

He remained astounded, last of all, that Hekili had wanted to remember the very early days so much that he had kept a memory cache at all. Imagine! The devastation that would have been everywhere around them, and the sheer scale of the task the first citizens had set themselves. For a start, they had to make themselves secure, and then collect all the resources they could. They worked on their plans for the policosmos, and created the Wereguard to assist with the building. All this before they had even begun their most useful project—his own creation. How difficult those early days must have been, Jaxon thought, without the benefit of a senior forecaster to provide a single information source, a reliable point of advice on every subject. Quite amazing that Hekili wished to think back on those days. On the other hand, perhaps the memory cache was less a fond recollection of the early years, and more of a statement of gratitude that those times were gone. Yes, that was much more likely.

He tapped the screen gently—mindful of its tendency to flicker into fizzing darkness—and traced one finger over the path of the teshniks' find-bots.

'They have reached the Acrocomplexa. They have made very good time.'

Adaeze sighed gustily. 'I wish we could see! I would love to look on the Acrocomplexa again.'

'My lady, when the plane is reconstituted, we may indeed have that ability restored,' said Teiuc. With his plan put into immediate action, the foremost ingeneer was enjoying a period of growing respect. After more than two decades of defending his staff and processes in the face of failing infrastructure, no doubt he was very glad of this opportunity to shine. Jaxon nodded, always ready to add his mite to the conversation. After all, it was his place to coordinate and lead any important project within—or Outside—the policosmos.

'We may indeed, my lady,' Jaxon intoned, his deep voice drawing all eyes back to him. 'We will know more in a very short time. Here we can see that the work party is now making its way into the Navel.'

'They will soon reach the parent plaque,' Quauhtli added with excitement.

Jaxon faced the screen again, his aspect quite stern. He folded his arms across his chest. 'A pity, though,' he said, 'that we did not know the situation and importance of this plaque earlier. We could have recovered it when we stripped all the valuable artefacts from the Navel, some months ago.'

A brief silence fell. Teiuc cleared his throat. 'Yes, Senior, that is a pity. We apologise for the time it took to perform the micron-by-micron investigation.'

'Not an unusual investigation, one would have thought. Quite within the scope of regular procedures, isn't it?'

Quauhtli shifted in his chair, and Jaxon smiled kindly at him.

'No matter, truly. If all goes well today, we can re-think our procedures to ensure that we never again experience such a loss.' After all, if the realignment of the plane was successful, Jaxon would have all the time he needed in the future to bring both the Chief of Teshniks and the Foremost Ingeneer to a proper sense of their dereliction of duty. But first, the plaque recovery.

CHAPTER 20

Feather, with Rasti tucked up around his neck, hurried over to the base of the enormous corrugation, where the other Shaking Lander had now bent to crouch even closer to the prostrate form of Helm. The man looked up as Feather dropped down beside him. He leaned back so that Feather could get a little nearer to his father, a sad smile on his face, his gaze keen and steady.

'I am glad we have found you, Feather of the Storm,' he said. 'I am Kaihoko, hearth partner to Kohu.'

Feather glanced at him distractedly, his mind taken up with the sorry state of his Helm, but he answered with all the courtesy of a tribal envoy. 'I am pleased to know you, Kaihoko of the Shaking Lands.'

The big man stood and took a step away. 'Look to your father. We are nearby should you need us.'

Feather moved in closer, one hand on Helm's shoulder, to study his father's face. Helm was lying limply, his body slumped and still. His skin was a sickly hue, his face pallid and his lips tinted blue. Feather had seen that look before. He could not contain the moan of grief that rose from the depths of his soul.

Helm opened his eyes and fixed them unerringly on his son. 'Feather?' he whispered. 'Feather? Is that you? We have been searching, Rasti and I, searching.'

At the mention of her name, the rat terrier whimpered and scrabbled to be let down. She licked Feather's face, but nestled in close to Helm, her pointy black nose sniffing at his neck. She tucked herself into a fold of his cloak and whined again.

'You have found me,' Feather said softly. 'Father, I am here.'

He took hold of Helm's hand, and despite the knowledge of certain death that crashed upon his heart, he was shocked at the papery feel of his father's skin, the slackness of his grip. 'I was on my way back to you. I wish you had waited at Newkeep! This journey has tired you.'

'Too long,' said Helm, with a twisted smile. His words were soft but it seemed his mind was still sharp. 'We waited too long. I should have left sooner. Rasti wanted to. Clever Rasti.' The rat terrier snuggled her face against his shoulder and closed her eyes. During all the words that followed, she did not once look up.

'I am sorry. We had to go further than we thought—all the way to the Pale and then beyond. Father, there is good news! We found Jarli's twins. The babies are safe. Jarli is with them now. The canini rescued them, cared for them. The canini of the ravine. They are friends of Callan's, you see.'

Too late he remembered that Helm had never run with the canini. Helm had not been present during those years following the great after-shock that threw the land into a new shape, that obliterated genera-tions of work as it destroyed every tribe's stores, their hunting grounds, their tents and clothes and weapons and cook pots and—Helm never knew that time in the tribe.

Helm had already suffered his own life-wrecking devastation.

Helm frowned up at him, confusion growing in his eyes, the focus less precise. 'Babies,' he said. 'My son.'

Feather leaned in closer. 'I am here, Father. I have been hurrying to get back to you. I want to tell you how much I love you.'

Helm gasped, an ugly, heart-stopping gasp that had the two Shak-ing Landers hurrying to see if they could help. As they watched on, Feather continued.

'I forgive you, Father. I understand, truly. I see the size of your love for Alia, you carry it still. The size of your love is the size of your heart. You are a great man, my father. I regret that I have not said this sooner. Father, I love you.'

Helm fixed his eyes on Feather's. 'I am sorry,' he said. 'I wish I had known you longer. My fault.'

'Hush, Father. No need to speak of fault. I love you, I say. Hear it, feel it. You are loved.' Feather had no more words, and he could barely see for the tears that flooded his eyes.

'Yes,' whispered Helm. 'I feel it. Know my love too, my son, know that—' He gasped again, this time a broken sound, half a cough, half a cry. He closed his eyes. 'Beautiful,' he said, and was still.

Feather crouched over his father's body, his tears flowing freely. Rasti shook herself free of Helm's cloak and wriggled her way between father and son, crying and whimpering. Either side of them, the Shaking Landers lifted both hands to the sky above, and sang thanks that they had known Kéhua, the spirit man who had lived with them for so many years in their time south of the Broken Ranges.

* * *

Callan was surprised that he had not given the equii any consideration for several days. He chastised himself as a poor friend to them, although he knew his time had been taken up with looking after Mashtuk and taking his turn at sentry. The equii lived at the far end of the ravine, true, but they often visited the meeting place, making their way through the deep to share thoughts and news with the ravine canini. The last he had seen of them was when Violeta and Pinto clopped in to see how the canini were enjoying the extra space and the blessed quiet that followed the Storm's departure. Nothing like humans, they said, to make unnecessary noise.

As he followed Hector along the well-worn track into the deep of the ravine, he made sure to mindspeak the hunters of their presence. The cubs of both packs—seven of them in all, half-grown, lanky creatures yet to reach their full size and strength—and their full common sense—were working with the hunters that morning. Nothing more likely than they would hear something coming and assume it was prey ripe for their attention. He looked for Enis, and found him at the stretch of his mindspeech, almost a league ahead.

'Hector and I are coming into the deep.'

'???'

'Not to hunt, Enis. We are going to see the equii.'

'I'll make sure Rhosyn doesn't attack you.' Enis tinted his mindvoice with humour, but there was a pull of annoyance as well.

Callan could almost hear Enis wishing that his parents were here to train their own cubs in the hunt. He could certainly feel the undercurrent of worry that coloured every thought. He sent back a wash of thanks and hurried to catch up with Hector.

'Watch out for cubs,' he said. 'They are on the hunt today.'

'What? Oh, yes. Thank you.'

Callan lifted his brows. 'You are more worried than I thought,' he said, wondering if Hector could sense something that he was missing. All the canini had now taken stock of Hector's enhanced powers and respected them, if sometimes a little grudgingly. The canini themselves had long ago been modified with thumbs and a deeper well of language, both of which they relied on as if such things were their birthright. In a way, those modifications were the birthright of the canini. They had been added so many generations ago—back in pre-Conflagration days—that it was only when in contact with the rat terriers of the Settlement that the canini even remembered that this was not the natural way of creatures of their kind.

Except the canini were not natural creatures and had not been for a number of centuries. The canini were simply canini, unique and marvellously fitted for life in the pre-Conflagration world. Which no longer existed. Callan checked himself. The canini were managing better than most in this post-Conflagration life.

Hector's modifications, unlike those of the canini, had been added after he was born, when he was a half-grown human. Human-humachine, that was what the tribesfolk of the Storm had called him. Callan wondered what it felt like, to be born one way and then to be made into something else. He checked his thinking. Today was for action, not thought. He quickened his pace again.

'Do you sense anything?' he asked.

'What? Oh.' Hector looked down. 'I'm questing. Let's be still a moment.' He went down on one knee and put a hand on Callan's back. Touching, Callan could now feel more of the busy hum of Hector's thoughts. 'The hunting pack, they are close, but you know that. Further, I'm not sure. I think I can sense the equii, but there's something else. Callan, are there other creatures in the ravine? Other predators?'

Callan tilted his head, thinking. 'Predators? No. Dangerous beasts, yes. There are wood-adders and scorpions and dart lizards. The panthera can't get in because we guard the path, and neither can ferals. Or those cursed vulpini.' He rubbed one paw over his eyes. 'Mammonites could fly in, but we've not seen any for some time. Thestia told me they once found a strikebeast, hiding in the deep. Years ago, but the mothers still speak of strikebeasts to warn their cubs not to stray from the den.'

'Strikebeasts?'

'Yes. Something between the size of a rat terrier and a canine, but with features of a panthera. Sabre teeth, razor claws, that sort of thing. Heads too big for their ugly little bodies.'

'Heads full of teeth?' asked Hector. 'Mottled coats, neither stripes nor spots? Shoulders higher than their hips?' He was not looking at Callan, but gazed into the darkness of the deep, where the thickest growth of the whole ravine formed a tangled and fertile jungle, full of small prey and marvellous vine fruits. But Callan could see that Hector was not thinking of these things.

'Can you sense one?'

Hector shook his head, rising to his feet. 'No,' he answered grimly. 'I can sense many, all around the herd. Call the hunters to follow, will you? And maybe call to the den. We must go and help our friends.'

He took off at a frightening pace, crashing through the jungle of the deep without consideration of the noise he was making or the smashed path he was creating in his haste. Callan could see that Hector's inbuilt weaponry had sprung out of his forearms, and that his skin had deepened into a metallic grey, as if his blood had formed some sort of armour under the pale skin. Then he was gone, and Callan roused himself to summon the pack's hunters.

'CANINI OF THE RAVINE! To the meadow sward! Strikebeasts have invaded! Tell the leaders!'

He waited only to be sure of a response from Enis, which came as a wordless shout of outrage. Leaving them to follow, he hurtled in Hector's wake.

* * *

'There may be a short loss of power,' Quauhtli said without heat. 'It is possible that the loss of power lasts some minutes.'

'Oh!' said Adaeze, her bronze skin flushing with surprise. 'I had not expected that. What will it feel like?'

Jaxon spoke over her bemusement in a stern voice. 'This is expected? Why were we not told?'

Teiuc answered him as the silence grew behind the question and Quauhtli stared like a feral hit by a stunner. 'We have never reset the plane before, Senior. It is possible that to remove the parent plaque from the abandoned districts and bring it inside our new walls, the ingeneers may need to disrupt the plaque interconnection.'

'But—you cannot—wait!' Jaxon fired queries all along his access points. A complete loss of power from the plaques would dismantle every system in the entire policosmos, and render every citizen helpless but for whatever liveware could function without an external power feed. 'Ah. I see that you have delegated this task to the lower level ingeneers and teshniks. I do apologise.' The haughty look he gave the Chief of Teshniks and the Foremost Ingeneer was anything but apologetic—indeed, they should be apologising to him!—but it did well to maintain the forms of politeness at these gatherings. Any bloodletting to be done was best accomplished beyond the confines of the regent's stronghold. These two, sure to be considered heroic if their plan succeeded, were proving to be seriously inconsiderate. No matter. He would have time, more than enough time, to reduce them to a proper sense of their place in the schema of the policosmos.

'In that case, my lady,' he continued, turning to put one hand over the regent's, 'you need have little fear. While it is true that those of us composed almost entirely of hardware may feel a certain weakness during this process, citizens with more liveware—such as yourself— should be less affected. Is that not so, Teiuc?'

The foremost ingeneer wriggled in his chair. 'We did not think—we did not plan—that is, we simply ensured that the work party included personnel with adequate liveware, so they could continue should the loss of plaque energy cause others to weaken too much.'

'Liveware being so much cheaper and more readily replaced than high quality hardware. I understand. It would have been appropriate, though, to give those of us with a majority of hardware a little more warning. The Wereguard, and myself, for example.'

As he and the Wereguard were the only members of the class of citizen optimistically labelled 'immortal', perhaps it was not surprising that the matter had slipped the mind of the ingeneers and teshniks. In general, Jaxon preferred lesser citizens not to ponder too closely on his construction. Over the decades of his life—he liked to call it life, no matter if he sometimes intimated that he was only a machine—he had gradually increased the proportion of liveware in his system, enjoying the additional sensations only liveware could experience. Of course, with his access to the highest levels of biofuel and upgrades, he had not suffered any of the less desirable traits of liveware composition, such as fatigue and pain and so on. It was quite likely that any disruption to the plaque power system would have less effect on him than on the Wereguard, most of whom were entirely machine-ware. Jaxon resolved to watch both Hekili and Hokulani carefully, and to mimic their reactions closely enough so as not to arouse any suspicions. The senior forecaster was known to be more alive than the Wereguard, but only just, only enough to render him a more pleasant companion for the reigning Patraena.

'I, we, that is, the teshniks apologise for any inconvenience while we carry out this maintenance,' Quauhtli said in a flat tone, as if reading from a script.

'Thank you,' said Jaxon, graciously lowering his head. 'My lady, perhaps if Hekili, Hokulani, and I could withdraw to the antechamber? We could more easily recline there, should the loss of power prove problematic.'

'But of course!' said Adaeze, sweet young thing that she was. Tiresome creature. 'Shall Ailani go with you, in case you need assistance?'

Hekili made a rumbling sound, which Jaxon interpreted as rejection of the idea. 'I thank you, no, my lady. We three shall be sufficient to the purpose. We shall return as soon as the plaques have been reset. I trust that will not be long?'

'As quick as we can, Senior. You can see, the team is at the site of the plaque now. Any moment they will disconnect it and bring it back inside the walls. Then it's a simple matter of aligning it with one of the others and pressing reset.' Teiuc radiated not only sincerity but an almost spiritual zeal in his belief in this rescue plan.

Jaxon merely rose, bowed fittingly to each of the senior officers and the regent, and led the two senior Wereguards to the antechamber. Here, low couches served as resting places for those wanting audience with the regent or the senior adviser. There were ten such resting places; the three senior officers of the Pale reposed themselves in anticipation of the imminent loss of power, Jaxon taking care to set himself where he could keep an eye on the reactions of the other two.

He need not have been concerned. While Hekili and Hokulani subsided into an almost comatose state, their biowires beeping ever more slowly and their limbs twitching in a steady, regular tic, he remained alert. Alert enough to adopt the same position as the other two when Ailani crept in to look, he supposed to make sure that nothing was needed. As the door closed behind her, Jaxon sat up. During the remaining minutes of what proved to be a very long hour, he ran various queries, ascertaining to his surprise that each more recent generation of citizens comprised more liveware and less hardware. As far as he could tell, this was a matter of economy and the vagaries of supply: live material—or rather, material that had once been live—was easier to come by than the metals and minerals needed for the creation of hardware. Metals and minerals were finite; liveware continued to procreate. Satisfied with this analysis, Jaxon was sure he had pinpointed the cause of the increasing faultiness among all classes of citizens. They had too much liveware! Liveware was notoriously unpredictable. He would look into it, he promised himself.

And this business with the plaques. He had never troubled himself to study the power sources too finely, for they had been created before him and had always appeared to be endlessly effective. He had never, until Teiuc and Quauhtli prompted him, even queried the schematics of the system. He supposed that it was inevitable that a fissure in the very fabric of the policosmos would have an effect on all its systems, but he had never—

Ah! Jaxon gasped as a current of energy pinged through every atom of his being. He blinked, his visuals suddenly enhanced to an almost unbearable brightness. Just in time, he sprang back to his couch and pretended to bound into renewed life at exactly the same time as Hek-ili and Hokulani. Like them, he gazed into every corner of the room, squinting at the brilliance of his vision. Like them, he bounced to his feet and flexed his body from head to foot, as if just now, like them, regaining that marvellous flexibility of multi-way joints. Then, like them, he grinned at the other two and hurried back to the regent's throne room.

The Pale was back online.

CHAPTER 21

'What is your rite? Your rite, for your dead?'

Feather blinked back into alertness. He was still holding his dead father's hand, and the hand had grown cold. Some time had passed; the light of the day had changed. He placed Helm's hand carefully on his chest. It was too late to close his eyes for him—one of the others had already done so. They had been waiting a good while in silence.

Feather rose to his feet, Rasti again in his arms. The little dog lay on his breast, her face hidden under her paws. She at least was not ready to face the world without Helm.

'Kohu, Kaihoko,' said Feather, glancing at each in turn. 'I thank you for your patience.' He took a deep breath. 'In the tribes we have two ways to return the bodies of our dead to the land from which we came, the land on which we travel. Most often, we burn our dead.' He had to stop, a sudden vision of the oily flames and dense smoke of a funeral pyre clouding his mind. Kilimanjara, was it? His mind insisted on Helm's body inside the inferno. He shook his head, clamping down on the roar of grief that shook his heart. 'Or,' he said, his breath returning only reluctantly, 'we may bury them if we can make the place safe from ferals.'

Kohu rubbed his chin. 'No way to make a pyre, I'm thinking. We would need a power of dry fuel.'

'Which we don't have and can't get on this sorry plain,' added Kaihoko. 'It'll have to be a grave.' With that, he wrestled a narrow hand-spade from his pack, similar to the one Feather carried for digging out edible tubers. He looked about for a likely place, and pointed with the spade toward the base of the ochre-striped ridge. 'Soil's deeper under the lee,' he said, and set off to mark out a space and begin digging. Feather watched, his mind quite empty, his hands absently stroking the warm curve of Rasti's back. Kohu touched his shoulder, making him start.

'Not to hurry you,' he said. 'Well, not too much, but this is not a good place to linger. Will you make your father ready? I'll help Kaihoko dig deep enough.'

Feather nodded. 'Yes. I'll be as quick as I can. Then I can dig too.'

The big man gave his shoulder a mighty pat as he went past. Feather went down on his knees again and took Rasti out of her nest inside his jacket, placing her on the ground. Here she sat upright, paying careful attention to what he was doing. As he straightened Helm's clothing, her soft whining kept any thoughts away. Almost like the tribe singing a lament, Rasti's sad whimpers kept his hands moving steadily. Helm's body and clothing set right, Feather checked over his father's gear. Tribal lore taught that the dead ceded their place to the living, a gift for the future. Had they been able to burn Helm's body, Feather would have stripped him to the skin, allowing a cleaner flame to return his flesh to the soil. As it was, some protective sense made him leave the body clothed. If Helm was to lie in the barren soil of Broad Plain, it seemed right to give him at least his clothing to define him as a tribesman. All his gear, however, would be shared out among the Storm. That was the way of the tribes in this after time.

First, though, Feather wanted to mark his grief. Helm's old knife, thin from many decades of whetting, was perfect for the job. He lifted one of his braids, and awkwardly hacked at the roots, nicking his scalp. As he pulled at the next braid, one of the Shaking Landers—Kaihoko it was—came close and put his hand over Feather's.

'Let me do it.'

'Please.' Feather's voice was choked with tears. He handed the knife to Kaihoko without looking at him, bent his head and closed his eyes. The Shaking Lander was deft and quick. In a brace of minutes, he set the knife back in Feather's hand.

'You should keep this.'

'Yes. I will.'

Feather turned and put out his other hand for the bundle of his severed braids. Together they walked to where Kohu was standing chest-deep in the compacted soil.

'We can go no deeper. See?'

Feather peered into the space. Perhaps half man-length in size, it was as deep as he was tall, but Kohu's feet were half-covered in water.

'Is it a soak you have found? A well-spring?'

Kohu shook his head, reaching up one hand to Kaihoko. They clasped forearms and Kaihoko pulled out his hearth partner with ease. 'No, Feather. It is the rising sea. It is what we have come to warn you about.'

'I do not understand,' said Feather.

Kaihoko patted his back. 'First your father, eh? Then we talk as we travel.'

None of it made any sense to Feather and he put it from his mind. Kohu tidied away his hand-spade and went over to Helm. He said some soft words and then lifted the dead tribesman into his arms. Helm looked tiny, although in life he had been a much taller man than Feather. In Kohu's arms he was as a sleeping child, his lolling head turned into the big man's chest.

Coming close to the site they had dug, Kohu kneeled carefully by the edge, and with even more care, lowered Helm into the space. Feather saw that the Shaking Landers used the same ritual as the tribes for burying their dead: the body curled like a sleeping infant, face to knees. He nodded his thanks and crouched down so he could scatter his braids into the grave. Beside him, Kaihoko and Kohu each cut a lock of their thick black hair and dropped those in beside Feather's. Rasti whined, asking to be picked up again, but Feather stroked her head instead.

'There, small friend, take heart. Say your farewell. Say—'

There was nothing more to say. The three men set to filling in the grave by hand. The place was deep, but even so, Kaihoko rolled rocks to cover it, large rocks too heavy for most predators to shift. With no further words, they collected their gear and made ready to move. It was well after the middle of the day, and nobody wished to be out overnight without shelter on Broad Plain.

'Where is it you are heading?' asked Feather.

'To the Settle Place,' said Kohu.

Feather frowned. 'Do you mean the Settlement?'

'That's it! That's the name we've been trying to recall. Do you know where we can find it?'

'Yes indeed.' Feather bent to share some mindwords with Rasti. 'A moment.'

'What is it? Kaihoko asked curiously. 'Is the little one talking to you? I thought only canini had mindspeech.'

'The canini were modified for greater language, true, long before the Conflagration. Are there canini in the Shaking Lands?'

'Alas no. The larger beasts no longer live in the Shaking Lands. But Kéhua told us many tales of this land and its creatures.'

Feather's brow was creased. He had so many questions, but a great lump of grief was lodged in his throat. He let the questions go and opened his mind to Rasti. She wanted carrying. She was not tired, but she missed him and wanted to be with him. Feather shook out the carry-sling that Jana had made for him, back at Newkeep—the one from Helm's pack, that his father must have been using on this journey that had cost him his life. Rasti scrambled in and, his passenger settled, Feather joined the two travellers on the land.

'I was heading for Newkeep, downriver from the Settlement. We can walk together.'

'That is well. We thank you, Feather, son of Helm of the Storm.' Kohu shook his head. 'Though we knew him as Kéhua, you understand.'

'I know nothing of that. My father and I have only met each other in recent months. Will you tell me the tale as we travel?'

'Truly? We thought he must have gone back to the tribe long since. Well, it is quite a tale,' promised Kaihoko.

Feather pressed his lips together, walking slightly in front of the other two as they made their way slant-wise across the rise of the first ridge. Many more would be navigated before the setting of the sun. He had no wish to speak, but he could listen as he led them toward the Settlement.

* * *

'You are back! Look, only look at all these screens.' Adaeze clapped her hands, and then danced across the room, pointing out all the comms features that had sprung into life. Carefully transported from the regent's tower back in the Acrocomplexa at the time of the abandonment, they had been painstakingly fitted into the remodelled regent's stronghold here in the building, which had for generations housed the forecasters, their trainees, and their equipment. Black and silent for months, a score of devices had sprung into new life. Some of these, Jaxon realised, he had not seen for many years. The gradual loss of power they had experienced could no doubt be traced back many decades. Definitely, the issue must have predated the PPA. Amazing, in truth, that the inexact plane of the parent plaques had allowed them to function with so much efficiency for so long. But this! This resumption of energy! Jaxon found it hard to recall when he had last felt so alive. He bit back a short laugh. A feeling of being alive, prompted by a surge of hardware power.

Hekili exchanged a glance with him, a look on his bright, silvered face that Jaxon had not seen for many years. He, too, like all the Wereguard, would be feeling this excess of wellbeing. Jaxon inclined his head, acknowledging their shared experience, and then replied to the regent.

'This is an excellent result. I had not expected such a great improvement in so short a space of time. Your staff, Foremost Ingeneer, and yours, Chief of Teshniks, are to be congratulated.'

Jaxon gestured to the table, and all the senior officers seated themselves. The youngest of them—the regent Adaeze and the head of recycling Ailani—who had never suspected the range and quality of comms within the Pale, were entranced and could not take their eyes from the screens. Those with more experience, who remembered the dark, shaking, dire days after the PPA, such as Teiuc and Quauhtli, were nodding to themselves, well pleased. The immortal Wereguard and the senior forecaster himself, who had all but forgotten what the Pale looked like in its full glory of function, could not supress the odd smile of satisfaction. The feeling was, Jaxon reflected, like giving a favourite trainee a present of the device they had most wanted in all their life but had never imagined possible.

'As to the timing,' said Hokulani, one finger resting on the reactivated hearing piece behind his ear, 'this has happened so quickly because the plaque has not been moved within our new enclosure. So the service personnel tell me.'

'What?' Jaxon was appalled. 'The Palatine parent plaque is still in the abandoned area?'

Teiuc cleared his throat. 'That is correct, Senior. When the placement was viewed, it was clear that it formed an integral part of the Navel itself. A kind of keystone arrangement, if you like. We were able to level the plane, but only with the plaque in situ in the foundations of the tower.'

Jaxon held up one hand, a burst of processing showing him the detailed plans of the massive building called the Navel, the first and foremost of the Pale's mighty edifices. When they designed it to house all their most precious artefacts, the first citizens had taken extensive pains to ensure its integrity. The Palatine parent plaque was clearly enmeshed in the fabric of the foundations. Probably this was what had enabled it to continue functioning to any degree, despite the undermining of the ground beneath the Navel's footings. Teiuc was right. To remove the plaque without damaging it, without bringing the whole towering Navel down on the rest of the policosmos, would be the work of decades, involving scaffolding and buttressing for which they had no materials, numbers of workers they could no longer afford to progress and to feed, and expertise that they no longer had. Jaxon nodded, confirming the arrangement, reassuring the others.

'That is satisfactory, thank you. The plane has been restored. That is sufficient. Master of the Wereguard, we must look to the security of the Navel. Beyond our new boundaries it may be, but its integrity is just as important as when it contained all of our treasures.'

'The Wereguard and the Service will see to it,' promised Hekili, and Hokulani nodded his agreement.

Adaeze, dragging her eyes from the brilliance of the largest screen— perhaps remembering her hours of instruction—spoke into the satisfied pause. 'Our thanks to all involved. This mission has brought untold benefits to our policosmos. We are very pleased. We are delighted!'

There was an embarrassed round of smiling and a couple of

suppressed laughs. Jaxon was content to have it so. Happy regents were very easy to manage, and happy senior officers rarely looked to their own safety. The time to replace Teiuc and Quauhtli, who had questioned the operational activities of himself and the immortal Wereguard, was close. But not today. Today was for celebrating. He joined the others in gazing at the large screen. Across its width was displayed a feed from the viewfinder on the wrist of the leading Wereguard of the raiding party. Hokulani muttered into his own wrist, and the view onscreen steadied and rotated to show a landscape that was fascinating and abhorrent at the same time.

'What are you showing us, Head of Service?' asked the regent. 'Is this a live feed? Do we now have visuals on our raid?'

'We do,' agreed Hokulani. 'I will allow the senior forecaster to comment. His command of language is ever greater than ours.'

'My thanks.' Jaxon lowered his chin, a familiar politeness between equals. Not that the Wereguard were his equals, exactly, but they were the closest beings in existence to his own status. He cleared his throat delicately, tapped into the direct link, and matched the vision with his extensive data on the Settlement. Interesting.

'What we see here is the lower courtyard, the fenced area closest to the Founders River on which the Settlement depends. The river gate has been removed and our service personnel are dismantling the palisades. Ah, yes, here we see some of the sanitariat collecting materials for our biofuel pits. Hmm, some of these bodies have been dead a while. Drowned, perhaps? That river looks to be in flood.'

He sent a command downline and the view shifted. 'Now we see the steps leading up to the High City, the more prosperous area.' Jaxon issued a query. 'There has been a flood, indeed. Our staff have collected all the livestock and reduced them into wagons for transport. They will need time to collect all the hard materials—wood, metal, stone work, and so on—but the convoy of carcasses will leave very soon to make its way back to us. Excellent.'

There were murmurs of interest and pleasure as the Wereguard's viewfinder relayed every corner of the lower enclosure, showing the piled ovines, a lesser pile of equii, and a makeshift coop stuffed with fowl. Some of these would survive the journey back to the policosmos, not that it truly mattered. Jaxon approved the system and economy that had directed packing the creatures tidily into as small a crate as could hold them for transport. There was no need to waste time on killing them first. Unlike the four-footed food animals, the fowl would create no trouble during the journey.

The vision moved up a steep path toward the upper sections of the Settlement. By the Wereguard's feet, sanitariat workers could be seen painstakingly lifting cobbles out of their beds, stacking them into hods they carried on their backs. As the Pale's workers picked their way forward, it was clear that they would leave very little of the Settlement behind. For all the mark it would leave on the land, it may as well never have existed.

Jaxon directed another query downline, and the big screen flickered as the Wereguard turned about. For a millisecond, everyone held their breath, frightened that the blinking indicated that the planar arrangement of the plaques had slipped again.

Only Hekili laughed. 'He moved too quickly. We must remember how to use these comms!'

'Indeed,' said Jaxon, again with the dip of his chin. Then the visuals shifted again, and the assembled senior officers of the Pale saw one flat-bed wagon loaded with neatly stacked human bodies, and roped between its yokes a detail of strong-looking settlers. Excellent. 'Master of the Wereguard, Head of Service, this raid has been most neatly handled.'

'It is true,' Hokulani said without pride or gratification. Truth was truth. 'Long though it is since we raided, we do not forget our procedures.'

'I thought there would be more humans,' suggested Ailani. 'I was hoping for more liveware, to sort for the gene pools.'

'Most of the settlers' liveware would be low quality,' said Jaxon, 'but your point is good. Hekili?'

The master of the Wereguard looked inward. Jaxon felt a thrilling shiver of satisfaction. He had not realised the extent to which the Pale had lost momentum. He was very pleased to once more witness the Wereguard and the service communicating across the better part of the entire post-Conflagration land.

Hekili grunted. 'The Founders River was in flood. The water is yet quite high. The settlers tried to escape it, but their way was blocked by landfalls. Most have drowned, but some returned.'

'And walked directly into our raid. Excellent!' said Jaxon.

Chapter 22

Hector arrived first at the meadow sward, his sensors giving him some warning of the grim scene he would find. The stench of fresh blood and ripped guts would have warned him in any case, even if he had not been alerted by every biowire in his body that a host of enemies controlled the ground.

The equii were packed tightly, the herd milling and snorting, stamping in an ever-diminishing circle. Around them, gangs of strikebeasts patrolled mercilessly, and even as Hector ran to the place, one of the gangs rushed at the heels of the herd and the panicked equii bunched and scattered, reforming as quickly as they could into their circle of relative safety. Too late for one of the yearlings, pulled screaming off his legs and dragged down into the midst of the strikebeasts. Several other gangs descended upon the successful one, but others—probably already sated by one of the too-many piles of hide and bone that littered the edges of the sward—continued their menacing round of the herd, their long sabre teeth bared, their blood-curdling snarls dreadful to hear.

Hector could not spend the time to look for answers to all the questions that pinged in his mind: how had they got into the ravine in such numbers? How long had they been tormenting the herd? Where was Pinto? Violeta? Little Mateo? Where was … How could …

He stopped abruptly a length from the nearest gang and ranged his blasts. He did not need to use the full power he had once deployed when he opened a chasm in front of the wild men who threatened Enis and Tsendi on their quest to the Storm. He no longer had that full power, in any case. Time was sapping the strength of his Pale weapons.

Strikebeasts, horrendous as they looked, were mere creatures of flesh and blood. They may have been modified back in the before-time— they could act as terrifying weapons—but they had no tech. Hector took out a dozen with his first blast, the ugly, snarling beasts somersaulting into death.

A dozen, but there were hundreds of the monsters, and he knew that each blast would be less effective than the first. No matter. Hector strode forward calling with all the power of his huge voice.

'Come to me, strikebeasties. Here I am. Attack me!'

Enough of them noticed him and answered his call to keep him very busy for the next little while. At some point he noticed that Callan was nearby, skirmishing with a handful of mottled attackers, and then the hunters arrived. He groaned when he saw Rhosyn dash past him, eager for the fight. Then he concentrated on the task he had set himself, to kill as many strikebeasts as he could. He had blast power for several dozen, and after that he would crush them with his bare hands, stamp them with his heavy feet, chase them down, and finish them with his bare teeth if he had to.

The equii herd was stampeding, running first one way and then the other, as the motley gangs of strikebeasts rushed at them from every quarter. Huh. The strikebeasts were smarter than he had expected, some of the gangs making sure to keep the equii between themselves and Hector's blasts. They were avoiding him now, concentrating their defence on the hunters of the ravine, intent on herding the equii away from these defenders. One of the canini screamed, and Hector roared as he fired another blast—and nothing happened. He flicked his weapons back into his forearms and strode into the fray.

Immediately sensing that he had lost his edge of danger, the strikebeasts swarmed him, clinging on with every tactic in their predatory repertoire. One sank its sabre teeth into his calf, another pierced his shoulder with its razor claws. More and more of the beasts ran at him and leaped on him, and although he managed to extricate himself from each one, crushing necks and cracking skulls, the numbers were telling. He could only kill one at a time while they attacked him in mobs, so he staggered about under the weight of them, losing his balance, losing his strength as again and again they swamped him. Their blood-curdling yowls and the horrifying sameness of each beast's ferocious body was overwhelming his sensors. Around him, the canini yapped and growled, screamed and yelped, and the equii shrieked in fear and pain.

Another strikebeast thumped itself against his back, stabbing its sabre teeth into the flesh of his shoulder. Hector fell to his knees, roaring and grabbing, smashing the beast's skull against the hard ground, ripping it in two. Its oily dark blood with its foul stench flooded his face. He shook his eyes clear of it, and something exploded in his brain.

He leaped to his feet. A mighty vein of power surged through his body, power he had never known himself to possess. He didn't waste time thinking about it. He just acted. Shaking his weapons out again with a powerful flick of both arms, he aimed, fired, aimed, fired, each blast obliterating a handful of strikebeasts as he stomped around the battleground, bringing every tussle to a close as he wiped out the mottled attackers. In a matter of minutes, he stood panting on the sward, piled corpses around his feet, strikebeasts lying like a harvest of stinking, disgusting blotchy fur. He looked up to see Callan, at the front of a handful of canini, regarding him with what looked like fear. Behind them, Freya and Jarli had arrived and stood staring at the carnage. He could hear the equii milling and squealing, so at least some of them still lived. Yet Callan did not speak, but stood unsteadily as if on guard.

Hector took a deep breath. 'What is it?' he asked. 'Are you hurt?'

Callan lifted his head, taking a step closer. There was too much blood on his coat, thick dark strikebeast blood and his own bright red blood. 'Hector?' said Callan, his mindvoice sounding unsure.

Hector shook his weapons back in and took a deep breath. 'What is it? What's wrong? Callan?'

The big canine stepped cautiously closer. 'You look … let me …' Hector felt the push of Callan's query inside his mind, and heard the delicate sniffing as Callan tested his scent. 'Ah. Hector. Well.' Callan sat close to Hector, but not touching. He looked up into Hector's eyes. 'Something happened, my friend. You changed.'

'Changed?' Hector looked down at himself. His skin was shining brightly, like polished metal. He put one hand to his face. He could no longer feel the stubbly beard that had he been growing. His face was smooth, his cheekbones sharp. His hair, too, felt wiry on his scalp.

Hector sat down. As the others began to move about the sward, clearing the dead strikebeasts for burning, tending the wounded, tenderly gathering the ripped bodies of fallen canini, he sat alone. Somewhere among the carnage and the wreckage of the battle, he suspected he had lost his humanity.

* * *

Talis carried Jasper most of the way back to Newkeep, though every now and then the boy insisted he could walk. There was no returning by the river path. Having made great incursions into the bank, the Founders River appeared to be growing in power, carrying even more water than in previous days, ripping away great swathes of soil as it thundered downstream.

Talis could not understand it. There had been no further rain for over a week, and they had all seen that the water level was falling. Such certainties were far from his mind now. The Founders River had forgotten it had any banks, or any normal flow. A mighty, untamed force, it continued to pour enormous currents down its new wider course, tearing down the earth, the trees, the rocks that stood in its path. Talis and Jasper headed inland and then further inland, their way continually blocked by new waterways that the Founders River was pushing through the land. They were now at least as far south of Newkeep as they were west of it. Talis could see the blunt, hulking shape of the Broken Ranges on his right. For the next few leagues at least, the land was higher, sloping gradually down to the river. As he well knew, the land continued its steady decline on the far side of Founders River, with most of Broad Plain lying well below the level of the surrounding territory. They had sometimes joked that it was like a huge lake of sand.

If Founders River continued to pour in tonnes of water at this rate, Talis thought, then the small billabongs and lakelets they had seen forming around Newkeep would be simply drowned beneath a new sea. Newkeep, the Settlement, the tribes—could they all be washed off the land by this flood?

'I want to go home,' mumbled Jasper, trotting beside him through the grey tussocks scattered all through the rocky terrain.

'We are going home, son, just as quickly as we can,' Talis replied. 'It happens that we're taking the long way around. Want me to carry you a bit?'

'No!' Jasper quickened his step, stumbling as he tried to hurry. Talis nodded approval, but kept an eye on him. The lad was close to exhaustion. Soon Talis would call a rest halt. They had a long way yet to go.

* * *

'Perhaps we should first say how we knew your father,' said Kohu. The big man matched his stride to Feather's neat pace, while Kaihoko ranged ahead, scouting the land in the direction Feather advised they should go. The rolling corrugations of Broad Plain formed a kind of prolonged ripple across the land, running roughly south to north. Travelling west, the trio had many up-and-down treks as they crossed the red sands, sands not as dry as they usually were. That surprised Feather somewhat. There had been no follow-up rain for some weeks, and even though the autumn had been unusually wet, he rather thought that the cold winds of winter would have scoured the plains dry. Not so. They came upon many surface puddles, some as large as a small lake. Most were shallow enough to wade through, for anyone who cared nothing about their boots and gear. Feather and the two Shaking Landers chose to go around such meres.

'We were only boys, you understand,' persisted Kohu.

Feather glanced sideways at him. Clearly there was a great deal to say, and he had noticed that the Shaking Landers liked to talk. 'Please, tell me all you can,' he invited. 'I am listening.'

Kohu grinned, looking about as he began his tale. 'It is well that we have the plain to ourselves. It is quite a tale. I would not like to interrupt it to fight with a feral, for example.'

Despite the sadness misting his thoughts, Feather felt a tickle of interest. 'Kohu, my friend, why not tell me of the Shaking Lands? We will not reach the Settlement this day. I wondered—would you mind leaving talk of … of Helm, until we are camped?'

'A good thought,' said Kohu, patting Feather's back heavily in what was no doubt meant to be an encouraging way. 'Are you sure you never heard of us?'

Feather concentrated on scanning the terrain ahead. 'As I explained, I only recently met my father. He lived away from us for many years. My grandmother, though, Kilimanjara—'

'Kilimanjara! It is long since I heard that name.'

'Well, there may have been a tale, once, of a people who crossed the bounding ocean in small canoes. We children had never caught sight of the bounding sea, and the canoe people seemed just part of a tale to amuse us.'

'Not seen the bounding ocean,' exclaimed Kohu. 'Has your tribe made its circuit only on the plain? Never crossed a mountain? Never ploughed the sea?'

Feather found himself rather affronted at the Shaking Lander's incredulous tone, but he had to admit that it was so. The tribes had never ranged south as far as the Broken Ranges, though everyone knew where they were, and they knew also that the Silver Mountains were to the north, beyond the dreadful Pale. There had never been a need to travel past either colossal barrier.

Kohu, his mouth set in a stern line, took hold of Feather's arm to hold him still. Rasti wriggled her face out of Feather's collar and licked Kohu's hand.

'What is it?' asked Feather, troubled by the sudden change of mood from light hearted tale-telling to grim foreboding.

'Feather, son of Helm of the Storm,' said Kohu. 'This is what we have come to tell your people. The tribes and the settlers, the wild men, too, should we find them. The bounding ocean is growling with new tides. The ice wastes are melting and the sea clambers over the land. Our Shaking Isles are already sinking. Here—' he gestured across the lifeless expanse of Broad Plain, '—here the Ruined Land will be swallowed whole. All of you must cross the Silver Mountains, as soon as you may. You must come with us to the highlands, or perish in the new ocean.'

* * *

Jaxon stood with Adaeze at the peak of the regent's stronghold, under the curved plexiglass that formed such an elegant dome over the newly installed garden. New the garden might be, and bare as the season was, they were perfectly content among the marvellously crafted metal trees and the arches hung with trailing vines of bronze and copper. A more pleasant place from which to enjoy the view, in this season, could not be found in the whole of the policosmos.

Well, Jaxon corrected himself, there was a better platform, one that allowed a full three-hundred-and-sixty degree view, but that was at the top of the regent's tower in the Acrocomplexa. Since the realignment of the parent plaques into their interlocked plane of power generation only a day before, Jaxon had toyed with a plethora of ideas. A head such as his, in which premium liveware partnered exceptional hardware, informed by the most complete sets of data surviving on the entire continent—perhaps the entire planet—was bound to be busy with ideas. One of those was the reintegration of the abandoned districts inside the policosmos.

'How long until we can see them coming?' asked Adaeze, straining her large, ebony-rimmed eyes toward the south.

Jaxon permitted himself a small joke. 'You may see them any time you wish, my lady, should you care to access the screen.'

Adaeze laughed. Such a comely sound, a glad tinkle with a hefty purr behind it. Jaxon was surprised at just how much his regent had improved after the plaque realignment. He should not have been so shocked, of course. Since the days of the first citizens, all the members of the Patraena dynasty had been magnificent creatures. Adaeze's youthful callowness, her scanty education, her immature tastes, now counted for nothing. How glad he was that he had stayed his hand, that he had waited for a more propitious time to promote a new regent in her place. He now found himself pleased with the regent he had selected, and more than pleased to leave her possible replacement— Ailani, head of recycling—situated where she was. The reinvigoration of the Pale's power into every hardware device and implant had done little for Ailani. Adaeze, now, was brimming with power, power that suited her panthera-like features, her purposeful movements. Jaxon counted himself happy.

'Beauteous as all our screens now are,' Adaeze reproved him, 'I would like to know the limits of my own viewfinder.' She held up her left hand, where a bulky leather band, in the vintage military style she favoured, made an artistic statement about the various sensing devices it housed. 'And even of my own eyes.' These she opened wide at Jaxon, and he could not suppress a smile.

'Soon enough, my lady,' he replied. 'We will see them. They are making good progress across the plain, difficult though it is. Of course, our raiders could move more quickly if they had proper paved go-ways to travel.'

'As we have in the policosmos.'

'Indeed, as we have in the policosmos, and around the perimeter walls for the collection details.'

They watched the light scudding across Broad Plain as the broken clouds scattered and bunched, chased by a strong, cold wind. Cold, but not freezing, Jaxon noted. As the autumn had proved unusually wet, so the winter was proving unseasonably warm. Any frost that touched their plexiglass windows immediately evaporated, and icy patches on the ground melted soon after each dawn. No further rain, no sleet, no snow. A most satisfactory season in which to cover several hundred leagues, husbanding a caravan of live—recently live, he should say—fodder for the biofuel pits, carts loaded with building materials, and dozens of human thralls to undertake the worst of the work in the policosmos and then be converted in their turn into biofuel. Very satisfactory indeed.

'Is it true, Senior, that once we had go-ways crossing the land in all directions? That we could easily zoom to any place on the continent?'

'In the very early days, my lady,' Jaxon confirmed. 'Many go-ways survived from the days before the Great Conflagration, and these we made use of in the first years of the Pale.' Jaxon himself had never left the policosmos, but the Wereguard had led many a successful service mission into the ravaged land. 'Our citizens, led by the Wereguard, ranged all over the continent, collecting all the materials we could possibly need to craft and then to maintain our wonderful home.'

'Building materials, such as the raiding party is bringing home?' asked Adaeze.

'Ah, not quite,' said Jaxon. 'You understand, the Settlement itself—in fact, every other edifice on Broad Plain and around it—was built of the substandard resources that we had not bothered to collect.' He shook his head. 'It is indeed a pity that we are reduced to collecting such low quality stuff, but the effects of the PPA, you see, are dire.'

Adaeze, peering to the south with her eyes screwed up and her left wrist held aloft, seemed not to be paying him any attention. 'What about there? Is that our army, coming now?'

'I think not, my lady. They were not so close just yet—' Jaxon gave a gasp, suppressed so quickly that the regent did not notice. He stepped up beside her and adjusted his own viewfinder. As the narrow band hummed into exquisitely clear focus, he had to work hard to shut down a further gasp. He had not thought ... this must mean ... He clicked his fingers to one of the servants hunched in out-of-the-way corners, awaiting the regent's pleasure.

'You there—fetch the master of the Wereguard! All the senior officers, in fact, at once. To the throne room.'

Adaeze turned to look at him. 'What is it, Jaxon?'

'We should go back inside, my lady.' He gestured for her to proceed ahead of him, and followed her down the spiral stairs with a look of concern that might have frightened her, had she been able to see it. Arrived at the throne room, Jaxon waited until all the senior officers were gathered to tell them the news. In particular, he fixed Teiuc and Quauhtli with a severe look.

'My lady, my fellow senior officers,' he began. 'Let me show you what the regent and I have just observed.' He waved a slim, elegant hand at the screen. The image changed from the channelled output of the raiding party's leading Wereguard, and switched to the long prospect from the viewfinder atop the Acrocomplexa, still the highest building in the Pale. They all watched in horrified shock as a mass of shambling, rusty metal creatures shuffled away from the policosmos, directly on the path of the returning army.

'The realignment of the plane,' Jaxon explained, 'would appear to have unintended consequences. It seems that every expired engine feral has been reanimated. Not only that, they are working in concert rather than attacking each other.

'Our revived parent plaques,' he went on into the stunned silence, 'have by some repulsive means given life and communication back to the ferals.'

Chapter 23

Hector roused himself. He had to help. Something had happened inside him, that much he knew, but how and why was more of a puzzle. That the Pale was involved he had no doubt, and he wished he could ask Tad what he thought, or even discuss it with Mashtuk. But Tad was a whisper on the wind and Mashtuk was shut inside the battered planes of his own skull. Hector himself was the one who knew most, and he was rather horrified to discover that he knew more than he wanted to. Multiple data sets clamoured for his attention, pinging hundreds of notices inside his mind. There would be time to sift them, to think about them, later. At the moment, there was a sorry battlefield to tend to.

He lifted his head to find Freya crouched beside him, a worried look on her face. He felt hot blood rush to his cheeks, but he imagined that she would not see his blush. All his feelings, all his Hector-ness, would be hidden behind the silvery angles and voids of his humachine face. His voice was unchanged, as was the affection he felt for her.

'Freya. You're not hurt, are you?'

She shook her head, its careful braids now loosened from the woven vines she had threaded through her hair that morning. That morning she would have been expecting nothing other than a quiet day in the ravine helping Jarli with the babies, preparing their food, taking a watch at the pinch point. She was teaching the hunters, too, some of the trail remedies that the tribesfolk used, which she had learned from Kilimanjara. Hector liked to listen in on those lessons. No doubt that was why she was here now, ready to help care for the injured. He hoped that was all it was. He hoped she hadn't run all this way to fight the strikebeasts. Now as the weak winter sun dropped beyond the rim of the ravine, the day had proven to be something completely different. Freya looked dreadful, white and shocked, as if she might faint any moment.

'I was worried you might be hurt,' she said as the silence between them grew. 'I can see that you have beast blood all over you, but I'm also pretty sure that's your own blood, there. I thought you might have been bitten.' Freya pointed to his shoulder, and Hector remembered hauling one of the strikebeasts from its perch there. Two of its sabre teeth had stabbed right through the muscle and slammed into the bone, he recalled. Of course, nothing of that remained. The sudden surge of power from the Pale had healed him, from the inside out.

'Didn't get me,' he told Freya. 'Must have missed everything important. Don't worry about the blood, it's no more than a scratch. Truly, I'm not hurt. Let's help the others.' He rose smoothly to his feet and smiled down at her, as much as his face could show a smile now. Freya met his eyes as though nothing had changed in him, and made a little grimace of her own. Her voice was rather shaky.

'It's bad,' she said. 'Over here.'

She led him from the bloody, trampled edge of the sward to where the equii were now gathered, clustered together by one of the ravine's little streams, with their heads hanging low. Most of the remaining herd had by now drunk their fill. Hector did not know how many hours, or days even, they had spent hopelessly circling in their defensive huddle, surrounded by tormenting strikebeast gangs. They would have been unable to drink or eat or rest, with the beasts constantly rushing and harrying them. He stepped up to Pinto, who, he was glad to see, was yet on all four feet, though he was shaking all over and still heaving for breath. Every rib showed through the crisp black and white patches of his coat, and even his backbone looked like a threaded collar of bare stones. Hector put one large hand on his shoulder, and Pinto leaned into him for a moment before righting himself again.

'Pinto, my friend, what happened? Why didn't you send someone for help?'

The parti-coloured equo lifted his head. 'That's what Callan said. Not equo.'

Hector looked around. Sure enough, Callan was nearby, sitting patiently while Jarli washed a great gash on his hind leg.

'He says it's not the equo way,' Callan muttered. 'He says they're a herd, not a pack. They stick together, whatever comes.'

Hector bit his lip. All around, he could see fallen equii—some of them hours-old heaps of bone and hide; another handful were fresh kills, taken just before or during the battle. The strikebeast gangs, though clearly they had joined together for this mighty hunt, had each tried to cull a prize from the herd and make off with it. From what he could see, none of the gangs had survived to escape the ravine. Maybe a couple of individuals. Nothing for the packs of the ravine to be too concerned about. The beasts had done more than enough damage already . He could see the purple-brown hide of Violeta, lying mangled and still, not far from where the survivors were drinking. He felt a howl burning up his throat.

Then he turned his eyes to the other shapes lying so still on the edge of the sward. His heart bashed like a power burst against the inside of his chest. Huh. He could still feel grief and pain, as he had when Tad had died, and when he heard of Zélie's death. But this! Hector went to his knees, trying to comprehend the size of the pain, the size of the loss.

Of the canini he had called to help the equii, he could see only Enis and Thestia and Tillie and Niccolò, and young Mishka from Thestia's pack, on their feet. And Callan having his hurts tended. And laid out carefully at the edge of the sward were old Tanno, his body in shreds, and Hippolyta, only recognisable by the thick sable fur of her tail, and all the other youngsters—Hippolyta's cubs Aled and Mared, the other two half-grown canini from Thestia's pack, and Rhosyn. All of them were bent in the twisted shape of bloody death.

Brave, reckless, warm-hearted, quick-thinking Rhosyn was dead.

How could they possibly tell Mashtuk?

* * *

Kaihoko knew himself to be better at explaining things than Kohu. The travellers found a likely camping place a little earlier than they would have preferred, but on Broad Plain it was wise not to take any chances. They settled themselves into a neat fold under the lee of perhaps the tenth corrugation they had crossed, a place from which they could see the land before them, with the protection of the ridge at their backs. There, out of the chill wind, they settled themselves in the last of the light. The days were still growing shorter, and winter's grip was only beginning to try its strength on the land. The sky was clear—as clear as nights ever were in this shattered post-Conflagration world—and there would be a light frost by morning. They would be warm enough, huddled close together and sharing their cloaks, without the need for a fire to alert anything unwelcome of their presence.

'Your father was a great man, Feather. He taught us many things in the years he travelled with us.'

'Kaihoko, I know very little of this. You would be surprised, I daresay, how few words he and I have exchanged in the weeks since his return.'

Kaihoko grunted. He had spent the best part of a day in Feather's company, and witnessed his pain at Helm's death. He had noticed the care Feather took over the comfort of that sorry little rat dog, and heard his careful, polite speech. Both he and Kohu now had a very good measure of Feather, son of Helm of the Storm. Added to their long knowledge of Helm himself, neither of them was surprised that there had not been an easy flow of words between the two. Helm was all warmth and energy, a man who felt everything to its height. Or its depth, true. Add to that the knowledge that whatever Helm felt was shown to the world, while Feather's feelings were kept inside. Kaihoko and Kohu had no doubt that Feather was a man of deep emotion just as Helm had been, but that he was very much quieter about it. Helm might bitterly regret abandoning his son, and Feather would doubtless forgive him from the bottomless well of his compassion, but the size of those feelings between them would be difficult to fold into words. Kaihoko patted Feather's arm and let one long finger reach to stroke Rasti's head.

'Life is not as full of surprises,' he said, 'as the elders say. I will tell you what I know. You will forgive me if I repeat some things that you have already heard.'

Feather nodded. They were making a meal from their combined journey foods; Feather was enjoying some of the Shaking Landers' dried salt fish, while they were much more pleased with his barley-grain flat cake and the strips of fresh hare the canini had gifted him. They had to share that with Rasti, true, but after all, she was only a small creature.

'Some years ago, we ventured across the bounding ocean. The Shaking Lands, you see, are small and fragile. In a bad season, the clans will starve. The bounding ocean is our life. From it we harvest the gift of fish. Yet we are human, and we wish for more than fish.'

Feather smiled. 'Your fish are delicious.'

Kohu looked sideways at him. 'You would not say so, had you eaten nothing else in your life.'

Kaihoko waved away the interruption. 'Hush, hearth mate. Now, we have travelled more than once to your Ruined Land. Yes, that is what we call this place. A little while ago we made a stay of some years, south of the Broken Ranges. There we met Kéhua, the spirit man, the ghost man. Your father Helm.'

'Why was he called a spirit man?'

'Ah, he was a mystery to us. A lone man surviving on the southern steppes? He might have been one of the gods of the place, you see. He was—'

'He was a wreck of a man. That's what my mother always said.'

Kaihoko elbowed his hearth partner. 'Hush. He was mostly starved, and he spoke so strangely. We never knew whether he talked of his own life, or told an ancient story, or gave us a picture of what our life might be after death. For some time, we Shaking Landers even debated whether or not he was already dead.'

Feather shook his head. 'This is a strange tale indeed.'

'Your father was a strange man. A great man, but strange,' Kohu put in.

Kaihoko spoke quickly, wishing to reassure Feather. 'Not so strange once we knew what had happened to him. Our people came to sift his visions from his history, his wishes from his certainties, his forgettings from his memories. Some days he told us much, and then the next day he would seem to know nothing about what he had said. His mind was a warren, you see, with twists and turns and dead ends.'

'Some of those dead ends he made himself.' Kohu sounded sad.

Kaihoko sighed. 'Helm told us of many things we had never seen in the Shaking Lands, as well as about himself. Thus we learned of Alia, and of you. We learned of the Storm, and we liked what we heard of your life. We learned of the Settlement and the settlers you trade with. We heard of the humachines of the Pale and how they squatted on this land like the worst of Conflagrationists, jealous of any other life, greedy only for themselves. We heard of Kestrel and of Kilimanjara.'

'Ah, Kilimanjara! She must have been quite a woman,' mused Kohu.

'She was our greatest ever huntmistress,' Feather said softly. His heart ached, but the ache was part of him now. Rasti licked his chin. After a moment, Kaihoko continued his story.

'Helm lived with us for many years, until at last we returned to the Shaking Lands. He would not come to the edge of the bounding ocean with us. He said he would rather walk into it and have it cover his head with its icy waves, than enter a canoe to be tossed across its white-laced hills. We thought he would go north to rejoin his own tribe.'

Feather gathered Rasti in close. 'He didn't do that. Not for many years. I only just told the Storm of his return. This journey I had planned to bring him home to them.'

Kaihoko and Kohu exchanged glances at the bleakness of his tone.

'Feather, son of Helm of the Storm,' said Kohu. 'He had found you. He was already home.'

'Thank you.' Feather's words came as a kind of gasp, but warmth flooded his heart.

Kaihoko extracted himself from the group and set about tidying the remains of their meal. Feather rose too, and went with Rasti beyond the reach of the folded overhang of sandstone that formed their shelter. Kaihoko watched as he put the little dog on the ground. The two of them walked up and down a while, but they never went out of sight, staying close enough to be discernible shadows in the dim light of the fading stars.

The two Shaking Landers waited, sitting close together with their backs to the ridge, for the tribesman to return. There was still so much they had to tell him. He had not even asked, in all the hours they had travelled together, more about why they needed to visit the Settlement.

Kaihoko greeted Feather as he returned to the shelter, making space for him and Rasti to huddle in close to him against the back wall. Kohu offered to watch for a while, and moved in front of them. Kaihoko whispered, in case Feather wanted to sleep now. 'Shall I tell you more now, or tomorrow?'

Before the tribesman could answer, an eerie, raucous scream tore the quiet of the night. Kohu leaped to his feet, and Feather quickly shushed Rasti, who had begun to bark in a frenzy of fear.

'What was that?'

'It sounded like a feral,' said Feather. 'But they have all … I don't understand! You will have seen them too, lying lifeless all over Broad Plain. We thought they had all died, that their engines had finally stopped working.'

The scream sounded again, and now that they were listening for it, they heard clearly the crackling, roaring sound of an engine feral making its way over the uneven ground of the plain. As they listened, they heard another feral answer. As one, they retreated further into the shelter, Feather keeping Rasti close and quiet. Their journey to the Settlement had just become even more dangerous.

* * *

Talis and Jasper had kept walking until night blinded them and forced them to a halt. There was little in the way of shelter, and it was even more difficult to find a dry spot to linger. Talis found a tangle of tumble grass piled against one side of a sand hill that seemed a little more solid than some of the others, and here he watched out the dark hours with Jasper gathered close against him. The boy was so exhausted that he sank immediately into sleep, wet and mud-covered and distressed as he was. They shivered together, their drenched clothing not even half-dried from the afternoon's walking. Over his son's head, Talis looked to where he hoped to find Newkeep. He could see nothing, not even a horizon where the hazed sky met the benighted land.

Long as the night was, to Talis it seemed shorter than those dreadful minutes when Jasper had disappeared under the roiling currents of Founders River. He found it hard to shake the horror from his mind, and his heart ached with the thought of Carlo, brave Carlo. He could not get Carlo out of his head. The picture of Carlo, his great dark eyes rolling in terror, struggling and sinking. He could not—

Talis knew he should have been worrying more about the settlers themselves. Trapped between the rampaging waters and the invading army of the Pale, they had little chance of survival. Any hope of escape that Talis had wanted to offer them with his warning was of no value now. Jasper had warned them; Jasper had led them on the path to safety; Jasper had almost died doing it. Talis did not see how any of them could find their way to safety now. So many settlers had already been swallowed by the river. He had seen them, sodden corpses tossing among the debris of baggage and clothing. How many more would fall as they tried to go back? How many would run directly into the cursed humachines? How many ... Talis shook his head. He had recognised Anielka, and maybe Olinna. Of Brettin he had seen no sign. Had she stayed in the Temple, minding the flame on the altar of Light? Was she there still, facing the dreaded humachines alone? Talis bit his lip. Brettin was alone as all the settlers were alone, as every one of them was all alone on the land with only a blink between life and death. There was nothing he or anyone from Newkeep could do to help them.

The night was long, but like other nights it came at last to an end. Talis found it hard to rouse Jasper at first light, although the lad struggled up gamely enough once he remembered where he was. He had not again said that he wanted to go home, but Talis knew the feeling.

'All right, son?'

Jasper nodded. Around his neck, the muddy collar of his tunic had rubbed the skin red raw, and he eased his shoulders. From the look on his face, Talis guessed that the movement hadn't helped. He placed on hand gently on Jasper's back.

'Let's go.'

As it happened, they had not much ground to cover. Before the morning light had grown strong enough to throw a shadow, and before the winter wind gathered itself to chill them too much, Talis saw the outline of Newkeep's boundary fences. Between them and their home, sheets of water mirrored the pearly sky. It seemed that some of the shallow puddles that the makers of Newkeep had encountered in their search for Jasper had joined into a lake-like expanse. To reach the gate, they would need to wade through that.

Just the thought of more water made Talis shiver, and he imagined that it was worse for Jasper, who after all had been submerged for longer than Talis cared to think about. But he was young, and it seemed he had more courage than his father.

'Come on! There it is,' he cried, and began splashing his way toward the half-made palisade.

'Take care, Jasper. There may be some deep bits. Jasper!' Talis found he was speaking only to his son's flying heels. He took off himself, aiming to keep within arm's reach, just in case the boy stumbled or slipped into an invisible hole, but the water was only ankle-deep. As they came closer, they were hailed by a shout from the gate, and within moments they were surrounded by people, all hugging and exclaiming. Valkirra, Cushla in her arms, pushed her way through, almost speechless with emotion. Talis pulled her close as they gathered their children into the embrace. Around them the makers of Newkeep cheered and talked, all at once, and all very loud.

'Talis! Jasper!' seemed the only words that Valkirra could say for quite a while, but before Talis was able to bring his own thoughts into words, she lifted her head. Around them, the makers grew quiet, and Talis noticed how their mood had grown grave.

'Talis, we have to move. You have no idea. We have to leave. I am so glad you have come back, both of you. I've been terrified that we would find your bodies on the bank, or see them sailing by.'

Talis looked at her in confusion. 'Our bodies?'

Branimir, always calm, put his hand out. 'The Founders River has turned rogue. It is eating our land and devouring our homes. Talis, it has washed countless bodies onto the bank and carried hundreds more past us. All we can see is dead settlers, dead animals, dead everything.'

Jana came up on his other side. 'We have come to another turning point in our story, Talis. Newkeep will not survive this flood that invades us from all sides. There is water everywhere, water all around us, bursting out of the river, rising up from the plain. The Settlement has perished, that much is clear. Newkeep will die. We must save ourselves.'

'What they say is truth,' said Valkirra, sounding much more like herself, with her partner and her precious children by her side. She was all decision. 'Talis, my heart, I know you are tired, both of you, but we must move now. Now.'

'What? I don't—where are we going?'

'We are going to meet Feather,' said Jana. 'We are going to ask the Storm for shelter. Their circuit lies on the far side of Broad Plain. Surely there we will be safe from this tide of water. With luck, Feather will be looking for us. Feather always returns. He will guide us across the plain. We must go now.'

After the disastrous events of the last two days, Talis found he was not surprised. With one arm across Jasper's shoulders, he followed the makers back into the flimsy walls of Newkeep to help with the hasty packing as they made ready to abandon their home.

Chapter 24

'So how did they get in?' Memandi asked Callan.

Hector sat beside the entry to Mashtuk's den, listening to the discussion. Somehow, with Hippolyta and both her cubs dead, it had not seemed right to gather at the pack's usual meeting place. All the survivors huddled together here, where Memandi and Tsendi had guarded the children when Jarli and Freya rushed to the emergency at the far end of the ravine. Romulo was sleeping in Jarli's arms and Remo was tucked against Hector's shoulder. On his other side, Freya leaned against him, her eyes wide and unblinking. Something had changed between them, Hector knew. The flaring power of his Pale strength and the fresh silver tint on his skin had somehow touched Freya, made her take pains to confirm his humanity. All her actions made him know he was Hector, after all, no matter how long it took this time for the influence of the policosmos to fade in the Outside.

Young Niccolò, who had joined the fight late and suffered only cuts and scratches, seemed to have laid claim to Hector and Freya too. Niccolò had his head in Freya's lap and was breathing a bit too slowly. He had not spoken since his sister Rhosyn had been carried to the farewell place, though every now and then a soft whine escaped him. Enis, too, was distraught, but he at least had Tsendi to think about. Tsendi was near to her time of birthing their first cubs, and the strikebeast invasion was the last thing she needed. She lay beside Enis and shivered.

Now that night had fallen, the pack had gathered to talk over what had happened and decide what to do now. Memandi was asking the questions, because of all the pack, only she and Tsendi had not seen the place, and Tsendi was not ready to speak. They had not been at the battle and had not joined in the cleanup. Hector thought that Memandi's questions were asked on purpose, to get the pack talking. Words might help the pack live through this time of disaster.

What was left of the pack, Hector thought.

'A rift in the walls,' Callan said softly, almost wondering, as if he was relating a dream he had experienced. A nightmare. 'Pinto showed me. Some underground river has broken through the ground and caused an avalanche.'

Callan was lying on his side, his breathing quick and shallow, with Thestia sitting on guard nearby. Young Mishka was there too, unhurt but exhausted. Hector feared that Callan's wound might go bad, but Freya had told him it was too early to say. They both knew that Callan's heart and mind were hurting more than his body.

The pack was broken, with Hippolyta the leader and most of their cubs dead. To add to their anguish, Mashtuk was nowhere to be found.

'The ravine is breached?' Memandi persisted.

'Yes.' Callan let out a long breath. 'Tomorrow we will have to think again. There is no longer any safety here. We cannot defend this space.'

They had spent the afternoon tidying the battle site as much as they cared to. The piled strikebeasts could rot. Any scavenger was welcome to them. Vultures, vulpini, mountain cats. Fire ants. Whatever could stomach their foulness.

Hector and the canini had been surprised to find that the equii, too, were content to leave their dead to lie on the ground. Pinto said it was natural, and better than being chopped into pieces for meat in the Settlement. The dead equii would return to the earth they had lived on for the brief months of their freedom. Callan had nodded his approval, but Hector found it strange. All through his life in the Pale, every scrap of any corpse had been recycled to make something—biofuel, fertiliser, fodder for the heaters. The canini preferred their dead to break down slowly, their bodies hanging high where the scavengers couldn't get them. He bit down on a groan of sorrow. Because of his great strength and reach, Hector had claimed the task of carrying the bodies of the dead pack members all the way through the ravine and up to the farewell place. It had taken him many trips, each one from the meadow sward, through the jungle of the deep ravine, past Mashtuk's den and along the meeting place trail. Then through the thorn forest to the top of the entry trail, and then onto the far side of the peak. Once there he lowered each of the canini into the farewell crevasse, alongside the metal skeleton of Tad and the bleached bones of Zélie. There the air and the sun would kiss them to eternity.

That was a comforting thought, he supposed, but it did not take much of an edge off his grief.

Jarli spoke up, his voice soft in the darkness. 'Our time in the ravine is over. We need to move on.'

'My father will be returning for me,' said Freya. 'He will look for me here in the ravine.'

Jarli replied, 'Feather, son of Helm, can find anything, anywhere. He could track us across bare rock. But what if we go to the Storm? Will he not easily find us there?'

Callan said dreamily, 'I would like to run once more with the Storm.'

Thestia yapped a reprimand. 'You'll run more than once, you lazy beast.' Her sharp voice was fractured with love and grief.

'I will. I will try.' Callan sounded exhausted, but Hector also saw a deep beat of warmth behind his words. Callan was not ready to give up.

'I believe that to be a wise course,' Thestia continued more evenly. 'Thank you, Jarli. It is a good notion. I myself have never run with humans, but my heart-mate Callan tells me they are to be trusted.'

There was silence for a moment. Thestia had just laid claim to Callan, spoken of him as if they shared a den. The big white canine did not correct her.

'I think that will work,' said Freya. 'The Storm are very good at taking in strays—not that we are strays—we are pack with them, are we not? Me, and Hector, and Jarli and the twins.' As she spoke, she reached out to put her small hand inside Hector's and left it there. Like a claim, thought Hector. Warmth flooded him, though he knew nothing would show on his burnished face.

'Callan and all the ravine canini are pack with the Storm too,' he added, feeling the flutter of warmth and hope in his heart. He took a breath to steady himself as Freya squeezed his fingers. 'And the tribe will welcome the equii, I am sure. Didn't they take some of the restless youngsters with them?'

'They did.' Pinto, standing off to one side, shook his mane and shared some sort of exchange with the half-dozen remaining equii, all of them huddled together on the little sward where Jarli's twins and the canini cubs usually played. 'Whatever your plan, we equii will not spend so much as another day in the ravine. We were born to run on the plain. We will not be trapped in walls or canyons. We prefer to face death some place where we can run.'

Hector glanced at Callan, who took a deep breath and closed his eyes. Callan had done all he could to protect 'his' equii, as Thestia called them, but it had not been enough. Most of them had perished in the strikebeast attack. Hector found it hard to see the pain in Pinto's great dark eyes. How dull the world must seem to him, with no Violeta, no Mateo. Their loss made the world dimmer for Hector too. He patted Remo's back and the sleeping child murmured Mashtuk's name.

Thestia lifted her nose to him. 'What does he say, our Hector?'

'Mashtuk. He wants Mashtuk.'

They looked at one another. Somewhere, somehow, on the very day of the battle with the strikebeasts, Mashtuk had gone missing. There was no sign of him around the dens, though Tillie thought she had caught a fleeting scent of him in the deep of the ravine. There was no sound of him, and nothing to be sensed of his mind. To every member of the pack, to every sense they had, Mashtuk had become invisible. They could only imagine that he had tried to follow them to the meadow sward and fallen into a crevasse or been taken by one of the larger passerines. Even Hector, with all his great range of sensors, could find no trace of him. Well, that was not quite true: he sensed a Mashtuk-trace in Enis and Niccolò, and, curiously, in Romulo and Remo too. There was even a Mashtuk-thread in his own tangled heart. But there was no Mashtuk.

He soothed Remo as well as he could. 'Mashtuk's not here, little one. Mashtuk loves you, but he had to go away.'

Mashtuk is a whisper on the wind.

Mashtuk is a tale from the before-time.

Mashtuk is a song of the canini down the ages.

* * *

The Storm wasted not a moment, packing their goods and readying their tents for a quick down-camp on the next morning. The word of Kiri Ana Rea was true, they all felt. There was no other reason for all the clans of the Shaking Lands to leave behind their homes, unless it might be a great disaster such as the one they wanted to warn the tribes about. Marin remembered, too, that there had been a strange smokiness in the sky some months before. Before the autumn rains, it was, and they had never found what caused it. They had suspected a huge bushfire, somewhere beyond the Broken Ranges, where scrub grew thick and the weather was harsh and dry, or so they had always been told. Kiri's explanation of the Shaking Mountains bursting into fiery life fitted in with everything the tribes had witnessed.

'Have the Shaking Mountains ever exploded before?' asked Marin.

'It is said. The Shaking Mountains made the land. It is also said that the Shaking Mountains will destroy the land,' Kiri replied.

Willow, seated by her partner, shook her head. Since the coming of the Shaking Landers, she had left off her sorrow over the twins and concentrated on the warning that now passed from mouth to mouth all through the tribe, and on to other tribes. The Shaking Landers, in their wish to give the people of the Ruined Land some chance to survive, had sent of pairs of runners all over Broad Plain. They had learned all the names from Helm, they said, and their messengers would do what they could to find and warn them all.

'The Settlement too,' explained Kiri. 'Kéhua—that is Helm you know—told us that they were good people, and good trading partners. We would not wish them to go on in ignorance of what is coming. Anyone who wishes to save themselves must move as soon as they can.'

'Sooner,' put in Paolo, who had spent the day talking with the hunters and scouts of the Shaking Land. 'We cannot wait on them to return, I am told.'

'That is right,' Kiri said gravely. She turned her face up to stare at the darkened sky. 'Our heralds go with courage. They hope to meet us in the Silver Mountains, but they know they may perish before they can even deliver the warning.'

'They are very brave,' Willow said softly.

Kiri smiled at her. 'They wanted to go. They do not forget Kéhua.

They wish to honour him by warning as many of his people as they can.'

Marin cleared his throat. 'They may well meet him, you know, if they go toward the Settlement. Feather told us that he waits just down-river, at the new settlement site.'

Kiri inclined her head. 'That would be good. Better yet if we all meet again in the Silver Mountains.'

Wisewoman Beris, who was sitting nearby listening intently to the strangers, reached to take a handful of Kiri's sleeve. 'How do you know of these Silver Mountains? We have scarcely heard of them, and you do not even live on this land.'

Kiri lifted her brows. 'We live on this land now, old one. Our own has sunk beneath the waves. But the Silver Mountains—yes, we have known of them for many years. There is much we know of this land and its shapes. For many generations our people have sailed the bound-ing sea and explored the new contours of the land. This we have done since the days of the Conflagration. Some say that this is how we lived in the before-time. As to that,' she shrugged, 'I cannot say for sure. But what is certain is that our only hope of surviving this time is to travel through the Silver Mountains and onto the highlands.'

'And that,' Marin said with calm decision, 'is where we will go. As we journey north, we will send runners to the ravine. Kiri Ana Rea, in the ravine we have dear friends, friends that Helm did not know of.'

'Friends of the Storm are our friends too.' Kiri spoke as if this fact was self-evident and that saying it aloud was merely a polite refrain. 'By all means, share the warning with all who deserve to live. But not, I beg you, not with the humachines of the Pale.'

The Storm nodded their agreement. The machine monsters of the Pale would be better off drowned. But mention of the ravine and of the Pale in the one minute had put another thought into Paolo's mind. He gave a little gasp as an idea struck him, and then addressed the visitor.

'Kiri Ana Rea, have your people walked much on this land?'

'I believe so,' she replied, with a gracious turn of her head. She had shining eyes, dark grey as a thundercloud, and they gleamed at Paolo as she spoke.

'What is it, Paolo?' asked Marin, intrigued by the thoughtfulness he saw on his scout's face.

'Huntmaster, I am thinking of Freya's friend Hector. Our friend Hector. I am looking at the young men of the Shaking Land and I am wondering—'

'Ai!' exclaimed Marin, his eyes opened wide. 'You are right, Paolo! Kiri, honoured visitor, there is a strange tale we must tell you, of a human boy adopted by the humachines of the Pale, and then thrown Outside to perish.'

'A human? Inside the Pale?' Kiri shivered. 'That must have been terrible. How did he survive?'

'That he will be able to tell you himself. But Kiri, we are looking at you, looking at your family, your clan, your people. Our friend Hector could be the brother of any one of you, by his looks. Is it possible that someone of your blood lived on Broad Plain? That they left a son at the gates of the Pale?'

'A boy of Shaking Lander blood? Gifted to the Pale? I do not think that at all likely.' Kiri Ana Rea sounded incredulous and even a little insulted.

'Only in desperation, only as a dying act. One slim, last chance for the boy to survive. Might one of your clan have done this? Might one of your people have lived here long enough to have a child, and to wish to make that child safe on a terrible day of death?'

Kiri turned her head, her eyes meeting those of some of her people. The Shaking Landers muttered and raised their brows. They exchanged some animated discussion in their own dialect before Kiri turned back to Marin.

'Yes,' she confirmed. 'Such a thing is just possible. As I have said, many of our folk have crossed the bounding ocean over the years. Not all returned to the place they left—indeed, not all returned.' She opened her splendid eyes wide and gave them her brightest smile. 'Now we cannot wait to meet this Hector of yours. Perhaps your Ruined Land truly is as full of wonders as our elders have always told us!'

* * *

The largest of the screens showed all too clearly what happened to the returning army of the Pale with its convoy of goods and slaves. Jaxon and his fellow seniors sat in silence as they saw the disaster unfold. For some of the time, they were able to follow the battle between the massed ferals and the raiding party by tuning in to the Wereguard wristscreens, but before long their only vision was provided by the long lens of the viewfinder at the top of the Acrocomplexa.

The sights they saw were horrible. Even Jaxon flinched as one by one, the shining silver of the humachines was submerged by a rusty tide of old ferals. These reanimated, vigorous ferals appeared to be entirely impervious to successive blasts of the Pale's best weaponry, weaponry at the strongest level it had enjoyed for decades. Or perhaps the ferals were not immune—perhaps there were just too many of them for the comparatively small raiding party to overcome. One thing was certain: the immortality of the Wereguard counted for nothing if he was torn into several pieces by ferals, his limbs shredded, and his inner workings ripped apart.

That was true for all of the humachines, whether of the higher Wereguard or service level, or the humblest citizens of the sanitariat. The ferals tore every one of them limb from limb.

'I cannot believe what I am seeing,' the regent said in a whisper. 'How can this be? I don't understand how this can happen. I thought the ferals had died.'

Nobody answered. As they watched, the ferals began to devour the corpses in the carts and to rend the terrified, chained settlers into smaller chunks they could consume with ease.

Jaxon cleared his throat. 'The realignment of the plane seems to have allowed the ferals to recover. They once more have not only their lives, but some sort of communication.' He shook his head. 'There is no mention of this in the data. We know that ferals were created before the Conflagration as mere killing machines. I have never known them to act in concert.'

'Perhaps,' Hekili said heavily, 'the first citizens programmed them in some way. Somebody at sometime connected them to the plane. After all, for many decades we have lived off the kills they drove against our walls. Perhaps that was part of the first citizens' plan for our survival.'

Jaxon shook his head, unwilling to believe it, reasonable as Hekili's idea was. 'There is no mention of it in the data,' he insisted. 'There are only defined ways to collect the bounty after feral kills.'

'Maybe—'

Whatever the regent was about to say was lost as the screen flickered, flashed green, and then died. No action of Jaxon's could revive it, and they spent a good few minutes making futile gestures at the control panels. Eventually Jaxon asked Teiuc and Quauhtli to investigate, and the meeting broke up in confusion and misery.

* * *

Fortunately, the route that Valkirra chose for their journey north led them many leagues to the east, well clear of the Pale's disaster on the plain. Branimir, who had some knowledge of the land between Newkeep and the tribal circuits, advised her about the general direction, and she herself scouted ahead while Talis managed the march. Both he and Branimir had often spoken with Feather about his journeys, and there had been that one occasion after the PPA when a caravan of supplies had been sent from the Settlement to help the tribes. Valkirra and Talis remembered that time well. They had every hope that the tribes would repay that one good deed now, in this extremity of need. If once the tribes had been left without shelter or resource on the ruined expanse of Broad Plain, the makers of Newkeep now had a very good understanding of that experience.

They could not move as quickly as they would wish, for the sands of Broad Plain were sodden and cratered with shallow lakes. In places, upwelling water marked the rise of new springs, and some of the irregular corrugations that crossed the plain's vast expanse had become unstable, collapsing into mounds of coloured dirt where once their peaks had shown a sharp edge of sandstone. Talis was worried there was something greater at work, something wider and more forceful than whatever tides were now driving the great Founders River with such force. To Talis, it felt as if the whole of the land was sinking beneath their feet.

Then there was the matter of the children, and the animals, and the elderly in the train. While they had two carts and their four remaining equii to pull them, these could only proceed slowly in the heavy going. Ovine had to be herded, fowls transported in cages, and the little children and old folk had to be carried in the wagons, by litter, or on the backs of the hale. Talis remembered the happy days when they had decamped downriver to Newkeep. He remembered the sense of a new beginning, their excitement at the freedom and the sense of danger, and the thrill and determination they all felt at leaving behind the only home they had ever known. On that journey they had shifted the most delicate of their goods by barge, unloading at the makeshift port of Newkeep, while the able-bodied had walked and danced and run and galloped along the river path. Now they struggled toward an unknown goal, pursued and surrounded by a sense of dread, in fear for their lives.

Fortunate they were, too, that Feather, son of Helm of the Storm, lived up to Jana's enduring expectations of him. Valkirra had only just mentioned to Talis, on her return from her latest scout ahead, that they should think about where and how to set up camp for the night, when a long, low whistle hailed them from the ridge ahead. Talis strode to the front of the convoy, which had walked on while he and Valkirra consulted, shading his eyes in an attempt to see more clearly. The sun was behind him and his shadow flowed across the sands like a giant of the before-time.

'If I am not mistaken,' he announced to the makers of Newkeep, 'we no longer need to look for the Storm. I believe the Storm have found us.'

Jana ran past him, her cloak lifting from her shoulders and flying behind her. At the same time, Feather—it must be Feather—dashed down the slanted side of the corrugation and staggered onto the level ground of the plain. He righted himself and came on unerringly. They ran into each other's arms, oblivious to the dulling afternoon, the dire Outside, the urgency of their travelling.

Valkirra put her arm through Talis's elbow. 'They make me feel old.'

'Give them a moment,' Talis advised. 'They will come to their senses soon, I expect. It is not so long ago that I gave Jarli this same advice. Feather and Jana do not see each other very often, and they love each other very much.'

They watched on for a minute, noticing that Feather was followed by two companions who also stood back, waiting on the tribesman and his partner. The two men were enormous, tall and wide-shouldered. For such huge fellows, their stance had something of gentleness—the way they tilted their heads to watch the lovers' reunion, the easy folding of their arms, the glances they exchanged that were full of love.

Talis pointed them out to Valkirra. 'We may not have met up with the Storm, my heart, but I believe we have met with friends. Come, let us go and greet with these good folk, and make our plans to move to somewhere safe and off this blighted plain.'

'Let's do that,' agreed Valkirra. She took her hand from his arm to straighten her jerkin and smooth the flying strands of her thick auburn hair, tucking in all the locks that had come loose from their braids. Talis waited with a smile on his face as she put aside Valkirra the scout and became again Valkirra Adelriksdottir, foremost of the Newkeep makers.

'What?' asked Valkirra, returning his smile.

Talis took her hand and together they began to walk toward the newcomers. Around them, all the makers murmured in relief, joining them to continue their journey northeast. Jasper ran to take Valkirra's other hand, and Talis called Cushla to climb down from one of the wagons so he could carry her. Valkirra pressed his hand.

'What is it, my heart?' he asked.

'Talis, my dear, do you think we should spend some time apart, so that our greetings could be just as warm as theirs?'

Talis grinned. 'Not a chance. All we need is a little more privacy than those two seem to care about.' He looked up, seeing that Feather, with Jana in his arms, was scanning the crowd to find him. Their eyes met and Talis gave the tribesman a nod.

'We may not get our privacy for a while,' he told his spouse, 'but we have our lives, our children, and our friends.'

'And for that,' agreed Valkirra, 'I am forever grateful.'

* * *

'What do you mean, Foremost Ingeneer? How can water make a difference, if it is not even touching the plaques?' asked the regent.

Far from her usual feline grace, Adaeze was moving about the room with a jerky impatience, touching first one non-functioning device and then another, over and over, until Jaxon grew tired of watching her. Neither the foremost ingeneer nor the chief of teshniks had been able to reanimate any of the communication systems. Their account did not satisfy the regent, and came nowhere near to explaining the situation to the rest of the senior officers.

Jaxon was more worried than he cared to say, and preferred to look out of the wide plexiglass window than to watch the bootless discussion among his peers. Clearly something momentous was happening to the base fabric of the Pale. He imagined it had to do with that thrice-cursed crevasse that the PPA had awoken under the Palatine district. For one of the rare times in his long life, he felt a stirring of anger toward the Conflagrationists. Their actions, it is true, had brought about his own existence, but the perennial repercussions of their futile, self-destructive war were likely to bring down the whole policosmos, the only remaining beacon of civilisation on the whole of this ruined land.

'My lady, there is water around the footings of the Navel, and it seems that one of the foundation pillars is … is …' the foremost ingeneer snatched at a word, 'is floating. Something is moving, beneath the lowest level of the foundations, and making the plaques unstable. The plane, my lady, is … is not … is not on the same plane.'

Fool! thought Jaxon. He discounted Teiuc's garbled description of groundwater rising and causing instability around the foundations of the Navel. The Pale was deliberately situated comfortably far from any river that might have flooded its footings; indeed, the closest such river, several leagues to the south, had been dry ever since the Great Confla-gration. If it had once had a name, that name was lost forever. The river systems were of no account to the mighty policosmos, and the bound-ing ocean was also many leagues distant. The Pale's water supply came from their own tanks; if autumn rains failed, there was always winter's snow and ice to be melted. It was even possible, although the occasion had never arisen, that the Service could source and carry water across Broad Plain if supply dwindled.

The senior forecaster looked down at the go-way beneath the

regent's stronghold. He was not surprised to find that a crowd of citizens had gathered there, gazing up in the hope of information or reassurance. He straightened his robe. That, he supposed, would be his role. As ever. He would stand beside the regent of the day and supply her with the words she needed to calm and comfort the citizens. Save the Pale, he thought. Good citizens, rest assured, you are safe. Be easy in your minds, he thought, we will save the Pale, as many times before.

He was still looking down, planning the regent's speech, when the first rumble reached their ears. Jaxon turned about, looking with surprise at the other senior officers as they all tried to interpret the sound that roared across the policosmos. It was the sound of the Navel, lifted from its foundations, crashing down first on the Palatine and then on the Capitoline district, sending shock waves that wobbled every other tower, every other building, within the walls. The rest of the Acrocomplexa sheared off its footings and arced outward, its considerable length smashing through the remains of Alpha Gate and down onto the sodden red earth of the Outside. One after another—sometimes two or three together—throughout the rest of the day, every one of the Pale's mighty buildings collapsed to the earth.

The regent's stronghold was one of the last to fall, but many hours before it did, all vestiges of life had ceased within the Pale's disintegrating walls. Jaxon Tangshi, Senior Forecaster, was luckier—or unluckier—than some of his fellow citizens. Having rather more liveware than most of them could boast, he survived the complete failure of the Pale's internal systems for several hours. Long enough to regret that he had not foreseen this event. Long enough to plan a number of ingenious schemes that would allow him to survive and rebuild the magnificent policosmos, to make it even better than the first citizens had ever managed to achieve.

Long enough to know those plans would never come to fruition.

SPRING

THE YEAR 230PC

Epilogue

Romulo looked over his shoulder, waiting for his brother to come up beside him. Remo always walked a little behind. He was naturally more cautious and preferred to follow, his eyes continually searching for any dangers that threatened. Romulo understood, and was grateful that his twin always came with him whenever the restlessness drove him outside the streets of Raki. He watched with characteristic patience as Remo took the last two steps in one graceful leap.

Below them the serried folds of Silver Mountain's foothills rose and fell in a descending sweep of dark grey rocks and fresh green shrubs. Contracting shadows echoed the shapes of the youngling trees, each drawing back into its own footprint as the milky sun rose toward midday. The shadows looked as if they were scurrying away from the ruined skeleton of the once mighty Pale. From here, Romulo could see dozens of shiny metal fingers rising aslant from the Plain Ocean, as if pointing the way north.

'Wait for me!'

Romulo faced about and watched Alys clamber painstakingly over the rocks that the two older children had run up with ease. Here at Parting Bluff, there were many places that allowed them to get a foothold for climbing, and wonderful views over the sea to the south. Just to the west was the less accessible outcrop of the farewell place, where the canini, and some of the tribesfolk, liked to leave the bones of their dead for the wind to scour clean. There were many bones there, but no fresh bodies. It was long since they had needed a ceremony at the farewell place. The winter just gone had been kind to them on the highlands.

As she reached the last step, a giant one to her young legs, Alys put up one hand. Remo, as always, reached down and pulled her onto the high ledge. Her two constant companions, Niccolò of the canini and her grandfather's treasured terrier Rasti, were content to wait on the lower level. Unlike the human children, they appeared to have no desire to study the land they had left behind.

Alys sat on the flattest part of the ledge, her legs straight out before her, and held the flying curls of her dark hair out of her face with both chubby hands. She had horrified her mother a few days earlier by taking the sharpest knife she could find, a worn old knife that was some sort of family treasure, and hacking off her beautiful braids. Too much trouble, Alys had explained. Freya just shook her head, but Hector had laughed. If his daughter wanted her hair short, then short was what she could have. He, alone of all the adults, never tired of Alys and her constant questions.

'What's that?' she asked now, pointing toward the oddly angled shapes that marked the place where the Pale had sunk beneath the waves.

'That's the Pale, remember?' Romulo said, glancing that way. 'We told you last time. Where the very last of the Conflagrationists drowned without trace.'

'I know,' said Alys, affronted by his tone. 'I don't forget. Not that, THAT!'

Looking where she indicated, both boys saw a huge dark shape lift off from one of the leaning struts that showed above the water. Romulo shaded his eyes.

Beside him, Remo gasped. 'A mammonite! It's a mammonite, it truly is!' He made as if to leap down from the high crag and carry the news back home.

Romulo put a hand on his brother's shoulder. 'Wait a moment, let's see what it's doing.'

Alys climbed to her feet and took a handful of Romulo's tunic. She wasn't going to let them go anywhere without her. As usual. 'What's a mammonite?'

'Something that Alys doesn't know,' Romulo said mockingly, but without heat.

'You don't know much about it either,' said Remo.

'Well, no, but at least I know its name.'

They observed the great flying beast for a few minutes longer, seeing the slow flap of its huge wings, the careful turning of its great head as it studied the sea below it, and finally the energetic flick of its long scaly tail as it picked up speed to fly south again.

'It's going away!' Alys cried.

'Well, they don't live here,' Romulo explained. 'Not anymore. Your father told us how the Pale's citizens used to hunt them. He'll be glad there are some left in the skies.'

'But what are they?' Alys persisted.

'They're a bit like passerines,' Remo told her. 'But not. A bit like crocodylli too. But not.'

'Can we eat them?'

'They're more likely to eat us. Especially little tasty ones with curly back hair,' said Romulo.

'But not!' said Remo before Alys could protest.

She laughed, reaching out a hand to be lifted down again, and then clambering ahead of them down the rocky path. Niccolò kept pace with her, watching closely to make sure she came to no harm, and Alys carried Rasti down the steeper sections that were too difficult for short legs. They came to the trodden path that led up and over the next of the folded foothills and back to their home at Raki.

Alys looked back at the two boys. 'Are you coming?'

'We're coming,' Romulo answered. 'You go ahead. Tell them about the mammonite.'

'I was the one who saw it!' Alys reminded them, already running away from them.

The twins didn't hurry after her. There would be plenty of time to talk about the mammonite. Everyone in Raki was sure to know something, or to think they knew something. It would be spoken of for days.

'I didn't think we'd ever see a mammonite,' said Remo.

'Me neither. Glad to, though.'

They walked in silence for a while, listening to the chirps of the small avians. As they came closer to the first of the huts, they could hear the murmur of voices. Alys would enjoy telling everyone of her find.

'I would like to see more,' confided Romulo.

'More mammonites?'

'More everything. They say most of the bigger animals didn't make it through the flood, but I don't know. Maybe, out there somewhere, there are all kinds of things we've never seen.'

Remo shifted his shoulders as if something itched his back. 'And you'd like to find them?'

Romulo looked sideways at his brother. As the years had passed, the bright red birthmark on his own chin had faded, so that people had to look twice to make sure which twin was which. Romulo couldn't understand it. He was sure his face didn't wear that permanent frown, that little crease that always sat between Remo's brows.

'Not for a while,' he reassured his brother. 'Not tomorrow, for sure. Not for years and years. But one day, maybe.'

'Years and years,' echoed Remo. 'That's all right then. Anything can happen in years and years.'

'True,' Romulo agreed. 'Anything can.'

ACKNOWLEDGEMENTS

A single book, let alone a three-book series, is never the work of one person. I'm eternally grateful to everyone who has supported and encouraged me on this journey: friends, family, colleagues, readers, bloggers, booksellers, the Oddies, the Savvies, and even Aeryn Spoodle, although she'd prefer I did more of my writing outside.

In particular I want to thank my publisher Michelle Lovi of Odyssey Books, who counts as one of the greatest believers of all times. She has a passion for stories and a dedication to bringing them into the real world as books. I am forever in her debt for picking up mine.

Thanks to Elijah Toten for another evocative cover.

To my dedicated beta readers, Aveline Perez de Vera and Kate Maher, you've made this story work across almost three hundred thousand words. That's not counting the several thousands now sitting much more comfortably in the cutting pile. I'm so fortunate to have your hands to hold along the way. The *Chronicles* are so much stronger and better for your wisdom and care.

My husband Bill, bemused as he mostly is by speculative fiction, has grown to love these fantastic characters and to cheer them on almost as much as he cheers for me. Thank you for your unrivalled love, patience and support, my dearest dear.

ABOUT THE AUTHOR

Clare Rhoden writes, blogs, reads too much, and reviews books.

Inspired by society, politics, culture, and history, Clare writes thoughtful stories about characters with heart and soul. From immersive world-building in science fiction and fantasy, to well-researched details in historical novels, Clare's books pivot on hope and love in the darkest of times.

Clare lives in Melbourne, Australia with her husband and their very clever spoodle.

www.clarerhoden.com